POISONING
EROS

MONICA J. O'ROURKE
WRATH JAMES WHITE

deadite
press

DEADITE PRESS
205 NE BRYANT
PORTLAND, OR 97211
www.DEADITEPRESS.com

AN ERASERHEAD PRESS COMPANY
www.ERASERHEADPRESS.com

ISBN:1-62105-095-5

Poisoning Eros copyright 2003, 2013 by Wrath James White and
Monica J. O'Rourke

Cover art copyright © 2013 Glenn Chadbourne

Printed in the USA.

Acknowledgments from Wrath James White:

Special thanks to Tod Clark for his thoughts and opinions, to my collaborator, Monica J. O'Rourke, for her crazy ideas and uninhibited passion and enthusiasm for this project. And to Deadite Press for bringing it to the masses.

Wrath James White:

To Mom

Monica J. O'Rourke:

For Mom—sorry!

INTRODUCTION
BY
GERARD HOUARNER

There's a path we take through life. It winds, climbs, dips and splits.

We make choices, doing our best or not, getting to road's end.

Supposedly, there's a road to hell, and one to heaven. You'll see how that choice turns out by the end of this tale.

Some stay to the straight and narrow, others meander, wander off, flee. Judgments are made, each path upon the other. There's a right path, and a wrong one. Judgments change with time, perspective.

Pig candy.

This is a choice.

You can buy it in the Essex Street Market, Lower East Side, NYC. Or www.roni-sue.com. Bacon. Covered in chocolate.

Dark, and milk.

There's something seriously wrong with the concept of pig candy. It disturbs the order of things: meat on one side of the dish, vegetables on the other, desert afterwards.

An offense to some. An epicurean transgression. A break from the consensual contract of what is good. The chain stores don't carry it. It isn't right.

And yet, for others, it is a delicious revelation. Enticing. Seductive. Smoky and sweet.

The path to wrongness can start with the most innocent of choices.

Pig candy. A step on to a slippery slope.

Here are a few more: listening to music, reading books, watching movies, experiencing expressive works that stray from the right path, the path of consensus, where everyone knows what is right and what is wrong.

These are all choices.

If you bought this book, you made a choice.

7

People choose the right path because it's safe. Boundaries are clear. Signs and signals proclaim danger. There is a sense of well being in the security of definitions, the protection of expectations.

On the safe path, the right one, everybody knows who they are, what everyone else is. Appetites are channeled, and then satisfied by processed and packaged goods and services. The right path is civilized. Nature is ruled by law and logic.

Definitions change. Expectations are circumvented. Inconvenient facts erupt.

Appetites break their bindings.

The right path, as happens so often, turns out to be wrong. Ruins and desolate places tell us so. Of course. Because, in the end, it is only people who travel that path. They're the ones who named it right.

So where does that leave the path of wrongness?

It depends, I suppose, on the person making the choices.

The wrong path, sometimes, serves to warn. Perhaps not everything on that right path is what it seems. It may be there are serious flaws in that consensual reality, cracks in the boundaries everyone is agreeing to ignore. Not all is as safe and controlled as one might wish.

The wrong path can offer commentary on the nature of those deciding what is right and wrong. Provides a reminder that staring desperately into the light we hope holds truth can blind us to what we seek.

Sometimes, in the darkness, in the wrongness, there are truths in whose presence we should not, as those wiser than I have noted, flinch. We might miss something.

And then how can we count the cost of being right and being wrong?

***

You hold in your hands a book that is wrong. It is a transgression against what many hold as a consensual agreement on that path of rightness. Part of that wrongness hits you right between the eyes at the beginning, but there are darker, deeper turns on the path.

But wrongness is not a judgment. It's only a sign pointing to a destination or, in the case of *Poisoning Eros*, a declaration of the city limits to a place you've never been to, population you.

Boundaries aren't going to protect you. The lines have been erased.

You saw the cover, you recognized the names of the authors, you read blurbs or reviews. You heard the knocking on the door. You've come to see what's on the other side, and what it means to the people living over there.

You made a choice to stray on to the path of wrongness.

Maybe you're going to see just how messed up, sometimes, in certain places, things can become between people and what else there is in the world they live in.

The work might make you wonder about lonely nights under the stars, in the hills and on the prairie, with the livestock nearby, and just what kind of blood runs down to you from those distant ancestors.

You might even taken a second look at certain individuals or family members in your life, or re-evaluate your web browsing habits, or change your party affiliation next time you go out and vote on what kind of consensual reality you're looking for.

If Monica and Wrath manage to make your stomach turn, your blood run a cold, if you have to think a little about what love means and how much sacrifice it takes, then maybe you've taken a walk on the wrong path along with them.

Look around. Take a deep breath. Hurl. Laugh. Discover a still and dark place in your heart. Or do all of it.

And have some pig candy while you're at it. Sweet, smoky, salty. Meaty, creamy, crunchy. Goes down smooth, leaves little chunks between your teeth so the aftertaste lingers.

You've come this far. Why not take another little step.

—Gerard Houarner
Author of *Road to Hell, Road From Hell, A Blood of Killers*
March 1, 2009

CHAPTER

I

Part I

"Christianity gave Eros poison to drink: he did not die of it but degenerated—into vice"
   —*Friedrich Nietzsche,*

Gloria was remembering the days when guys would line up two-hundred deep at the conventions to get her autograph on plastic casts of her clean-shaven vagina, or copies of her "Suck, Swallow and Smile" movies, or just to have their pictures taken with her.

She was thinking back to the days when some of the best-looking and well-hung men in the business were clamoring to work with her. When some of the most sought-after actresses were hitting on her in the dressing rooms, and keeping their faces between her thighs for several minutes after the director yelled cut just to taste a bit more.

She'd been a star then—the hottest adult film star around. She thought of all the money she'd made; the expensive cars, the semi-custom house on the golf course with the Olympic-sized negative edge pool, all the coke she'd snorted and pills she'd popped, all that good weed she'd smoked, and bottle after bottle of Moet, Crystal, and Dom dumped down her amazingly deep and wide throat.

She relived all the moments from her glory days as she gagged on twenty-four inches of donkey dick, and winced at the Great Dane's claws digging into her love handles as it thrust its hairy cock into her distended snatch. Lately, the business just hadn't been very kind to her.

The donkey fucked her face as the internet geeks filmed her live, the digital video camera plugged directly into their website for all the other internet geeks who paid five dollars a minute just to watch these bestiality gang bang videos. The animal's cock disappeared further and further until a full twelve inches of it found its way down her gullet. Gloria would have shamed a sword-swallower. Like her dignity, her gag reflex had disappeared after she'd sucked her thousandth or so cock many years ago.

The beast thrust deeper, speeding the rhythm of its hips. Gloria tried to retract the enormous mule-cock from her throat but was too slow, and what seemed like a gallon of donkey semen erupted into her throat, filling her stomach. Copious amounts of thick salty white ejaculate continued to spill as she withdrew it from her mouth. Her belly and mouth were full and the beast was still cumming. The computer geeks zoomed in to show what seemed like another half-gallon wash over her face, down her neck and between her impossibly large, surgically enhanced breasts. Gloria began to regurgitate and they filmed that too as a bucket-load of cum worked its way back up her esophagus and onto the barnyard floor.

No sooner had the donkey shot its load then the massive canine followed suit. Again it happened so suddenly that she didn't have time to pull away, and the Great Dane ejaculated inside of her. The geeks zoomed in to show the doggy semen drip out of her swollen red gash and run down her inner thighs.

The Great Dane withdrew its cock and began licking its own semen from Gloria's snatch. Gloria started to pull away.

"No, no! This is great! Stay right there!" She allowed the dog to perform cunnilingus on her and was surprised when she started to get aroused. She was close to orgasm when the stupid dog stopped licking and stooped to lap the donkey semen by her feet.

"That's perfect! You get down there too."

"What?"

"Get down there with the dog and lick the cum off the floor! Don't worry, we'll pay you for it."

Gloria knelt nose to nose with the Great Dane and lapped up the lukewarm donkey semen from the barnyard floor— which was already covered in horse and chicken shit—as the camera rolled.

"That was fucking awesome!" The geeks cheered as they high-fived over her back. "We can run this clip for a week. Word of mouth alone should get us like twenty or thirty thousand hits."

The two geeks were going to make hundreds of thousands

on this film. For her part, Gloria made a thousand dollars, about a twentieth of what she'd commanded in her prime. But Gloria was not in her prime. She was in her late forties—fat, drug addicted, AIDS infected. Doing the doggy and donkey shows was about the closest she'd ever get to real work again.

When she'd first begun her downward slide there had still been plenty of work, even if it paid less. After she'd been kicked off a film shoot for nodding off with a cock in her mouth, then the following week went into convulsions during an anal scene and had to be rushed to the hospital after overdosing on a speedball of cocaine and heroin, she'd found herself not only thrown off another set but out of the elite class of porno actresses. She'd slipped from the A class down to the B level where anal scenes and gangbangs were the only way to get work.

Somewhere during this time she'd managed to meet a man and even to have a child. But she had been so determined to fuck her way back to the top of the porno industry, even convincing herself that she might have a career in straight films, that she had abandoned both her daughter and the father of her child to throw her legs up for strangers while cameras absorbed her soul from every angle. Sometimes she still thought about the life she might have had with Ryan and their daughter Angela in their Park Avenue apartment. It was usually at times like these when she found herself on all fours gargling the semen of some barnyard animal.

After leaving her family for drugs and sex, she'd continued to snort and shoot up most of her profits, and soon even the B producers wouldn't touch her. Doped up on a cocktail of street level pharmaceuticals, she broke one gangbang record after another, trying to drown the memory of her lost family in cocaine and cum, until people grew tired of seeing how many cocks she could stuff into her various orifices, and she was dumped by one producer after another. Then she'd found herself doing S&M and bondage films, fake snuff and fetish videos, and then finally she'd been diagnosed with the HIV and her career in legitimate porn was over. Now at age forty-six—twenty-seven years after starting in the business—she found herself doing zoo and farm sex videos.

Gloria packed herself with ice cubes and prepared for the next take.

"Can you really take this thing's cock in your ass? I mean, we don't want nobody dying on the set," Jordan asked.

Jordan was the money behind ZoologicalPorn.com. He looked like Buddy Holly on crack. Glasses as thick as bulletproof glass, and you could see all the bones in his face, as if he'd had one too many liposuctions or snorted one too many lines of coke. He and his portly longhaired partner Colin filmed all the movies for their website.

"Trust me. I've had bigger cocks than this in my ass. In 'Stuffed' I took the business end of a baseball bat and a stuffed elephant penis. Just get that donkey over here and start rolling."

"You'll have to get him up again."

"No problem."

Gloria knelt down between the donkey's legs and took the thing's massive organ into her mouth, and within seconds it had achieved the desired length and rigidity. She shot half a tub of AstroGlide into her ass and slathered the donkey's penis in it, then bent over and spread her ass cheeks, revealing an asshole big enough to toss a baseball through.

"Roll camera!"

It hurt like hell. But Jordan had promised her another thousand bucks if she could do it. The ice helped but still it felt like she was being split in half as she eased the thing's massive cock into her anus. Having the harness break, and the thing's full weight coming down on her back was more of a concern than having the donkey's dick ripping through her distended rectum. She was so high that she was practically numb.

The donkey thrust three of four times into her asshole, stretching her wide and causing her stomach to cramp. Then it shot another geyser of cum into her asshole. The fit of its cock in her asshole was so tight that semen sprayed out like an open fire hydrant. The two geeks zoomed in to catch the mule semen erupting from her vandalized anus.

"You're a fucking star, Gloria!" The geeks high-fived again and then took out their own cocks so that Gloria could fulfill the rest of her contract. After the donkey it was almost a relief for Gloria suck on something so small, something that she didn't have to pick hair out of her teeth when it was over. She sucked them both off, and when they finished jacking off on her face, they paid her.

"Good job, baby. We'll see you again next week." The geeks left, gibbering about the possibilities of getting a hold of something bigger for Gloria to fuck, like an elephant or a giraffe.

"We don't want to kill her, though," Colin reminded his partner.

"Did you see her take that donkey's cock in her ass? She barely batted a fucking eye. An elephant couldn't be much worse. She said she already had a stuffed elephant cock in her ass. How much worse could a live one be?"

"I don't think I've ever seen an elephant's cock, really. How big are they?"

"I'm not sure. Maybe we should go to the zoo and check it out."

Then they were gone. Gloria shrugged back into her dress and, still covered with cum and blood, AstroGlide and donkey semen leaking from her ass, she stumbled out to her car.

***

Gloria showered as soon as she got home. After she dressed, she went to the corner and waited beside a trash container to score some heroin from one of the local dealers. She couldn't find heroin though—everyone was selling crack, meth, and xstasy. She didn't want to be up though; she wanted to crash, to forget about her sick and diseased life.

She turned the corner. A fleshy little man in an obviously expensive suit surprised her by offering her heroin out of the blue, before she'd even asked. Not that she'd been intending to ask. The guy looked like a child molester. There was something disconcerting about his smile. It looked too confident to be coming from a face so homely.

The man's skin was the color of raw calamari; thin blue

17

and green veins crawled beneath the surface. The ends of his handlebar moustache curled up like ram's horns. Thick, curly hair surrounded a splotchy bald spot in the center of his head. With all that red hair, she'd expected his eyes to be green but noticed that they were as black as a starless sky.

"What are you, a fucking cop?"

"No. I'm a fan, Gloria."

"I'm not a prostitute. I'm an actress. So whatever you've got planned, forget it." She started to turn away but he reached into his pocket and pulled out three small balloons filled with heroin. Gloria's gaze latched onto them, and she began to sweat. Saliva trickled out of the corner of her mouth.

"Actress. That's exactly what I'm looking for, Gloria. An actress to star in my next film." He smiled, a repulsive contortion of facial muscles that she assumed were meant to be comforting but instead made her flesh crawl.

"What kind of film? If you're such a big fan, then you must know that I'm HIV positive. That's why I've been doing the animal videos. They can't catch it."

"Don't worry. You won't be fucking anything human in my films."

***

Gloria was pretty sure the man with the flaming red hair was insane. Not only had he given her the heroin for free, he'd promised her fifty thousand dollars for her services. All she'd have to do is lie on a bed in a run-down old house and just "go with it", as he put it. Did he get his kicks from creepy old houses? Gloria once spent a weekend with a guy who could only get it up inside a coffin. Liked to pretend he was a corpse. Maybe a run-down house was a way for this guy to get his rocks off. Whatever his hang-up, he was paying way too much for her to give a shit.

He'd told her that the house was haunted by the spirit of a convicted serial rapist who'd been stabbed to death in prison, and that he was paying her to have sex with the ghost.

Gloria smiled. "Whatever." She slipped the spike into the

vein behind her knee and shot herself full of dope.

Once high, she stripped off her clothing and lay back on the piss-stained mattress. The heroin kicked in, and shortly after she no longer cared about much of anything.

***

Gloria slowly woke from a drowsy, semi-conscious state. She felt hands crawling over her skin, kneading her mountainous silicone stuffed breasts, and struggled to open her eyes, to bring her vision into focus. She wanted to know who was attached to those rough hands. He spread her legs and thrust a finger, two, three, until his entire hand was inside her. A mouth clamped down on her left breast, panting heavily, hot steaming breath almost burning the flesh. He bit so hard her nipple bled, and her eyes flew open.

She was staring at an empty room—empty except for the redheaded pervert behind the video camera. Empty except for whatever was still running its hands and mouth over her body. Some invisible thing, hot misty breath on her inner thighs, licking the flesh there. The invisible thing that was now gnawing at her clitoris even as it punched its fist up inside her. Gloria screamed and tried to push the thing off, surprised when her hands actually encountered substance where her eyes beheld only dead air. Still, even though she could touch it, she couldn't seem to move it. Whatever the unseen entity was, it was all rock-hard muscle.

"That's it, Gloria. Wonderful work. Keep it up, so to speak."

Hard, invisible fingers twisted into her hair and jerked her head forward. She could feel the unmistakable push of a rigid cock against her lips, forcing them open to allow it inside. She could smell the musky aroma of pubic sweat. Taste the salty drops of pre-cum as the throbbing erection slid past her tongue and down her throat. Still, she could see nothing. Nothing but an almost empty room.

Vlad moved in closer with the camera, and Gloria wanted to turn away, repulsed by Vlad, by the invisible thing fucking her raw. Disgusted with herself for allowing this debasement, sick of what she had become.

Vlad looked up from the camera, grinned, shook his head. "What has it all become, dear sweet Gloria? 'Christianity gave Eros poison to drink. He did not die of it but degenerated into vice . . .' Nietzsche said that. Apt, I think."

Gloria groped, her nails passing over large hairy testicles as her invisible rapist attacked her throat. She felt the cock swell in her throat. Felt it jerk and the warm spray of molten semen fill her mouth. The ghost withdrew and she spit his seed out, felt it dribble down her chin. Still she saw nothing. Even the thing's cum was invisible.

Once free, she tried to crawl away but invisible hands threw her back down on the mattress, wrenched her legs apart again.

His erection felt even longer and thicker than the one she'd had in her throat. It ripped its way inside of her and began pounding into her at a manic pace. Hands clamped down on her throat and began to squeeze. Long callused fingers crushed her windpipe, cutting off the flow of oxygen as the poltergeist continued to assault her slack vaginal walls with its brutal penis. Spots began to dance in front of her eyes and everything started to go black.

"Fucking slut! Whore! Jezebel! Harlot!"

The words assaulted her, words spoken from lips she could not see. Gloria began to cry and that seemed to both anger and excite her assailant. A fist collided with her jaw with an audible *pop* and Gloria's eyes rolled back in her head.

Her body bucked and rocked as the ghost rode her hard, flipping her from one position to the next and entering her from every angle. Whenever she failed to moan and squeal appropriately she was smacked or bitten or strangled nearly unconscious. The assault went on all night and the redheaded man behind the camera filmed it all.

***

The next morning, Gloria was back in her apartment. Fifty thousand dollars in her purse hardly seemed to make up for the countless bruises and bite marks on her breasts, face, thighs, and buttocks.

She rolled over onto her side, faced the night table, snatched the half-empty pack of smokes and shook one into her mouth. Too much heroin last night. Now her head pounded like someone was keeping time with a sledgehammer.

The best way to get rid of the headache was to shoot up again. Her thoughts flashed back to the night before and she tried to bring it into focus. Whatever had attacked her, there was no way it could have been a ghost. She was so wasted she must have imagined it. Imagined an invisible rapist. Maybe she'd been blindfolded and just couldn't remember.

That little redheaded freak, she thought. *He must have drugged me, raped me himself.* "I hope that fucker catches AIDS and dies!" Then there was the money. She'd never made that much on a single film, even at the height of her career.

Her asshole, sore from the donkey's attack, was turned nearly inside out, inflamed hemorrhoidal tissue bulging out of her anus. It looked like a baboon's ass. Gloria snubbed out the cigarette in the overflowing ashtray and went back to sleep.

That night she dreamt of Ryan and her daughter and woke up feeling guilty and ashamed and in desperate need of another fix. Her daughter's face lingered in her mind; her conscience always wore Angela's face. That sweet, angelic, dimpled smile telling her what a worthless slut she'd become, what a degenerate junky, screaming at her to stop killing herself. Another hit of H and her conscience slipped back into the coma in which it had so often languished for most of her adult life, until motherhood had awakened it with anguished shrieking. If only she could pull the plug on the damned thing once and for all. But even after years of degradation, drugs and abuse, she still knew right from wrong. The drugs just helped her not care.

***

This was not the path Gloria had once dreamed for herself. As a child she'd imagined a world of dancing and painting and marrying into happiness, as little girls are wont to do. When she was older she would envision stardom, rising to fame in movies, appearing on all the talk shows.

She'd been a beautiful and popular girl in high school. Then she dropped out to hitchhike her way to Hollywood, to become a star. She'd been raped by one truck driver, and offered a choice of being dropped off in the middle of the Nevada desert or giving a blowjob by another. But she'd survived, and in her mind it had been worth it. Almost.

Gloria knew that she'd never make it through college. Only her long blonde hair, long legs and large breasts kept her from being doomed to minimum wage jobs for the rest of her life. But with her body she soon found that she could make more money than she'd ever imagined . . . in the porno industry.

She'd been an instant success. She didn't mind all the cocks she'd had to suck or pussies she had to lick. She was famous and getting paid to do what her body had been made for. Then came drugs, and age, and the long fall from glory.

She could have gotten out but she hadn't saved any of the money she'd earned—so much of it went up her nose or into a vein—and she couldn't imagine herself as a truck-stop waitress or crawling back to Ryan with her tail tucked between her legs and her red blood cell count plummeting. So instead, she made her way back east and fucked animals and whatever the hell that thing was she'd been ravaged by the night before. It was a living, and thanks to the heroin she hardly felt the pain in her body or her pride.

***

A week passed, and Gloria had managed to put the strange ordeal behind her, for the most part. Her bruises had all but healed, and so had her torn and partially prolapsed anus and vagina. The fifty thousand was almost gone. Converted to hard liquor and hard drugs.

The two geeks called. "Hey, Gloria! We found a giraffe! We're trying to figure out how we can rig up a harness underneath it so that you can fuck the thing. Its cock is like three feet long! If you can do it we'll pay you a thousand dollars a foot!" He apparently found that immensely funny. "But seriously. If you can't fuck it you can give the thing head for the usual thousand. We'll call you tomorrow."

Gloria hung up, fell back onto the bed in tears. Her life had become a horror show. A giraffe? Those sick fuckers! But she knew she'd do it. Soon she'd be out of money, out of drugs. She was almost broke again and in the last week her habit had doubled. Whereas she previously only made just enough money to keep herself from getting sick, with the fifty gees she'd had enough to actually get high again and so she had, two or three times a day. Those fucking geeks could make her do anything now as long as they could keep her in horse.

The phone rang again. Gloria rolled over and hesitantly picked it up. "Yes."

"Gloria?" His unctuous voice crawled over her skin like a bucket of leeches.

Gloria shivered. "Who is this?" But she already knew.

"Bill Vlad. You made a film for me last week. It was sensational! I've sold almost a million copies already. You're a star again!"

"Are you serious?" Gloria's vanity reawakened.

"Absolutely."

"How come I haven't seen it on the shelves in any video stores?"

"Most of my clientele don't frequent video stores. They're clamoring for more, Gloria. How'd you like to make another fifty thousand?"

The answer was never in question. She called the two geeks back and told them to fuck the giraffe themselves.

***

The teenaged boy was lying on a bed, chains wrapped around wrists and ankles. His thin body was covered in welts and bruises, and his breath was a cloud of steam, despite the oppressive heat and humidity of the room.

"Whoa! What the fuck is this? How old is that kid? I don't

do kiddy porn!" Gloria turned to leave. Bill Vlad stepped in front of her to block her exit, twirling his moustache like some silent film villain.

"And I don't do kiddy porn either, my lovely. Stuart's seventeen. The age of consent in this state is sixteen."

Gloria looked at the boy, who was writhing on the bed, growling, tugging at his restraints. "It doesn't look like he's consenting to me. Why's he tied down?"

Bill Vlad smiled. Gloria noticed that his teeth were filed to points. She shuddered, remembering the invisible thing that had gnawed at her breasts and clitoris.

"Because he's possessed."

"What?"

"Stuart there has a rather nasty demon inside of him. I want you to have sex with that demon."

"My god. You're crazy."

"No. Not at all." Bill smiled again and pointed at Stuart. "Don't you want to be a star again?"

No, she thought. *Not like this. It's not worth it.* She was sure Stuart was a child. Even if he was of legal consenting age, this was wrong. It was disturbing and nauseating and probably illegal. She glanced up at Vlad and believed it very unlikely he was going to let her leave without doing what she'd been paid to do. But too much of that new payment had already been promised to her dealers even before she'd touched the money. She couldn't afford to quit now.

Gloria pulled her dress over her head, her massive breasts slipping from a bra sized somewhere in the middle of the alphabet. Vlad smiled, wiped the back of his hand across his bottom lip and set up the video camera.

The bed leapt off the ground nearly a foot and skirted three feet closer to Gloria, sliding across the splintered and warped hardwood floor like a Ouija board planchette. She felt her legs wobble as she stared into young Stuart's eyes, which had rolled up into his head, revealing only the whites. Those white orbs followed her movements; it was clear that he could still see her.

She crossed her arms over her bare chest, nipples tickling

her skin, her body trembling in cold and fear and excitement. This was new territory; there was no mistaking that. Even if this was some kind of trick, it sure as hell was convincing. Gloria has never been particularly religious—she'd given up on God years ago when it was clear He'd given up on her first—but this was just too . . .

Vlad cleared his throat but didn't say anything. He obviously wanted to give Gloria some time, but she guessed he didn't mean forever.

It was time to earn her money. The drugs had kicked in and were earning their worth. Gloria slipped out of her underwear and moved onto the bed. *Never mind*, she thought. *Tricks. All tricks. Fuck this already, I need my money.*

Gloria crawled up the boy's hairless torso, kissing his flesh along the way. Her saliva boiled wherever it landed on his skin and her tongue began to blister. She moved back down his body. Her face was inches from his cock when it began to elongate, ripping the skin as it swelled to a length nearly that of the donkey she'd fucked little more than a week ago.

Sallow fat and strawberry-red muscle fiber oozed through the tears in his skin as his cock swelled, now thicker than a wrist and as long as a child's arm. Blood and semen ran down the sides like lava from an erupting volcano.

Gloria slid her tongue over the head, and the cum was thick and chunky, like curdled milk. The boy howled and his skin began to tear everywhere, his body leaking blood onto the mattress.

Gloria jumped up. "I'm sorry, but I can't do this! What the hell is wrong with this kid? Does he have some kind of disease or something?"

"I told you. He's possessed. Now climb up on his cock and fuck the devil out of him!" Bill Vlad laughed, and licked his razor sharp teeth until his tongue bled.

Gloria turned back to look at the boy's enormous suppurating cock, then at his body, which was now crosshatched with slashes and welts from his forehead to his groin.

"Jesus," she muttered, climbing back onto the bed, visions of dollar signs dancing in her head. Disease or no disease, she had to fuck this kid. She straddled his engorged muscle and slowly lowered herself onto it. It burned into the center of her body as it slid deeper and deeper, skewering her. The boy began to convulse, thrusting up into her so hard she could hear bones snapping in his back and pelvis, could feel her own organs shift. Blood trickled from her own mouth as the boy's cock thrust deeper and deeper. She tried to climb off but was trapped, impaled on the massive organ.

The boy's breath reminded her of the time a meth-amphetamine lab had exploded in her old apartment and the entire place had burned down, with half the tenants still trapped inside. The smell was death, smoke, burned flesh. It was disease and decay, like cancer patients rotting from the inside out. He coughed a cloud of noxious smoke into her face. His tongue snaked out of his mouth, extending nearly a full ten inches and coiling around her gumdrop nipples.

She looked at his eyes. Bulging, bursting blood vessels created a kaleidoscope swirl, and the pressure proved to be too much. His eyes exploded, leaving only bloody craters in his face. Gloria sobbed and turned away but continued to ride the boy's massive cock, still unable to climb off of it. His tongue raped her face as his cock pulsed within her, scalding her like a white-hot poker, like drinking gallons of boiling oil, like a rampant fever turned inward. She was beyond screaming. Smoke billowed out of her mouth.

The boy's nose exploded, one nostril resting on each side of his face. His smile stretched until the corners of his mouth tore, his cheeks ripping all the way back to the hinge of his jaw. His chest split, the ribs cracking and tearing through his torso, displaying his intestines, his pulsing heart.

He broke his restraints and grabbed Gloria by her hips, pushing her onto her back. He thrust harder, deeper, even as his skin ruptured, even as he literally fell apart, still he fucked the aging porno queen. His insides poured out onto her body, and still he fucked as if on remote control, his face an unrecognizable mash above her own.

Gloria found her voice again and screamed, over and over. Bill Vlad was right beside her with the video camera, grinning like a boy watching his first stag film, taping everything.

Something huge tore its way out of Stuart's body, finally disengaging Gloria from the boy's cock, knocking her to the floor.

"You're mine," she heard Vlad say. "You work only for me. Understand?"

She passed out after glimpsing the dark shadowy thing that was fleeing the room.

***

Back inside her apartment. She woke up staring at another fifty thousand dollars stacked on her nightstand. Her lips curled into something of a smile, despite the headache—although it was nothing compared to what she expected to have. She had no delusions that last night had actually been a dream (*nightmare?*), that it had been some extraordinarily bad trip from a dust-laced hit of whatever the fuck she'd taken. The dull aching in her cunt was too much of a reminder that last night had been real.

But real *what?* She could accept that something had happened, and all she knew was that she didn't want to dwell on it. Heaven and Hell were the farthest things from her mind these past twenty-odd years. The spiritual, and whatever trappings went along with it, were overshadowed by the poignancy of her everyday existence. Some part of her believed that the previous night might have been a supernatural experience, but her pragmatic side refused to believe it was anything more than a drug-induced hallucination.

And he'd call again, she knew. The man who called himself Vlad—how quaint—wasn't finished with her. She was sure of it.

Gloria fingered the stacks of money, stroked it like a lover, inhaled its perfume.

Fifty gees were no longer enough.

But she also had to admit that she was intrigued on some level by what Vlad might offer next.

27

***

The terrible happened. Vlad didn't call. Not the next day, nor the day after that. Two weeks passed, then three, which eventually morphed into months, and Gloria gave up on ever hearing from him again.

Poverty was a strong incentive for desperate moves. Her landlord had threatened eviction—she was months behind in her rent now—and she was blowing dealers for dime bags of pot. So she thought about the geeks and their giraffe and wondered if they'd hire her again. She couldn't wait for Vlad any more.

Their apartment, where they did most their filming outside of the barn, was a huge loft in the West Village, in an industrial area where they wouldn't be disturbed by neighbors or police. The door was unlocked for her, as always, and she entered the building.

"Here's our star!" Jordan took her hands and pulled her inside the room. "How've you been, Gloria? We considered taking your advice but didn't want to fuck the giraffe ourselves. Thanks for offering though."

She didn't bother responding to that. Instead, she said, "So what's the deal?"

"Animal gangbang. Think you can handle it?"

She shrugged, then nodded. "I've done worse."

Colin looked up from working on setting up the camera and laughed. "Worse? That I'd like to see."

"How much?" she asked.

"Two thousand."

"Not enough. I need ten."

Jordan shook his head, flashed his charming (so he seemed to think) smile. "No way, Gloria."

Gloria waited before responding, knowing this stall tactic often made people uncomfortable. Jordan didn't seem to care. "No one else on this planet will do the shit that I do. And you know you can't turn back from here, can't go back to simple doggy fucks. Your audience will never accept that."

His smile faltered. "Three thousand."

"Seven."

"Five. Final offer."

Gloria nodded. "Five." She was playing with him. She'd do a few things with the animals but would hold off a bit. There was a lot more money than five thousand dollars to be had—these guys were making a fortune off of her. Time to share the wealth.

Jordan took her hand and led her across the room. Gloria had already heard the various noises coming from this side of the loft, so she had a general idea of what sort of animals were back here. A pack of dogs? A cow? She wondered how they managed to get their hands on these animals. How was she supposed to fuck a cow? Maybe they'd just have her play with the teats or something.

"Start off with the dogs," Jordan said. He went over to the dog kennel and released three of them onto the set.

Several cameras had been mounted on tripods, and Colin went around the set, checking them all.

"Let me know when you're set," Jordan said to Colin. To Gloria: "Time to get undressed. Right?"

She rolled her eyes, nodded. Ready as she'd ever be, she supposed. She was way past the point of modesty or embarrassment, had been for two decades now. This was a job for her, nothing more.

"Ready," Colin said. All cameras were running, catching the set from various angles.

"Get in there," Jordan said. "Do your stuff."

"Anything specific?"

He shook his head. "Just see if you can get into a gangbang with them. Try to take as many at once as you can."

Gloria entered the set and knelt beside the dogs, two German shepherds and a Doberman. She just hoped they wouldn't rip her apart trying to get at her.

One of the shepherds entered her from behind, and at the same time she reached the Doberman's cock and took it into her throat, bobbing up and down on it. The dog seemed confused and tried to pull away, but Gloria held tight and followed him as he backed up. The dog fucking her from behind slid out of her snatch and mounted her again, wrapping his paws around her abdomen. The second shepherd was kneeling below Gloria, sniffing her crotch, his tongue licking her clitoris. He seemed to be trying to find a way into the middle of all the fucking. His paw batted at her thigh and he whined.

"Beautiful," Jordan mumbled. "You're so good at this. Keep going."

The shepherd fucking her from behind came inside her and pulled away. She released the Doberman, his cock rigid, the dog not yet satisfied. The Doberman ran behind her and straddled her, but she moved before he could enter, moved to the shepherd that had been trying to get her attention, and took his cock in her mouth. The Doberman was finally able to enter her from behind. The shepherd in her mouth didn't seem to care what hole he was fucking and started to thrust his hips, fucking her mouth.

The dog came in her throat, and he ran off. The Doberman was still going at it, and Gloria realized she was going to cum as well. She managed to orgasm right before the animal shot his load, and she moaned and bucked, and Colin and Jordan whooped and laughed.

The Doberman pulled out and ran off with the other dogs to the other side of the loft.

"God *damn*," Colin said. "How'd you learn to do that? Bring out the cow. Just lick the cow's pussy and suck its teats for the camera."

Gloria knelt beneath the huge bovine and stuck her face up into its sweaty snatch.

"No. Not like that! We can't get a shot like that. You'll have to lick it from behind."

Gloria scowled but knelt behind the cow and began lapping at its swollen pink labia. The cow moaned and shuddered as Gloria lapped at its clitoris, bringing it closer and closer to orgasm.

"It's about to cum! Stick your tongue in its ass!"

Gloria dragged her tongue from cunt to ass-crack in one deft motion and the cow trembled and convulsed as it climaxed. It backed up trying to force Gloria's tongue deeper into its rectum but knocked her onto her ass instead.

The geeks laughed.

Gloria glared up from the floor at them. "Can I have a towel or something?" she snapped.

Colin tossed her a towel. "Sorry."

"I need a break," Gloria said.

"All right, and then we'll do some more. Okay? We just acquired some new . . . uh . . . creatures. We're eager to try them out."

"Do you have any coke?"

"Sure." Colin reached into his pocket and pulled out a small plastic vial. He then added a small pink pill to it from another pocket and dumped them both into Gloria's outstretched palm.

"Here's a hit of Xstasy too. It'll really get you going."

Gloria scooped the cocaine out of the plastic vial with one long, garishly painted plastic nail and shoveled it into her nostril. She then dry swallowed the Xstasy. The combination of the two sent an immediate jolt through her nervous system and nearly counteracted the effects of the heroin. There was so much speed cut into that tab of X that Gloria could feel her heartbeat gallop like a fucking racehorse. Every nerve in her body came alive. The humid air crawled over her skin and the air conditioning fought to beat it back. The two sensations were somehow arousing. She knew that it was just the effects of the X magnified by the cocaine but suddenly she was ready to fuck. She wished she had one of her former male co-stars to mount her. Someone like Lance Mannion with his beautiful nine-inch ramrod or even one of those fresh-faced up-and-cumming starlets who'd always been so eager to lick her well-worn twat for more airtime. Instead, she would have to content herself with whatever farm animals the geeks had lined up for her. Right now she didn't even care. She was so horny all she wanted to do was get fucked by something.

"That sure got her going. That's some great fucking X, ain't it? My cousin makes the stuff himself. He's a chemistry major at Princeton. He said all the chem students sit around all day trying to see who can make the strongest designer drugs. I can get you more if you like it."

"Yeah, get me more." Gloria's eyes had glazed over with want and she had already slipped a hand down between her naked thighs to finger her suddenly swollen clitoris.

"Man, incredible! We need to pass that stuff out at the nightclubs. We'll start orgies everywhere we go." Colin smiled and shook his head. "Okay, let's get her in there with the worms."

"Worms?" Gloria looked up.

"Oh, you're going to love this, sweetheart. We got them from this exotic animal dealer. He only handles rare and endangered species. He's the one who was going to get us the giraffe, then yesterday he approaches us with these . . ."

Jordan swung open the door and Gloria caught her breath. There was a large Jacuzzi—big enough to fit six people comfortably—in the middle of the room. Within it seethed huge serpentine creatures slithering through the bubbles in slow peristaltic undulations. A humid stench wafted from the hot tub, clogging Gloria's nostrils. It smelled like a septic tank, like some loathsome thing shat out from the bowels of the earth.

There were nearly a dozen of them. Pale larval vermin covered in a sheen of greenish mucus that not even the steaming water seemed capable of washing away. At least five feet long, none seemed to have eyes, ears, or even a mouth. One end of the things contained an orifice that resembled a vagina and the other end contained a human-looking cock, complete with testicles. Midway between their bodies was a nest of little snake-like appendages that they were using to cling to each other during copulation. As Gloria watched, the creatures found each other again and again in the bubbling water, sliding their penises into one another's vaginal orifices while simultaneously allowing themselves to be penetrated. An orgy of slithering slime-covered invertebrates fucking like sex-starved speed freaks. Had the eel-like creatures possessed backbones their corybantic thrusts would have snapped them in two.

"The *fuck* are those?"

"How the hell should I know? The guy just called them worms. Said they came from the center of the earth or some shit."

"I'm not getting in there with those things! They'll . . . they'll eat me alive or something."

"They don't even have mouths. I don't even know *how* they eat." Colin stared into the hot tub and scratched his head, a perplexed expression on his chubby, pockmarked face. "Look, you wanted ten thousand? You get in there and fuck those worms and we'll give you ten thousand. As much as we paid for them, we're not about to let them go to waste. Here— have another hit of X to loosen you up."

Jordan reached into his pocket and withdrew another magic vulva-pink capsule. Gloria could tell by the pathetic bulge in his paisley shorts that he was eager to find out what those things were going to do to her.

Gloria tossed the pill down her throat. She didn't really need it; she was already horny as hell, but she wanted to be beyond horny, past caring. She wanted to be a mindless animal when she did what she knew she was about to do, what they all knew she would do: take the money and fuck the worms.

Gloria climbed into the hot tub.

They swarmed her. Tiny tentacles slithered across her breasts, thighs, buttocks, stomach, throat . . . tickling and probing, looking for ways inside of her. One of the unctuous vermin wrapped its wiry appendages around her waist and entered her from behind, the lubrication oozing from its skin easily allowing its man-sized cock to slide into her distended asshole, thrusting in rapid-fire strokes that only the horniest teenaged sex-fiend could have mimicked. Another entered her vagina, ramming up into her with the same relentless enthusiasm as the creature pounding in and out of her asshole. Still another wrapped itself around her face and began fucking her throat so vigorously that Gloria nearly drowned as she gasped for air and thanked god for the absence of a gag-reflex.

She couldn't see but could feel two more mucus-slickened cocks being thrust into her hands, which she began to masturbate. The worms didn't last long—they came within minutes, filling her with a thick gooey tar that she assumed was some type of semen. They recovered quickly though, their erections resurrecting moments after each orgasm. No sooner did one ugsome vermin spill its seed, ejaculating a copious deluge of heavy bittersweet slime, when another rushed to fill its place.

The creatures smelled like they lived on vomit and excrement. Gloria choked on the stench, tried to keep herself from regurgitating with one of their penises in her throat because she was pretty sure the worms would not pull out but would continue fucking her face. Besides, the second hit of X had kicked in, and all the attention she was getting from the worms was starting to build one hell of an orgasm within her.

"Man, look at her go! She's getting off on this shit. Those worms are fucking the shit out of her. We are going to make millions off this!"

The digital video camera continued to record Gloria's latest debasement.

"This is like Fear Factor with one hell of a fucking twist! I wonder where that Vlad guy got these things?"

Gloria heard the name and froze. She tried to speak but one of the worms was still thrusting deep into her esophagus with its man-sized cock. She grabbed hold of the thing and torn it off of her face, ripping its soft squishy body in two in the process and filling the tub with an inky red-black blood.

"Who did y—"

Before she could finish the question, another worm insinuated itself into her mouth. She bit down, severing its cock, and spit it into the tub. Blood sprayed from the ragged hole where the creature's sex organ had been as it convulsed in agony, squealing a high pitched death-shriek. Where the noise was coming from, Gloria didn't know—the damned things didn't have any mouths.

"Did you say Vl—"

Another worm mounted her face and Gloria tore that one apart, too. She speared her fake nails into the worm wrapped around her waist and shredded its body. Its lower half continued to pump in and out of her weathered cunt as the rest of its body sank to the bottom of the tub. Gloria speared her fist up inside of herself, squashing the rest of the creature and scooping it out in handfuls of brackish goop. She then reached around to tear off the one still digging into her rectum. No sooner had she freed herself than all her holes were immediately filled again. Gloria attacked these as well, adding their cries to the symphony of terse shrieks echoing from the hot tub.

The noise was like metal scraping bone. It made Gloria's hairs stand on end. But there was almost a pattern to it. As if they were trying to speak. She could almost make out the words. But that had to have been in her head. Another side effect of the X? These filthy things couldn't have been intelligent. They were just horny, mindless animals and she had to get them off of her. If they had gotten them from Vlad then they had to have been evil in some way.

"What the fuck is she doing? She's killing them!" Jordan covered his ears to drown out the pealing screams of the dying worms.

"Maybe we can edit this part out. We've got plenty of film from the beginning to make a great movie," Colin said as he stared at the carnage taking place in the Jacuzzi.

"Just keep filming. I know people who'll pay extra for this shit. You ever hear about those perverts with the bug-squashing fetish? They'd kill to see a woman fuck and then smash a worm."

"Man, Jordan you're one sick sonofabitch. You've got all the angles covered." Colin looked up at his twisted little anemic friend with an expression of near reverence.

The worms had been completely decimated. Blood, thick black semen, and whitish gray chunks of wormflesh clung to her as she rose from the blood-red pool like Aphrodite rising from the sea foam. She was breathing hard and her eyes were wild with panic as she lunged toward Colin and Jordan, seizing both geeks by their polo shirts and pulling them closer.

"You said Vlad gave you those things? Bill Vlad? Do you mean Bill Vlad?"

"Yeah. Why? You know that weirdo? Let me guess. You fucked him, right? What's he like, one of those Ron Jeremy types? A big fat dorky guy with a yard-long cock?"

"Where is he then? Why isn't he here?"

"He didn't want to be here. He just made us promise to

give him a copy of the tape so he could sell a few copies himself. Why? Who is this guy?"

"Nobody. Just give me my fucking money and get me the fuck out of here." Gloria grabbed her clothes and began pulling them on over the tacky crimson and black effluence still coating her skin. She was pretty sure they wouldn't be asking for blowjobs tonight. Colin and Jordan looked as if they were about to lose their lunch. She snatched the wad of cash out of Jordan's hand and stormed toward the front door.

"Hey wait! We've still got that giraffe thing going! I'm telling you, that would absolutely make your career."

"This is not a fucking career!" Gloria shrieked. Tears streaked her face, and she suddenly felt as if the world were closing in on her. Something about Bill Vlad, knowing that he was involved in what she'd just been put through. It freaked her out. She felt haunted. Trapped.

"I don't know what the fuck this is—" She looked back at the overflowing Jacuzzi, at the bubbling waters that had turned completely black. Something broke the surface of the water and slipped silently below the murky waves. A shudder shivered up her spine.

"—But this is not a career." She slammed the door and sprinted to the subway without looking back.

***

The money was going fast. Gloria was getting stuck deeper and deeper in a cycle of damnation and chemical oblivion from which she could see no possible way of extricating herself. Fuck something hideous and terrible. Get money. Get high. Run out of money. Get sick. Fuck something more hideous and terrible. A self-perpetuating downward spiral.

It had been less than two weeks since Gloria's conqueror worm orgy. The geeks were calling every other day about that damned giraffe and Gloria was almost desperate enough to do it. It couldn't be much worse than the shit she'd already done. Like they'd said, a giraffe's dick couldn't be that much bigger than a donkey's and she'd taken that mule's entire cock in her ass. Gloria was thinking more and more about the giraffe as her stash dwindled.

Then Vlad began calling again. His voice always made her feel as if she were covered in slugs. Now it reminded her of six-foot worms hung like stallions that screamed when you squashed them. Gloria could still hear their cries. They had almost sounded like words but sped up like a record playing at double speed. But that couldn't be, because that would have meant that they were intelligent. She was pretty certain they weren't.

"No, Vlad."

"And what is it you think I was going to ask you?"

"Whatever it is, it can't be good."

" . . . *It is better for thee to enter into life maimed, than having two hands to go into Hell, into the fire that never shall be quenched. Where their worm dieth not, and the fire is not quenched . . .* You're in Hell right now Gloria. Your fire is not quenched. It still burns within you, consuming your soul. I can ease that pain for you and set your worm free. I just want you to meet an old friend."

What the fuck is he talking about? What the hell does that mean, "set my worm free"?

"Just want me to meet an old friend, huh? And fuck him?"

"Of course."

Gloria could sense him smiling through the phone.

"What is it, a werewolf or something this time?"

"There's no such thing as werewolves. I want you to fuck a demon, the one you helped me release from that teenaged boy whose flesh he was imprisoned in. He was quite impressed with your talents and wants more. It would be worth a lot of money."

"No way, Vlad."

"What are you going to do? Go back to fucking donkeys and cows? You work for me now, Gloria. Me and only me!"

Gloria hung up the phone and tried to shake the slimy trail of Vlad's voice off her skin. The memory of the boy who'd unraveled beneath her as she rode his bloated and ruptured cock came slithering in from the dark edges of her memory.

She remembered how the boy's soul had screamed from deep within him, only to be drowned out by the roar of the demon as it ripped him apart in its haste to be free. She could still see the innocence in his eyes wink out like a candle flame as his soul expired and the evil came blazing to the fore. She'd played a part in the destruction of that boy, had taken away his innocence with her diseased twat, allowing the demon to take full control, allowing it to enter the world. And now it wanted to fuck her again. Cringing inside, Gloria stumbled up from the couch and into the bathroom to find her heroin works.

She wrapped the surgical tubing around her left bicep and heated up her last balloon of heroin in a spoon held over the stove. To hell with rationing out the little junk she had left, just to keep from getting sick. Gloria needed to get high, as high as she possibly could. She shot her veins with all the heroin she had left. Minutes later she was drifting away. She'd figure out what to do for her next hit after she came down.

If only I had enough heroin to never wake up again, she thought, as she fell into a deep haze.

Slowly the sun slid from the sky and crashed against the horizon, bleeding fiery oranges, yellows, and reds across the sky and drowning Gloria's roach-infested apartment in shadows. She watched the pyrotechnics through a slowly dissipating drug-haze. By the time the darkness had completely taken over the sky, she was sober. That's when the geeks called again.

"How about pigs? We've got a whole kennel full of pigs that you could fuck for a grand."

"A grand?"

"That's all it's worth. The novelty has pretty much worn off the farm sex thing. People want to see women fucking more exotic animals. Now if you'd do the giraffe, then we could talk."

"I'll take the grand. When and where?"

"Back at the loft. Where else? Meet us here at midnight."

"Why so late?"

"Because it's already ten o'clock. It'll take you an hour just to get here and I'm sure you want to freshen up a little for the camera."

Ten o'clock? Had she really been out for that long?

"Yeah . . . uh . . . sure. I'll be there at midnight, but no more surprises. If I see anything that looks like you got it from Vlad, I'm out of there—right after I kick both of your asses."

"Don't worry. That guy freaks us out too. I don't think we'll be dealing with his ass anymore. He wanted us to hand over all the copies of that worm tape to him. We told him to go fuck himself. So you've got nothing to worry about."

Somehow Gloria doubted that. Vlad wasn't the type of guy to just go away. Not when he wanted something. If there was one thing being a smack-addicted porn queen had taught her, it was that there was always a reason to worry.

By the time Gloria's fifteen-year-old BMW pulled up outside the rundown old building, she was in the first stages of heroin withdrawal. Her skin felt as if a legion of ants had crawled beneath it. Her body temperature rose and plummeted. Gloria's teeth rattled while she simultaneously shivered and perspired. Her legs wobbled as she stepped from the car and walked into the loft/makeshift barn.

"Jesus, Gloria, you look like shit. How much weight have you lost?"

Gloria hadn't even noticed her body wasting away. She looked at herself in the mirror as she undressed. Her cheekbones were sharp and prominent, her ribcage jutted from her skin, and her eyes had sunken deep into her skull. Even her knees and elbows looked sharp and knobby. She couldn't remember the last time she'd eaten. All the drugs she'd been consuming had completely sapped her appetite.

"You look sick. Are you all right?"

"Do you have any toot? Any blow?"

"Sure. You want some X too?"

"Why not?" She shrugged.

Gloria snorted the blow and dry-swallowed two pink tabs of X. The geeks led her to the pigsty where three four-hundred-pound hogs wallowed in mud and excrement.

"Just get in there and do your thing. Oh, and afterwards you get to suck us off too. Just like old times."

Gloria turned away to stare at the pigs. Somehow she

found them less distasteful.

It took a while to get the pigs in the mood. Gloria sucked their mud-streaked cocks and jacked them off until they finally got the hint and began trying to mount her.

"Okay, roll camera!" Jordan shouted as the largest of the hogs clamped his hooves around Gloria's waist and slid its long slender cock inside of her.

"Suck the other one off while that one is fucking you!"

"Look like you're enjoying it, will you? Let it cum on your face. Now lick your lips!"

"See if you can get it to tit fuck you. Get the big one to fuck you in the ass. Turn and spread your ass-cheeks for the cameras so we can see. Stick out your tongue. Yeah, perfect. Hold that pose. Don't wipe it off. Let it drip down your chin. Perfect!"

They filmed for nearly an hour, with Gloria taking inch after inch of hog-dick in her mouth, ass, vagina, and between her big plastic tits. The camera zoomed in on her as she rose from the hog pen to show the mud and swine semen dripping from her various orifices.

"You know, that was pretty good. I think we can sell this," Colin said.

"Yeah, it's okay. But it's not going to make us rich. They show this type of shit on every other website. People come to our site looking for something special, not just another slut sucking up pig sperm." Jordan looked at Gloria with disgust and disappointment etched on his face.

"Are we done now? Because I'm tired and I really need to score before I crawl out of my skin." Gloria was standing naked in the middle of the room, trying to clean the mud and semen off her body with two filthy beach towels.

"I need something to wash that taste out of my mouth. Those fucking things tasted terrible. I'll never eat bacon again."

"Get her something to drink, Colin. Then maybe we can discuss the next scene."

"What next scene? You wanted me to fuck the pigs—I fucked the pigs! Now just give me my thousand bucks so I can get out of here." Gloria was starting to get that claustrophobic feeling again, like enemy forces were ringing her in.

Jordan nodded. "Just relax. It's not about the giraffe. I've got something else lined up and I'm willing to pay you almost as much. I'll get us some coffee and we'll discuss it." He looked across the room, then back at Colin. "Who's that?"

Gloria glanced up, looked across the room to see what Jordan was talking about.

Oh no.

She hadn't seen him in more than three months, but she'd heard his voice crawl through her phone just last night, aurally molesting her. The ring of red hair around his bald head, the ridiculously oversized gut hanging over his belt, that handlebar mustache, those cold black eyes, and those sharpened teeth were unmistakable. Her own personal Satan. Suddenly Gloria felt as if the air within the barn was beginning to cook, the oxygen being sucked out. She swooned and fell back against the pigsty.

Colin glanced up from watching the recorded footage on the tape and shook his head. "It's that fucking Vlad guy. The one who sold us the worms."

"What the fuck's he doing here?"

Colin raised an eyebrow, shrugged.

"Hey, man—I told you we don't have any more use for your services. So what the fuck are you doing on our set?" Jordan hadn't moved at all, and Gloria suspected Jordan must have sensed something. After all, Vlad was rather formidable.

Vlad approached them, ignoring Jordan's question and focusing directly on Gloria, shaking his head as he walked. "I'm very disappointed. Very. Gloria, my sweet. What did I tell you the last time we spoke?"

Gloria pulled the towel closer to her body, almost hugging it, as if it could shield her. It draped across her breasts, covered her torso.

"I seem to remember telling you that you work only for me. Am I mistaken? Did I not say this to you?"

"I, um." Gloria swallowed. She didn't know what to say to him—was his question rhetorical? Did he know exactly what he'd said to her—as she knew? Of course she remembered him saying that, had thought it strange. But should she admit it to him?

Colin approached Jordan and stood beside him, arms crossed over his chest, facing Vlad. "My partner asked if he can help you. You haven't answered."

Vlad smiled, revealing his razor-like fangs, and Colin backed up a step. "I was talking to Gloria. Surely you fellows have better manners than that."

Colin nodded, lower jaw unhinging slightly.

"Good. I was beginning to worry." Vlad turned back to Gloria. "Let's go."

She rose up from the floor and snatched her folded clothing from a chair.

"Hey, wait a sec," Jordan said, shaking his head as if waking from a deep sleep. "Gloria's working for us. I don't know if you're her pimp or her goddamned father and I don't care, but you can work out the money with her later. Right now we're making movies."

Vlad cocked his head. "Is that so?" He walked over to one of the tripod-mounted cameras and looked through the lens, then turned the camera toward the men and switched it on. "Let's film then."

Vlad slowly turned his head until he was facing the three hogs that had been released from the pen. He raised his hand and nodded, and the hogs raced across the room, sliding along animal feces and piles of straw, their hooves clicking when they made contact with the hardwood floor.

The men barely had time to scream as the hogs attacked in a mad frenzy, knocking Colin and Jordan to the floor, tearing at them with frothing jaws, biting into their faces, ripping out their throats. The men were shredded into unrecognizable pieces.

Gloria's shock was broken and she doubled over to vomit.

When the hogs were finished, they sat obediently beside the body parts and waited, as if for Vlad to make another command.

Vlad ignored them, took Gloria's hand, and led her into the street and away from the loft.

***

"You smell like pig shit," Vlad snapped, pulling Gloria through darkened streets, tripping over litter strewn about on the sidewalk. "Is that what you like? To smell like pig shit?"

Gloria stopped, yanked her hand away from Vlad's grip. "Fuck off!" She pulled her hand against her body and massaged the wrist. "You don't own me. No matter what you think."

"Oh, but I do. I do own you. I know everything about you, Gloria. Everything."

They stared at one another, a bizarre showdown in a dark alley, two urban gunfighters.

It unnerved her that he wouldn't look away, that he held his gaze far longer than she ever could, and she averted her eyes, studied the mound of dogshit smeared across a discarded sheet of newspaper. Her cheeks burned, and she glanced up again. He was still staring.

"You're like a goddamned serpent. They don't blink either."

Vlad's mouth curled into a smile.

Then she realized that he'd somehow gained the upper hand, that she had leaned forward almost in supplication and was looking up at him from that position. Almost as if she were bowing before him. Or cowering, like a whipped puppy.

"What do you want from me?" she whispered, afraid of his answer.

"I want you to stop with the drugs, first of all. I want you fresh, clear-headed." He held out his hand. "This isn't a good neighborhood. Let's go."

Stop with the drugs? Who's he kidding? Just a moment's hesitation before she gave her hand again, let him pull her down the alley.

***

He brought her home, made sure she was inside the building before disappearing into the night. He hadn't wanted anything after all, she guessed. Just for her not to be with anyone else.

When she was sure Vlad was gone, Gloria left her building, intending to score. There was the money from the two dead freaks, but it wouldn't get her far. She knew she'd end up doing whatever Vlad wanted. That goddamned addiction was strong than any repugnance she might have felt.

The geeks were dead—there went her X connection. Pot did nothing for her. The only thing she could really afford was crack, but she hated messing with that shit. It wasn't even that effective anymore.

Even at that hour, Times Square was lit up with neon signs and harsh streetlamps. Even cleaned up—Disney-fied—it still was a shitty area. She stepped inside the headshop on the corner of Forty-first and Eighth Avenue. The tiny store was adorned with magazine racks filled with porn, bootleg videos and DVDs in piles near the floor, and a glass-covered counter sporting the latest in drug paraphernalia.

"I'm looking for Manny," she said, leaning over the counter.

"Busted," the man working the store told her. "Earlier tonight."

"Fuck." Gloria rubbed her hands over her face. "Who's around?"

"No one. They all got busted."

"What do you mean, 'all'? How can that be?" She knew these guys didn't hang out together. There was no way the cops could have rounded them all up, not on the same night.

He shrugged, looked around. "Just go home, Gloria. Things are weird right now."

She tried the liquor store next door, the deli, the bodega. They all said the same thing: the dealers were gone. Busted.

This was bad. So bad . . . and she had the feeling that no matter where she went, it would be more of the same. Her head pounded, vision blurred. She managed to make it to the curb before throwing up into the gutter, spewing remnants of a dinner that had consisted of cheap booze, expensive drugs, and pig semen.

God! What had she done with her life? She stared at the vile mixture draining away in the street and began to sob, hanging on to the back end of a parked taxi. When did she become *this*? When had this become her life?

The vomit was burning her chin, and she wiped it away with her palm. Even the front of her jacket was coated with it.

She once had a life . . . Had someone who loved her, someone who knew who she was, what she did for a living but was willing to love her anyway. Ryan.

When she'd first met him at the Adult Film Awards in Vegas she'd thought he was just another sleazy producer. One of the hordes ogling the talent, trying to get sucked off beneath the table by a few of the more impressionable young actresses, in exchange for the promise of a starring role. It turned out he was just the old college friend of a porn producer who'd dragged him to the awards ceremony to show off for him.

She remembered taking an almost instant dislike to the fat, overdressed producer in the sharkskin suit and snakeskin cowboy boots, who sat wobbling around in the chair next to the handsome young man like some Irish-mafia version of Humpty-Dumpty. The producer's breath had smelled like cigar smoke and rotting pork and he had greeted her with a familiarity that suggested they had done business before, snaking one of his chubby ham-hands around her waist and pulling her close. Planting a clammy kiss on her cheek and a pat on her ass. Gloria had been so enamored by his companion that she'd endured the awful man's sophomoric groping and allowed herself to be dragged over to his table.

"Gloria! You look absolutely delicious, as always. I have a friend I want to introduce you to. Gloria, this is Ryan. He's flown all the way from New York just to meet you. He's a big fan of your movies. I tell you, Ryan, this little gal has got the best head in the business, and I've seen them all. No one sucks a cock like her. She won Best Oral scene two years in a row."

The overly gregarious butt broker had practically shoved Gloria into the chair next to Ryan, who looked just as flabbergasted as she felt. Ryan had risen as she sat and then settled back into his chair like a man is supposed to do when a lady joins the table, but it had been so long since anyone had treated Gloria like a lady.

Gloria was touched by Ryan's almost charming shyness.

He tipped his hat to her and even called her ma'am like some type of southern gentleman. His friend the producer made sure to whisper in her ear that Ryan had just sold a computer game for 1.5 million dollars, as if this news was supposed to make her drop to her knees instantly. Gloria was impressed again when Ryan appeared to be even more annoyed by his friend's brazenness than she had been.

"Gloria? Do you think you'd like to go out with me sometime?"

Something in his eyes had seemed so afraid of rejection that there was no way she could have turned him down. That night he'd flown her to New York on a chartered plane and there she'd stayed for the next ten years. Six of those years living with Ryan, sharing his wealth and his bed while still maintaining her career in porn.

If what she did for a living had bothered him at all, he never once gave indication of it. It had all seemed too perfect. She'd even been close to marrying him until he'd asked her to give up the drugs. She'd have rather he'd asked her to stop sucking cocks and licking pussy on camera.

"I just can't stand to see you destroying yourself like this. You're killing yourself with that junk"

"You've got it wrong. This is how I celebrate life. I don't want to die without experiencing the highest highs life can offer."

And so she had. The highest highs and now the lowest lows. Ryan had loved her and she'd thrown it all away in order to keep the party going. She'd thrown away all hope she'd ever had of having a normal family. It was after leaving Ryan that the drugs had really begun to take control and her career had nose-dived.

Sometimes Gloria would visit that old neighborhood—upper Manhattan, a decent neighborhood, certainly better than the one she lived in. A neighborhood where she once belonged. And where he still lived. She wondered if he would even recognize her. Or worse, if he did, would he shun her, treat her like shit, pretend to not know her? That terrified her, so she never sought that answer. The chance of it was too painful to imagine.

She began walking. North. And east. She knew where she was headed, even if she didn't understand why. Sometimes she just had to be there, pretend she still belonged. Pretend the fantasy was still her life.

Central Park didn't scare her, even in the middle of the night. There wasn't much she hadn't been through, not much left anyone could do to her short of murder that would make much of an impact. So she cut through the Park, crossed fields of grass just starting to sprout, past bronze statues of horses and dogs and heroic men riddled with graffiti, past a carousel long in need of a face-lift, until she reached the Seventy-second Street entrance. Fifth Avenue. She could barely remember having lived here, among the elite. In clean buildings with large apartments and no rats or roaches. Greeted by doormen who knew her name and handed her mail and dry cleaning. Waited on by maids who did the laundry and cleaned the dishes and made the beds.

She glanced at the cheap watch she had bought in Chinatown for five bucks. Almost seven a.m. She'd been wandering the streets for hours. Wooden benches lined the shoulder-high stone wall surrounding the park, and she sat, watching the building across the street, waiting for the flurry of commuters, an exodus of tenants heading for work.

She knew his routine better than he did, even though it had been months since her last trip uptown. Every day at seven-thirty, like clockwork, he left the building. So many times she'd wanted to follow him, get up the nerve to approach, but the idea of rejection terrified her. Better to watch from a distance.

He was late this morning, but only by ten minutes. God, he looked good! So handsome . . . so *normal*. That's all she wanted. Normal.

And there she was, across the street, holding his hand. Looking adoringly at him as he wrapped his arm around her shoulders.

Gloria leaned forward, unsure of what she was seeing. What the hell was *she* doing here? Gloria tried to swallow but her mouth and throat had gone dry, tried to seize up. The cobblestoned ground rushed at Gloria as she stumbled to her knees, climbed back up to her feet and moved toward the street. She crouched behind a car and stared at them across the avenue.

She looked so beautiful . . . her long blonde hair tied behind her head in a ponytail. More like a photograph. Too perfect to be real.

Just like her mother, once upon a time.

"Why isn't she at school?" Gloria muttered, covering her mouth with a hand that still smelled faintly of vomit. Angela had been in one of the country's finest boarding school since she was six years old—right before Gloria left her family— ten years earlier. And as far as she knew, that's where Angela had stayed. In the years she had been coming back to watch Ryan's daily activities, she hadn't seen Angela, except during summer vacations or holidays. It was April now—Easter break had ended weeks earlier, and school wouldn't let out for the year until mid-June. Maybe someone had died, maybe that's why the girl was back. Maybe it was a special vacation she and her father had planned. Maybe Gloria was hallucinating and Angela wasn't there at all. What the hell did it matter? It wasn't so much that it mattered . . . it was the shock of unexpectedly seeing the girl, being unprepared for it. Feeling that aching want return, that incredible need to be with her daughter, her only child.

And knowing it would never happen.

She drifted away, sneaking back into the park before they spotted her, and made her way home.

***

Vlad had gotten his way, yet again. She'd been unable to score anything at all, not even a goddamned Vicodin. She spent the morning vomiting, fighting fever and chills and a massive headache, all thanks to her addiction trying not to flee her body. *Just one hit, Gloria . . . that's all we need. You'll feel good again. Trust us!*

Too weak now to even crawl to the toilet to puke, so she used a bucket at the side of her bed. Not much left to throw up anyway. Her stomach was empty, and all that was coming up was yellowish bile. This didn't worry her—if she started spewing blood, then she'd worry.

With fever-swollen eyes she stared across the room, looked at Vlad sitting in a chair by the window. She was about to yell at him and realized she had to be imagining it, he couldn't have gotten into her apartment. The building was old, the doors constructed of steel back when builders knew how to make things that last. Several locks and a deadbolt made break-ins impossible.

"You're not hallucinating," he said, snapping his newspaper as if gearing up to turn the page.

"How'd you get in here?" she mumbled, still not sure she was talking to the actual Vlad or to his apparition.

"You look awful. How long before you get over this withdrawal? I'm a patient man, but my customer isn't."

She groaned and fell back onto the pillow. "Get out of my apartment."

"Get up, Gloria. I have something for you."

She couldn't get up if she wanted to—and she didn't want to. Oh, here was something new for her personal enjoyment: the headache had intensified to such a degree that she could see auras surrounding the objects in the room. She squeezed her eyes shut until it hurt, until she thought blood vessels would rupture.

"I'll come over there, then."

She heard him approach, heard his feet padding across the worn, filthy carpeting. Seconds later he had crossed the tiny bedroom and sat beside her on the bed.

"Look at me."

Slowly she opened her eyes, fighting against the pain, against the burning blur that had overtaken her vision, blinking back tears that had formed because of the heat and pain and nothing else.

He offered her a glass of water—and two pills. She licked her lips, almost started to salivate at the sight of those pills, accepted them eagerly and dry-swallowed, not caring what the hell they might be. He could have slipped her cyanide and it wouldn't have mattered.

"Get up, Gloria."

She was about to protest—to complain about her pain and suffering when she realized that this was no longer true. No more pain. No more headache and burning eyes and shivering body and crawling flesh.

"What did you give me?" She sat up, crossed her hands over her throat. "My God, what did you give me?"

That weasel-grin formed on his face again. "I don't have time to watch you suffer, as much as I would have enjoyed that. I told you, my client is not as patient as I am. And I know you would have suffered for at least a week. Maybe some other time for that, eh?"

She sighed, nodded. Didn't know what else to do, what to say. How could she be grateful to a man she utterly despised, one who repulsed and terrified her—but had saved her from so much agony?

The addiction was gone; she was no longer trapped in its stranglehold.

"You couldn't have gotten hold of anything stronger than baby aspirin anyway. Trust me." That vile grin turned into a laugh. The expression on his face was happy enough, but she saw that his eyes remained cold. Empty. The smile never touched his eyes.

"It *was* you, then? The dealers?"

"Of course it was me. You think the police are capable of doing that much? They can barely do their own job, never mind doing something so extraordinary." He leaned over until he was resting on his side, head cupped in his palm. "I always get what I want. Always."

"So what do you want?" she asked quietly, unsure that the words had come from her own mouth. She certainly hadn't meant to ask; the words just popped out on their own.

"Get dressed, put on a nice dress. But shower first. *Please.* You still smell like pig shit. And now you smell like vomit as well." He shook his head. "You're quite a classy lady, Gloria."

***

She followed him out of the building and into the taxi he had hailed.

"Where are we going?"

"It's a surprise," he said, leaning back into the seat.

Surprises weren't something she much enjoyed. A surprise didn't have to be something good—and in her experience, they usually weren't.

"How much are you paying me?"

"You mean over and above that miracle cure for your addiction?"

"You only did that for your client, not for me. You don't give a shit if I suffer, you said so yourself. So don't try to pass that off as payment—I'd rather go through with the withdrawals."

Vlad chuckled. "At last you know how to negotiate. All right. You're getting a hundred thousand for today's work."

Gloria was torn between feeling absolutely ecstatic over that amount and extreme terror at wondering what she'd have to *do* for that much money. Traffic outside the cab whirred by as the driver took them north along the East River Drive. The normally congested Drive was unusually clear that evening; their cab always seemed to get around the rest of the vehicles. Almost seemed to float past them.

"Where are we going?" she asked again as they got off the Sixty-ninth Street exit and headed west, toward Central Park. There was no reason to worry, yet a lump lodged itself in her stomach as she realized where it appeared they were headed. But that was impossible. Even if Vlad knew where they lived, why would he bring her there?

He stroked her cheek with his forefinger and shook his head. "We're almost there. Don't ask so many questions."

The cab stopped on Fifth Avenue and Seventy-second Street, and the blood rushing to Gloria's head made her dizzy. "Why did we stop here? Please, we have to go. I can't go here."

Vlad took her hand after he paid the fare and led her out of

51

the cab. And she followed, filled with dread and terror as they entered her former building and moved toward the elevators. When he pressed the button for the seventeenth floor, she thought she was going to pass out. She wished she would drop dead.

"I can't do this," she said, reaching for the Door Open button, but he took her hands and pushed them down.

"You can and you will."

They reached the floor and exited the elevator, and headed down the hallway toward a world she thought she'd never see again, even in her dreams. An existence foreign and frightening to her now. To people she no longer knew.

They entered the apartment, and it was as if she had never left. The same art adorned the walls, the furniture had obviously been replaced through the years but the style was remarkably similar to what she had been used to. Same hardwood floors leading from the foyer to the living room and den, buffed and waxed to an almost blinding sheen. Even the umbrella stand by the front door was the same. It was as if time had stood still in this place.

"Have a seat in the living room," Vlad said. "We'll join you in a moment. I trust you remember where it is?"

She nodded and wandered toward the living room, sat on the sofa beside the fireplace. A small pile of wood was stacked haphazardly against the wall.

"We're ready," Vlad said, entering the room. "Come with me."

Still used to commands, especially for money. Gloria followed without thinking, without considering the consequences, the thought of a hundred grand propelling her. What did she care what Vlad wanted? Maybe Ryan had turned kinky. Stranger things had happened.

They entered the room that had once been the master bedroom but now appeared to be something else. It was bathed in darkness, so it was hard to tell what was in there, but there didn't seem to be a bed or other furniture. In fact, all she could make out in the extraordinarily dim light was a large table in the center of the room.

She could hear breathing, from someone other than Vlad. Some *ones* other than Vlad.

A mewling noise filled her ears, and she wondered what a cat was doing in the room. She also wondered just how strange this was going to become.

"Vlad?" she whispered, groping in the darkness for his arm, but he was no longer by her side. "Vlad?" she said louder, stopping where she was, afraid to move any further.

Matches were struck, and several candles were lit. The room was awash with flickering, faint light, but enough so that she could now see the room more clearly.

Vlad stood by the table—a table that she thought had been their dining room table, a large mahogany piece they had gotten from the Ethan Allen gallery. He was covering it with a sheet.

Across the room stood Ryan—and beside him, Angela.

Gloria clamped her hand over her mouth and stifled a cry. This was too bizarre, and she didn't know why she was here, what they were planning. Her legs refused to obey and stayed fused to the same spot.

"Ryan?" she said through splayed fingers.

"Hi, Gloria." He smiled at her, even gave a little wave.

"What . . . what are you doing here? Are you involved with him too?"

"You mean Vlad? He and I go waaay back. Don't you remember? He's the one who introduced us."

That was impossible. How could she not have remembered? It had been a long time ago, sure, but you didn't forget someone like Vlad. But on some level, Gloria did remember. When she'd first seen him on the street, she'd thought he looked familiar but figured he was probably just a john from her long and sordid past. Now it was coming together.

How long had this evil fat fuck been messing with her life?

She wanted to approach Ryan and Angela, had even tried to move her foot in their direction but something compelled her to remain where she was. Still too afraid to approach them. Still terrified of that rejection, even though she was standing in the same room with them.

"Go give your mother a hug," Ryan said, and Angela walked across the room and approached Gloria.

Gloria gasped, choked back a sob as her daughter threw her arms around Gloria's waist and squeezed. Gloria buried her face in Angela's hair and inhaled the sweet scent of her child. Unable to speak. Unable to do anything but sob into the girl's blonde hair.

Angela withdrew from the hug and returned to her father's side. Her face was devoid of expression, as if she were sleepwalking.

"All right," Vlad said. "We ready to begin?"

Ryan smiled, nodded. "We are."

Gloria looked from person to person and tried to get a feeling for what they were planning, but they weren't giving any clues. What could they possibly want from her, with her child in the room? With *Ryan's* child in the room? Surely he wouldn't let anything happen to Angela.

Vlad motioned for Gloria to join him at the table, and slowly she walked toward him.

"Here's the thing," Vlad said. He chewed his lip and looked like he was trying to choose the right words. "First of all, there's no backing out of this. Not that you had a choice in the matter to begin with, but I'm telling you now that you can't leave.

"Second, you will do exactly as you're told. If you try to disobey, not only will you be forced to do as you're told, but you won't be paid. Am I clear?"

Gloria opened her mouth, shut it. "Well yeah, but—"

He interrupted her. "That's all you need to say. That you understand what I've told you."

"What exactly do I have to do?"

His grin would have been better suited on a jackal. "Ryan—would you like to give dear Gloria the details?"

Ryan stepped forward and moved close to Gloria. "It's simple. But first, let me give you a little background." He rubbed his hands together as if he was trying to spark a fire. "You're a grandmother, Gloria. Your daughter gave birth to your granddaughter."

Gloria's head snapped in Angela's direction and studied her sixteen-year-old daughter. The girl looked bored, even yawned and cocked her head.

"How? How could you let that happen?" she yelled at Ryan.

"How could I let that happen?" He laughed. "I'm not exactly pleased with this development myself. She was supposed to have Vlad's child."

"What? No. *No.* Tell me you didn't let that pervert near my baby. Tell me he didn't touch her."

"No, he hasn't touched her yet. But I have."

The room started spinning, and Gloria gripped the table for support. She looked at Ryan and whispered, "Is the baby yours?"

"I doubt that. Among other things, you gave me a rather nasty case of syphilis that went undiagnosed just long enough to make me sterile. The little ankle biter isn't mine and she won't give up the father's name. I tried to get her to tell but she's every bit as stubborn as her whore of a mother. So off she goes, back to boarding school, carrying that little parasite inside of her. Then the school calls me—Sir, do you know that your daughter is pregnant? Heh. They ship her home with her stomach sticking out like a fucking beach ball. I was so fucking mad I wanted to rip her open and pull the bastard right out of her. But too many people had seen Angela pregnant, so we had no choice but to carry it to term."

Gloria sucked in a breath. She looked at Angela, who still looked bored, like she wanted to be anywhere but here. This little routine was apparently a major inconvenience for the teen. Vlad's Cheshire grin spread even wider.

"So we don't want the kid." He reached down and lifted up Angela's shirt, revealing the cigarette burns around her areolas. "I've convinced Angela that she doesn't want it either."

"You sick son of a bitch! You're worse than this fat freak. She's your own daughter!"

Ryan shrugged.

"So—what does all this mean? You want me to take the child?"

"Not exactly." Ryan turned to Angela. "Get her."

Angela moved to the corner of the room and approached a basket that Gloria hadn't noticed before, and lifted the infant out. It (*she*) started to cry, and Gloria recognized that mewling bleat as the noise she had thought belonged to a cat.

Angela placed the baby on the table.

Vlad reached beneath the table and pulled out a butcher knife, offering it to Gloria. "Remember what I said. You have no choice in the matter. You will do as you're told, or you will be *made* to do as you're told."

Gloria shook her head, started to back away from the table. "You're crazy. You're out of your fucking minds!" She stared with bulging eyes at the infant wriggling on the table. "Why me? Why do you want *me* to do this?"

Vlad templed his fingers beneath his chin. "You see, my dear, there's a demon waiting for you in Hell, waiting to fuck you raw for the rest of eternity. You kill your granddaughter and you're guaranteed a trip to inferno where your demon lover will greet you with open arms and bulging cock. Or you can let Angela kill her and she can go to Hell in your place. I don't think her young pussy can accommodate a cock that size. She's tight as a virgin, not like momma's old stretched-out snatch. But I'm sure he won't mind tearing it a little to make it fit."

What little color that remained in Gloria's anemic complexion drained away as she stared in horror at Ryan. This was not the man she had known. Her sweet, shy, loving Ryan, who had always seemed so awed and intimidated by her. This evil thing could not have been the same man.

"But why? Why would you do this? I loved you."

"Because I'm dying too, you filthy fucking slut! You killed me with your diseases! You've killed us both! But I don't want to die. I'm not going to die. I refuse. And Vlad is going to cure me. As soon as I help him get you. You or her." He pointed at his daughter and for the first time Angela showed a hint of genuine emotion, flinching away from Ryan's finger as if it were the barrel of a loaded gun pointed at her face.

"You mean . . ."

"Yes. I have AIDS. You gave it to me. I loved you—and you killed me." His lips twisted into a sneer of profound disgust, as if he had a mouth full of bile and was looking for a place to spit it.

"I didn't know. I swear I didn't know. I hadn't been diagnosed when we were together. We'd been separated for almost three years before I found out."

"I don't give a fuck if you knew or not! What does that change? You want me to forgive you or something? Fuck you! You want my forgiveness? Then kill that little bastard and give me my life back!"

There was a desperate madness in Ryan's eyes. Fear of his own extinction had driven him right out of his mind.

"But if you have it, then . . ."

"Yeah, Angela's HIV positive, but so far she doesn't have any symptoms, and her kid appears to be fine. But who knows? We all might be dying anyway."

Gloria turned toward Angela, her eyes brimming with tears. "Oh my god. No! Not you too!"

Angela nodded, stared at the floor. "I was diagnosed last month. None of this matters now. You might as well just do what they want." The little teenager stared at both mother and father with an expression that boiled with hatred and a bitter resignation.

Gloria's eyes swept the floor as she turned away from that fearsome gaze. What could she say to defend herself? She had left her only daughter in the care of a rapist and pederast who had molested her and given her AIDS; a disease he had caught from Gloria herself. She was just as guilty as Ryan.

"You'd let your whole family die just so you can live a while longer? Even your own daughter?"

"I can always start a new family. I'm young. I'm fucking rich. I can meet a new woman and start a new life without the taint of your filth and disease to ruin it."

"Then what?"

"What do you mean?"

"I mean, if I kill the baby, then I'll go to Hell, but eventually you'll die too, and where do you think you'll be headed?"

57

"That's not for a long time, sweetheart. All I'm worried about is the here and now and right here, right now, you need to decide which one of you is going to spend the rest of time in Hell getting their insides dug out and rearranged by that demon's dick."

Unclouded by narcotics for the first time in years, Gloria's mind struggled to find a way out. Ryan and Vlad flanked her on either side. And in front of her stood the daughter she'd abandoned—and the granddaughter she was supposed to murder. There had to be a way out of this. But she couldn't imagine what that was.

For the first time in years, she began to pray. She fell to her knees and began to cry. "Our Father, who art in Heaven . . ."

Vlad stepped forward. "Stop that."

" . . . Hallowed be thy name . . ."

"I said stop that!"

"Thy kingdom come, Thy will be done, on earth as it is in Heaven."

"*I SAID STOP!*"

Vlad's fist collided with Gloria's jaw, spinning her around like a piñata. She collapsed on the floor in a heap. Eyes closed, facedown on the polished hardwood floor, she feigned unconsciousness. More time to think.

***

How did things turn out so wrong? she wondered for the millionth time.

From her prone position on the floor, hovering above her, Vlad and Ryan were discussing her fate—and the fates of Angela and the child.

"She'll never do it," Ryan said. "She may be a whore and a drug addict but she's no killer."

"Everyone has their price. Besides, she has no choice. She may not care about her own life, but I'm betting she cares about those little girls over there. Did you know that she's been coming by here almost every week for years, just to catch a glimpse of the two of you? She knew your schedule better than you did. She's even gone to Angela's school a few times. She loves you. Both of you. Even now. And she knows that I won't hesitate to tear you, little Angela and her little bastard apart to get what I want." Vlad's voice billowed out in a dense humid cloud of halitosis that made Gloria's eyes water.

Gloria's head was turned in an awkward angle, and it ached. But if they knew she was awake, she'd be out of time again. She cracked her eyes open, trying to get the tiniest hint of her surroundings. Vlad and Ryan were flanking her other side, and when she peeked out, she caught Angela's attention. She was afraid her daughter would give her away, but Angela didn't change her expression.

Gloria licked her lips and mouthed the word *run*. She prayed her daughter would understand, and would act on it. How, she couldn't imagine. Was there even a way out of that room? Could she get past Ryan and Vlad?

"Dad?" Angela's voice cracked.

"What? Why are you interrupting us?"

"I need to change her." The baby was cradled in Angela's arm.

"Stay put. The baby can wait."

"No she can't. She smells."

Ryan sighed. "Fine. You've got three minutes."

Angela disappeared from Gloria's sight.

"Let's get this bitch off the floor," Vlad said. "Put her on the table."

She felt their hands beneath her armpits and she was lifted into the air. The table was cold beneath her clothes, and she suppressed a shudder.

"I'll just make her do it," Ryan said. "Even if I hold her hand, force her to kill the baby."

"No. Won't work that way. If you help her, you might as well do it yourself—she won't burn in Hell, you will. She has to do it herself, using her own will. Otherwise the deal's off."

"Fuck you, then." Ryan slammed his hand on the table. "You know I won't be able get her to kill that fucking kid—so I might as well kill this bitch right now."

She felt the cold steel blade resting against her neck, and

she began to tremble. Tears flowed into her temples from the corners of her eyes.

"I *knew* she was awake." Ryan laughed, withdrew the knife.

Gloria opened her eyes, looked up at Ryan. "Please don't do this," she whispered. "I'll do anything you want."

"Oh, like what? Have sex with me? Kill me all over again?"

"No, Ryan . . . I loved you."

"You have a funny way of showing love, Gloria."

She sat up, rubbed her aching head. "Can't we work something out?"

"Where's that kid of yours?" Vlad asked. "She's been gone too long."

"She's changing the shitty diaper." He glanced at his watch. "I'll go check."

Gloria was sitting on the edge of the table, legs dangling, and Vlad slid between her thighs. He leaned into her until their foreheads were touching. "I can make this miserable for you. I can make you suffer."

"Your breath already is."

"Very foolish to make jokes right now, Gloria."

"Who's joking?"

He leaned his head back a few inches but stayed between her legs, pressed himself against her. "You know what I'm capable of. You've seen what I can do."

She nodded. "But I also know that you need me. Otherwise you would have killed me by now."

"I'm just making your transition to Hell complete, Gloria. Don't think you ever had any hope of anything else—not with your past."

"So that's it? I'm an easy target? What, do you get bonus points for every soul you condemn to Hell?"

He smiled. "Something like that."

"She's gone," Ryan said, rushing into the room. "They're gone."

"What do you mean, 'gone'?" Vlad snapped.

"I searched the fucking apartment. They're gone."

Vlad stepped back, his eyes slitted, his upper lip twitching. "Where the fuck would she go?"

Ryan ran his hand over his hair and dropped his head. His way of producing deep thoughts, Gloria knew. Or his way of attempting to, at least. "The park, probably."

"Central Park? At this hour?"

Ryan nodded. "Shouldn't be that hard to find. Young girl carrying a baby."

"Let's go then. What can we do with her?" Vlad jerked his head toward Gloria.

Ryan dropped his head again, scratched his scalp this time. Then grabbed Gloria's wrist and yanked her off the table, pulled her behind him down the hall and into another bedroom. He threw her inside a small closet and slammed the door.

The closet was pitch black. A small crack of light tried to sneak in through the bottom of the door. She heard something scrape along the floor, then bash against the closet door. She assumed it was a chair or a large piece of furniture.

There was no point in yelling or crying or protesting. They weren't letting her out of that closet. She sank to the floor and rested against a pile of shoes and boxes, pulled her knees against her chest. She thought she would be terrified right now but found herself numb, found that she was resigned to her dreadful fate and just wished they would get it over with.

There was no way she was going to kill that baby. She didn't care what Vlad did to her.

About ten minutes had passed, she guessed, when she heard the noises outside the closet door. Scraping sounds, grunting. And a minute later, the door opened.

Angela held out her hand, and Gloria took it, got up off the floor.

"Where's the baby?"

"In her crib. We were hiding when Dad was searching the apartment. I left the front door open a crack so he would think I had left."

Gloria hugged her daughter, held her face in her palms. "I always knew you were a smart girl."

Angela smiled, a blush blossoming on her cheeks. "Where can we go?"

"Anywhere but here."

Gloria followed her to Angela's bedroom, and they gathered the baby from the crib.

"Let's get the hell out of here," Gloria said, leading them to the front foyer. She threw open the door, and Vlad and Ryan were waiting on the other side.

"Good try," Ryan said. "But I'm not stupid you know." He pushed his way into the apartment before Gloria could slam the door shut.

Angela began to scream, and Vlad wrapped his hand over her mouth.

Ryan shoved Gloria, sent her reeling down the hall. They were headed back in the direction of that black room, the room where they expected her to murder a baby.

Vlad threw Angela into the room, and she went tripping in until she stopped herself against the far wall. Vlad had already taken the baby from her.

Ryan had his hand clamped on the back of Gloria's neck and pushed her inside the room as well.

Vlad lay the baby on the table, unwrapped the blanket, her small legs kicking, small hands groping air. He lifted the knife, turned to face Gloria.

"Games are over. No more stalling. No more bullshit. If you try to pray, I will cut out your tongue. I swear to God I will." He smiled at his little joke. "Listen to me, and listen very carefully. You *will* do this, and you'll do it now. I'm out of patience. Do it now!"

He handed the butcher knife to Gloria, and she dropped it to the floor. "I won't do it." He couldn't stop her from praying in her head. *God, it's been a long time since we spoke. Since I've asked you for anything at all. Please get us out of this. Please save Angela and her baby.*

She didn't expect an answer. God had remained strangely silent for most of her life. But if He was there, and if He was listening, maybe He would help her. Though she knew better.

Vlad nodded. "I expected as much. I really can't understand

why you would choose to fight me when you know I always win."

His calm demeanor was more frightening to her than his anger was.

She tried to lick her lips but had no spit. She sucked in a breath, took a step back.

Vlad picked the knife up off the floor and slowly approached her. Gloria had backed up into the table and clutched it now, digging her nails into the wood.

He grabbed her shoulders and pulled her to the floor. When she was flat on her back, struggling beneath him, kicking her legs, he planted his knees on her shoulders, pinning her down. Grabbed her by the hair and pressed the knife against her face.

"The Lord is muh-my Shepherd . . ." she said, her body shaking, her breath seizing in her lungs.

"No atheists in foxholes. Right?" Vlad dropped his head forward, leaned in to Gloria's ear. "And if thy right eye offend thee, pluck it out, and cast it from thee: for it is profitable for thee that one of thy members should perish, and not that thy whole body should be cast into Hell.

"One thing at a time, I always say."

He lifted the knife and laid it against the outside of her eye. She cringed, tried to move her head but he held her too tightly. She squeezed her eyes shut and felt the point of the blade touch the lid. Less than a second later it penetrated; she felt the blade digging around inside her eye, felt the warm fluid pour from the wound and trickle into her ear. Heard a slight squeaky plop.

Then the pain hit, and she screamed, writhing beneath Vlad, wanting to escape him, wanting to comfort her wounded eye. Then he climbed off, and she pressed her hand against her eye. Eye *socket*, really. Nothing there but blood streaming from a hollow point in her head.

"Mom!" Angela screamed. "No!"

Gloria leaned forward and vomited. On her hands and knees, she tried to get up but slipped in her own blood.

Vlad handed her a towel and directed her hand to it, pressed it against her wound.

The eye couldn't be missing. Couldn't be. This couldn't be happening.

She managed to look up using her good eye. Vlad was in front of her, his feet planted wide. On the end of the knife he still held was her eyeball.

"Get up, Gloria. Let's get this over with."

"No . . ." she moaned, using the table to pull herself up on quivering legs.

"All right. It appears that torturing you won't make much difference." He turned his head in Ryan's direction. "Fuck her," he said, indicating Angela. "I'll fuck her when you're finished."

Not even a moment's hesitation and Ryan was unzipping his pants.

Angela started sobbing, begging her father not to.

"Wait," Gloria said, extending her hand toward them. Speaking was difficult, exhausting. "Don't do it. Please."

Vlad pulled the eyeball off the blade tip and popped it into his mouth, chewing slowly, viscous fluid oozing from between his lips. He flipped the knife around in his hand and offered it to her shaft-first. "Do it now, Gloria."

"Please don't, Mom . . ." Angela cried. "Please!"

She raised the knife over the infant, stared with her one eye at the innocent child lying on the cold table. As horrible as the rape of her daughter would be, this was worse.

She slowly lowered the knife.

Vlad nodded, and Ryan pushed his hysterical daughter to the floor. Gloria turned away, away from the noises of zippers and tearing clothes and sex-grunts from her daughter's muffled cries from beneath a hand over her mouth. Then Ryan was moaning, breathing hard. And Angela was sobbing.

"We can do this all night," Vlad said to Gloria. "And after we fuck her a while, then the real fun will begin. Can't you see yet? You can't win."

Gloria sobbed, pressed the towel against her eye. The pain was excruciating but she would go through it again if Angela didn't have to suffer like this.

Vlad handed Ryan the knife as Ryan stood, then replaced

Ryan between Angela's thighs.

"No!" Angela shrieked, and Vlad was inside her, slamming hard, moving her along on the floor with his thrusts. He reached up and viciously squeezed her breasts.

Gloria couldn't feel her legs anymore and slumped to the floor.

Vlad finished even faster than Ryan had. He pulled away from the girl and stood beside Ryan. "You ready for another go yet?"

"No. Not yet."

"Okay then. We'll have to do something else."

Gloria looked up, shook her head. "No more. Please, no more."

"We're just getting started," Vlad said. He went back over to Angela and dragged her across the floor by her hair. The sobbing girl was dumped by Gloria's feet.

Gloria reached down and stroked Angela's hair, wanting to comfort the child.

Angela cocked her head until she was facing her mother, and said through hitching breaths, "Maybe you should do it . . . I don't think I can take any more of this."

Gloria nodded. "I understand, believe me. But we can't kill the baby. We can't!"

Angela cried even harder and wiped tears from her cheeks.

"I think you're ready for another round," Vlad said, standing over them. He had retrieved an item that he was now hiding behind his back. He grabbed Angela's thigh and pulled her toward him, put the object on the floor so he could flip her around.

In Gloria's line of work, she had seen thousands of sex toys, including some custom made, some homemade, but she'd never seen anything like this. An oversized dildo, at least twenty-two inches in length and half a foot in circumference with thick veins that appeared to be coursing with blood. Studded up and down the shaft with small thorns that seemed to be growing out of it rather than grafted on. It pulsed like it was alive, breathing, in apparent synchronicity with Vlad's own panting breaths.

"See, Gloria? We've got things much worse than donkeys and giraffes in Hell. Those worms were nothing compared to what's waiting for you. They're the lowest life forms. What most of *your* kind become when they pass into inferno. But some become other things. Bigger, nastier things."

Gloria remembered the worms screaming as she tore them apart, how she'd thought their cries sounded almost like words. She'd attributed it to the drugs. Now she knew better. Still, she felt no remorse for them. They must have been real scum to wind up as giant maggots in Hell. If only she was so lucky. Whatever her destiny in the afterlife, it was bound to be far worse. She looked back over at the dildo as it seemed to swell even larger, growing more erect with anticipation.

She shook her head, couldn't pull her attention away from the huge phallus in Vlad's fist. "You can't do this," she whispered. "Oh god, you can't do this."

"Me?" Vlad laughed. "No, not me. You." He lifted it higher, and the strap-on harness dangled below his wrist. "If you don't do it, then this thing goes up her ass, then down her throat. Am I clear on this?"

He tossed the dildo into Gloria's lap. "Get going."

Angela shut her eyes and turned away her head, but she didn't protest, didn't squeeze her legs tighter together.

Gloria tossed it away. "I'll do what you want," she said. "I won't do that to Angela. I can't hurt her."

"You'd rather kill the baby?" Vlad asked, sounding suspicious.

"I'd rather do neither," Gloria said icily. "But you're not leaving me with much of a choice. I know you won't stop torturing her. And I can't watch you do this to her any more. I won't."

"Do it then. If you fail me again—"

"I won't fail you." She took the knife from him after standing, and moved to the baby. Crying so hard she could barely get in enough air.

She raised the knife over her head with both hands. The towel fell to the floor, and the air hitting the wound brought a fresh bout of pain.

66

"Do it!" Vlad shrieked. "Do it now! I won't accept deception one more time."

Gloria tilted back her head, starting at the ceiling. "God forgive me for what I am about to do . . . I'm sorry. I'm so sorry." She brought her head down again and looked at her daughter. "Please forgive me for this. I'm too weak."

"Mom, please—" Angela stretched out her arm, but Vlad wouldn't let her move from where she was standing.

Gloria brought the knife down, hard. Blood sprayed from the wound, covering the table, the baby, her. She slumped forward, her head resting against the baby's chest, and dug the knife in deeper.

"No!" Vlad screamed, rushing toward Gloria.

"Mom!" Angela cried, grabbing Vlad's arm, trying to keep him away from her mother.

Gloria collapsed, leaning against the table leg to keep her upright.

The knife still protruded from her stomach.

Vlad slapped her hard across the face, and she tumbled onto her side. He kicked her in the ribs, kicked her again. "Bitch!" He started pacing, muttering unintelligible words, throwing his hands up in the air.

Angela slid across the floor until she was beside Gloria. She took her mother's hand and pressed it against her cheek. "I'm sorry, Mom." She looked up at Vlad, at Ryan. "Did I do okay?"

"You were wonderful, sweetheart," Ryan said.

"What?" Gloria strained to ask.

"Same deal as before," Vlad said. "Only we didn't think you'd actually kill the kid, so we came up with an alternative to the original plan. Suicide works as well as murder, Gloria. If it's any consolation, you really did save Angela from Hell. But at this rate . . ." He chucked Angela's chin. "She'll be spending lots of time with you. It'll be quite a family reunion."

"Go to hell . . ." Gloria said.

"After you, my dear."

Angela retrieved the grotesque dildo from the floor and handed it to Ryan. "You promised we could try this out."

Ryan wrapped his arm around her shoulders and led her

from the room.

Gloria felt her heartbeat slowing, had given up trying to cease the flow of blood from her wounds. The chilly room suddenly became a comfortable warmth, like a favorite blanket.

Gloria closed her eyes and her face settled into an expression of serenity and peace . . . even as her immortal soul began to scream.

Part II

"Nothing begins and nothing ends/That is not paid in moan;/
For we are born in other's pain,/And perish in our own."
—Francis Thompson, *"Daisy"*

"Today is bad, and day by day it will get worse—until at last
the worst of all arrives."
—Arthur Schopenhauer, *On the Suffering of the World*

Gloria's knees shook. The pain in her thighs wound tighter
and tighter, cramping, burning with lactic acid, melding with
the pain in her lower back, her neck, shoulders, and calves
into an absolute agony that washed away all other conscious
thought. Her world was only pain and confusion.

She knew where she was. The agonized screams that
echoed endlessly from all directions and her own ceaseless
torment told her all she needed to know about her surroundings.
Even though she could not see, Gloria knew she was in Hell.

She was imprisoned in some sort of cage. A small iron
cell into which her body had been tightly packed; squeezed
into in an uncomfortable squatting position, sitting almost
on her heels, her knees pressed up tight to her chest, breasts
squashed flat against her. The confines of her prison were
too cramped to allow her to shift positions and take some of
the pressure off her calves. The muscles burned, the tendons
strained beneath the weight of her body. Her body shivered
and shook. Perspiration trickled down her skin in a steady
stream as she bit her lip against the pain.

"Help. Help me. Oh God, I'm so sorry. I want to go home.
I'll do anything, just let me go home." Her voice was barely
more than a whisper. She'd been repeating the same prayers
for days, screaming them first at the listless walls and her
hostile tormentors until her vocal chords failed and she was
reduced to a hoarse squeak.

The bars of the cell were hot. Bits of her skin stuck to it,
sizzling and blackening from where she'd leaned against it in

exhaustion. She wasn't allowed to sleep; perpetual exhaustion was part of her torment. Sleep was a luxury of the blessed. Gloria was damned.

Gloria's head hung down between her knees from both the pressure of the scalding hot cage lid pressing down onto her cervical vertebrae branding stripes into the back of her neck and the weight of the ghastly necklace locked around her throat.

It was a thick iron collar hung with tiny putrefying corpses... fetuses. Another insult. Six in all. Each a different size representing the trimester in which they'd been aborted. Unwanted pregnancies had been an unfortunate occupational hazard. Gloria could smell the fetid reek of their decomposing flesh but could also feel their heartbeat fluttering against her chest. Their tiny hands and mouths groped for her nipples, starving for sustenance. Somehow they were alive, even while clearly rotting away. Their touch was an abomination that made Gloria's skin crawl.

She had no idea how long she'd been in her cell. It seemed like days. Her head was covered in some type of animal-skin sack cinched tight around her throat with twine. In its sweaty animal musk, she could smell the pain and fear the animal had died in. If it had died. Perhaps in this place animals lived on without their skin; raw muscle, and nerves exposed to the cruelties of Hell. Just as her own soul lay naked and exposed.

When she'd awakened in the darkness with the sack on her head and her body folded nearly in half, she'd screamed in terror, believing she would suffocate. She imagined that she could feel her own breath steaming back in her face. But Gloria wasn't breathing. She was dead. And where she was there would not have been enough oxygen to breathe even without the sack on her head. The flames consumed the oxygen breathing nothing but carbon dioxide back into the thin polluted atmosphere. Gloria's lungs expanded and contracted out of habit. She no longer needed oxygen to fuel her body.

Gloria's eyelids were pasted shut with tears; still she was awake. Not once since she'd woken in her cage had she been allowed to sleep. Whenever she dozed, she was cracked with a whip or poked with hot metal. The harsh voice of her demon lover barked orders at her, spittle flying from his lips and coating her in its vile spray. Sometimes he cooed softly and seductively, then would slide his enormous cock between the bars of the cage and masturbate on her. Sometimes he would urinate or defecate on her. The thick toxic sludge of his excrement coated her skin in a crusty shell. She was grateful for the sack over her head. It at least offered her face some measure of protection.

Gloria could not remember how long she'd been left to rot in that cage before the sack was finally removed from her head. How long it was before the day the demon released her from the cage in order to rape her. How her relief at being able to stretch her stiff tortured joints had turned to horror as the thing had assaulted her, tearing up her insides, fucking her for hours at a time until her body broke and bled. Then tossing her back into the cage to wait for her to heal so that he could break her again. Once it had begun, it seemed to go on forever. She could no longer distinguish the monster's first thrust into her torn and lacerated vagina from the last.

She knew that she was no longer flesh, yet still she bruised and bled, organs ruptured, and bones snapped and burst through the surface of her skin. The spirit was not at all what Gloria had expected it to be. It was not some ghostly wisp of ectoplasmic energy. It had substance and weight. Lighter than her flesh had been but still not the ghost she had imagined she would be. Her soul remained in the shape of her body and seemed to have all the vulnerabilities of flesh. She felt fatigue, nausea, anguish. Everything seemed to bring pain. Matter and energy cannot be created or destroyed but merely changed from one form to another. This soul could not die.

After every assault, her spirit body gradually resolved itself back into its original shape. Sometimes it took hours or even days but eventually, regardless of the severity of the injury, her body would reshape itself. Open wounds and shattered bone knitted back together. Severed appendages reattached or were regrown. Everything healed except the mind, which forever screamed in anguish.

71

Gloria's astral body seemed to feel pain so much more intensely than her flesh ever had. This she hadn't expected. No nerves, no skin, no muscle, yet still pain. All her senses in fact seemed to be heightened in this place. The smell of burning souls scalded her nostrils. The screams and prayers and curses were almost deafening. The taste of demon sweat and semen made her retch. And her own agony and fatigue was like nothing she'd ever experienced on earth.

It was as if her flesh had formed a protective cushion around her, dulling her perceptions and now, without it, she was exposed and vulnerable, a raw naked nerve screaming out beneath the assault of myriad sensations. The sensation of that yard long cock drilling up inside her, piercing and tearing deep into her soul. The sensation of the monster's acidic breath and saliva steaming in her face, sizzling on her skin as it slathered her face and body in thick pus-like saliva, tasting her terror. Gloria had been screaming for what seemed like years. The thing never seemed to stop fucking her, and no matter how many cocks she'd taken in life, not one of them had ever burrowed deep enough inside of her to touch her immortal spirit. No matter how much she'd thought she'd loved Ryan, he hadn't touched her soul. Her spirit had been a virgin when she'd come spinning into Hell. It had been pure and untouched when the demon had split it wide with its enormous cock. Now it was completely tainted. Its light, soiled and muddied, tacky with the monster's semen.

There were souls burning in the lake of fire that still believed they had a chance for forgiveness, that they might one day enter Heaven. Gloria had no such delusions. She looked at herself in the mirror through a dripping mask of black demon seed and knew that no God would ever take her now. She was a slut straight through to her eternal soul.

The demon was waking again. She could tell because his cock was stiffening even before his eyes fluttered open. Its urethra yawned wide like the mouth of a sleeping baby. Gloria began to whimper at the very sight of it. The pain was about to start again.

"No. Oh God, please don't hurt me again."

72

The soul did not acquire a tolerance for suffering the way the flesh could. Physical pain was something the spirit had never been meant to experience. Once liberated from the body, the spirit was supposed to ascend to paradise where all pain would forever be forgotten. The agonies of Hell had not been incorporated into its design.

This fragility was the very thing that made eternal torment possible. Each new intrusion of the demon's megalomorphic penis into one of Gloria's bleeding orifices was like the first time for her. The rape of a near virgin. Like a donkey fucking a ten-year-old . . . or a giraffe for that matter. Gloria grimaced. That was her one regret in life: not fucking that giraffe. If she had just fucked the animal, none of this would have happened. But then again, if she had never taken that first snort of cocaine or that first shot of heroin . . . If she'd never taken that first job when they'd said all she'd have to do is have sex with this gorgeous man that she'd have probably dropped her panties for anyway if she had just met him in a nightclub or a bar somewhere only this would be on camera and she would be getting paid. If she had never moved to Hollywood in the first place. If she had just stayed in her little town flipping burgers and sucking off the occasional truck driver in the hopes that he'd stay and marry her, none of this would have happened. But now the demon was rising and his cock looked more threatening and more lethal than the twin barrels of a shotgun.

The already massive organ swelled as the demon stroked itself. It gave the iron ring pierced through its urethra a tug, and it shivered in some sensation between pain and ecstasy. Its cock gleamed with steel and iron, like a piece of battlefield artillery.

"Please, don't. Don't hurt me again. I can't take anymore. Please, no more." Gloria sobbed, her eyes fixed on its hideous phallus.

The pierced, perforated, surgically altered and tattooed penis was as long as the arm of a basketball player. The head of its cock was as fat as a child's skull and encircled just beneath the mushroom cap with sharp barbs, so that once inserted, withdrawing it resulted in shredded tissue. Iron rings

73

hung from the underside, and a chain ran through it down to a steel rod pierced through the demon's perineum. At the base of the shaft, two more rods had been run clean through at an angle so that they criss-crossed in the shape of an X. It was lumpy with little iron balls that had been inserted beneath the skin. Gloria had never seen anything so ghastly.

She squeezed her eyes shut as he approached and prayed that all her tormentor wanted was a simple blowjob. She could manipulate her mouth to avoid the barbs as long as he didn't thrust too deeply into her throat. However, the taste of his molten black seed was worse than the taste of worm semen, and it burned like battery acid as it went down or splattered her face and breasts.

The barbs at the end of the thing's cock and the sharp horn-like protuberances of bone that lined the length of the shaft like a French tickler had shredded her lips and tongue like fajita meat as the beast had raped her throat just hours ago. She could still feel the thick caustic sperm boiling in the pit of her stomach, causing her intestines to cramp. She had swallowed as ordered, chugging half a gallon of the vile ebon effluence as it spurted into her gullet. To spit it out would have meant a severe beating, and if she dared to regurgitate she'd only be forced to lick it up off the cave floor.

The demon stood above her now, carrying a cat o' nine tails made out of thick chain and tipped with dog skulls. Gripped tightly in his other hand was a smaller one, made of chains that ended in nearly a dozen tiny rat skulls. He had used it once before to whip her breasts and clitoris. The miniature skulls had beaten against her vagina like clubs and occasionally one of the rodent's long front teeth would gouge a chunk out of her labia. Once her vagina had been beaten bloody, her clitoris a swollen and bloodied ruin, he had introduced his brutal phallus into it, further lacerating her already injured sex, matching his violent thrusts to her shrill cries for mercy.

There was already a sheen of oily black cum glistening on the head of the monster's thick pulsating organ. It dripped from the bulbous glans onto the volcanic rock floor and sizzled there like oil in a skillet. Gloria licked her lips enticingly but the demon was not interested in her mouth anymore. He ordered her to turn around. Gloria tried to scream but could only emit a helpless whimper.

Her new master was an arch demon, one of the original fallen angels, tossed into the lake of fire by the hand of the Almighty back when mankind was first summoned from the protoplasmic stew to walk upright across the earth. At times Gloria imagined she could see glimpses of the radiant angel he had been beneath the self-inflicted scars, burns, piercings, tattoos, and other body manipulations. The ram's horns grafted onto the side of his head. The rhinoceros horns that formed a neat row down the center of his spine along his coccyx. The gruesome smile that dominated his face where his lips and cheeks had been first cut away and then singed until they curled up tight around his gums, revealing a gleaming row of shark's teeth and wolf fangs. The bisected nose that splayed across his face, one nostril pinned to each cheek with a silver ring. Even his titanic sex organ was a bit of the demon's own artistry, the cock and balls of some antelope, a moose or a bull, with animal horns and spines embedded into it to further increase its capacity to injure. None of the creature's horrifying features were original. They had all been modifications inspired by eons in Hell as the torturer of sinful souls. Form followed function and his hulking form had taken on the shape of man's fears.

The demon reached out for Gloria with one massive hand. Each finger ended in a long claw or talon stolen from an alligator, large jungle cat, or some bird of prey. There was dried blood, some of it perhaps several centuries old, caked beneath the nails.

Her body shook when she felt the creature's touch. A hand clamped down on the back of her neck and bent her over until her head touched the cave floor. The first crack of the cat o' nine tails felt as if she had been kicked by a small crowd of people. The dog heads punched into her back with enough force to break ribs or shatter vertebrae. The chains raked her skin, tearing at her, drawing blood.

She landed face-first on the gravelly floor, the skin on her palms and knees and chin abraded raw. She tried to crawl away, to pull herself along on her fingertips but was crushed to the ground under another blow from the cat o' nine tails.

The gravel punched into her skin, left a trackwork of scars. "Please!" she shrieked.

The demon remained silent as he flailed at her with the dog heads.

"God please help me!"

God wasn't listening.

The demon grabbed her ankles and dragged her back along the floor until she was beneath him. His cock pushed against her ass. His clawed hands raked her back, grating the skin, exposing her spine. Massive fists crashed down on her, and she felt the vertebrae crunch, bits of bone exploding, crumbling down her sides. The pain was immeasurable, and to her horror she realized she was paralyzed. Every nerve ending was alive, sizzling like hornet stings, but now she couldn't get away.

He lifted her legs and forced her into a squatting position, her ass pointed up, exposed, her forehead crushed into the gravel floor. Lungs frozen . . . unable to scream, unable to beg for mercy that never came anyway. Tears dripped onto the floor.

Hands on her hips. Cock pushed into her cunt, slowly at first, and she knew he was toying with her, prolonging her agony. Entering wasn't the problem . . . the barbs decorating the base of the glans was the problem. He gripped her sides tighter, claws slicing her flesh. Drool dripped onto her back, searing the already tortured flesh.

He pushed harder, his twenty-two-inch cock digging deep, filling her cunt, entering her uterus. She screamed, her already damaged throat and lungs searching for more. As he pulled out, her cunt was stripped raw; she could feel the skin flayed, her insides burning like a sea of fire.

And he repeated this, slowly, slowly, until his motions increased in speed, until finally he came, his thick, viscous semen like battery acid. When he withdrew, he wiped his cum on her back, fingered her crushed spine, licked at the blood and shattered bone.

He dragged her back to her cage. She was an unrecognizable

76

lump of mutilated flesh, a pile of pulverized bones. Unable to move, he tucked her into an awkward, bent shape and slammed the door shut.

***

This time they let her sleep, though she didn't know why—there wasn't any compassion here.

Several feet below her cage the demon slept, its massive chest rising and falling with breath that she imagined didn't really exist. If she wasn't breathing, why would it? Probably the same as her—habit.

Her body was restored again; she was able to move. She couldn't imagine an eternity of this . . . the nonstop assault, the repeated agony. She knew she deserved to be punished, but hell—she hadn't done anything so horrible to deserve this. Had she? Even her suicide had saved another life. Surely there had to be some forgiveness . . .

But the demon wasn't talking. Refused to answer her questions, refused her mercy when she begged until her throat was screamed raw. Yet there had to be a way out of this.

The demon stirred, and her bowels cramped, her heart dropping into her stomach. But it didn't wake, and she sighed relief, her body trembling.

The bars of the cage singed her skin, no matter what her position. Kneeling left grooves like barbecue tracks in her knees and calves, her forehead seared by the bars.

She tried to reshift her position in the cramped cage, at the same time avoiding contact with the cage, but movement was impossible. The thick iron collar around her neck weighed her head down, and she tried to ignore the needy, rotting fetus corpses that reached out to her. Her shoulder bumped into the bars and scorched her skin, and she covered her mouth to keep from screaming. Leaning back, trying to stretch her aching spine, she bumped into the cage door. It creaked open, the rusty hinges screaming. Gloria glanced over her shoulder, shocked.

The door was unlocked.

But why would it have been locked? The demon slept right below—why would anyone even think of trying to escape?

But Gloria thought of escape. The idea of it actually made her salivate.

She glanced down. The floor was several feet away. Not an impossible distance, but she was squashed in that cage, unable to maneuver, unable to gain the leverage she needed. And if she fell the wrong way, she'd land on top of the demon. The only way to do this was to grab hold of the scorching bars. But a few moments of pain would be worth it if it meant freedom from this hellhole.

Gloria moved backwards until she was at the edge of the cage, until her ass hung out the door. Now squatting on her feet, the tender flesh there in agony. Leaned forward and gripped the bars on the floor, and swung her body out of the cage. Legs dangled in midair until she lowered herself, her feet scrabbling for purchase. A bit lower and she found the ground, and let go of the bars. Her fingers were unrecognizably mashed and bloodied stumps, burned nearly to the bone.

She didn't care. She knew she would heal, the pain would eventually subside.

But now—she was free.

***

Gloria crept cautiously out of the cave, trembling with every step, afraid the demon would awaken and drag her back inside. She reached the mouth of the cave and looked back over her shoulder at the sleeping demon. Then she ran, as hard and fast as she could down the long dark passage that led away from that torture chamber, unsure of where she was going. Dashing without direction through a vast labyrinthine honeycomb of caves and tunnels. Just trying to put distance between her and the demon. Gloria fled, stealing down the corridors, the only light on the pathway small human skulls fitted with dripping candles, hands caressing the cold, wet stone walls. From every corner came screams and wails, pleas for mercy, the hideous laughter of broken minds that had lost all hope and reason.

Sounds of whipcracks, of acetylene blowtorches popping into life, chainsaws, thuds like something hard hitting something squishy. Her mind raced, imagination working overtime. There was an exhilaration coursing through her as her naked feet pounded down the corridor and her sweaty, blood and semen soaked body parted the dense humid air. She was scared, terrified, but she was free. She almost felt like laughing, like shouting, but she was still in Hell, still in danger.

She wrapped her arms around her cold, naked flesh, repressing shudders. Nothing was following her at least; glances over her shoulder confirmed that.

Up ahead: brighter light. She wished there was some place to hide in the corridor, but the walls climbed endlessly, and she couldn't see any alcoves. So she had to press on, and hope that whatever was ahead wasn't worse than the torture she had just escaped.

A hundred feet ahead, she came to the entrance of a cavernous room. In the center was a bubbling river of lava. Thousands of people were thrashing about in it, clawing at the air, trying to reach the bank. Every time they moved, they were whipped back into place. As the fiery lava consumed their feet, they sank lower, until it dissolved their calves, thighs, torso, until nothing remained but a screaming head, begging for help as their flesh and bone melted down into that boiling sludge.

Naked souls shrieked in agony in that boiling lake. Their flesh had already been melted away and now only their spirit remained, burning there for all eternity, or until one of the demons took an interest and singled one out for special attention in the caves.

The demons controlling the room were as horrible and terrifying as the one that bastard Vlad had sold her to. They were massive creatures, adorned with chains containing dangling skulls, some of babies, some of animals; ram's horns, antlers, and tusks sprouted from their foreheads, curlicues of sharpened bone, jutting toward an intended victim. Huge, thickly muscled legs that ended in hooves, talons, or claws, thick black toenails clacking on the hard dirt floor.

79

Each carried a weapon more ornate than the one before it. Clubs studded with what looked like gigantic fishhooks, swords of sharpened steel fitted with razors, cat o' nine tails made of thick leather and bulky chain, axes heavy with dripping blood.

With all the horrible shrieks and screams and curses from the damned, the demons were perfectly silent. Just like the one she'd left back in the cave. Their eyes gleamed with lust and passion as they meted out brutal punishment in mute ferocity. Occasionally one of the demons would reach down into the boiling lake to wrench free a bit of loose flesh or skin from one of the burning victims before it was consumed by the flames. There were piles of such liberated tissue along the river banks.

"Oh, Jesus," she muttered into her hand, plastering herself against the wall. Praying that nothing down there had spotted her. Gloria could only guess what the re-appropriated material would later be used for. She searched the room with her eyes, hoping to find a place to escape, another door perhaps, but the room was surrounded by stone walls. The only way in or out was behind her.

The screams coming from this room—the pure anguish, heart-wrenching suffering—tore her heart from her chest. What had these people done to deserve this? What could anyone do to deserve this?

Several feet away, a demon worked relentlessly, using its razored claws to flay the skin from a woman's body, the layer of epidermis pink and pulsing and dotted with blood. Slowly it tore away the dermis, first from fingertips, moving back to wrists and arms, the skin separating in long, bloat-white strips, then moved to her shoulders, gouging claws into the flesh, creating chunnels, something for it to grab onto. Peeled back another layer, the flesh exposed now on her breasts and ribcage and stomach. The demon continued until the woman was a throbbing mass of blood-specked soft tissue and exposed nerves. It tossed the long strips of meat and skin onto a large pile and then threw the woman back into the burning lake. Then it reached in to grab another victim.

Around the cavern, countless images of torture, suffering.

Gloria sucked in, searching for a breath that no longer mattered. Her skin tingled as if attacked by insects. Several feet away, a man dangled from the impossibly high ceiling. Chains had been imbedded in his flesh, and he hung spread-eagle. The demon beside him lifted its weapon, a long, slender knife shaped like a cobra, its tip spread out as if the snake were about to strike. With surprising agility and speed, the demon impaled the man's bowels and lifted, dragging the knife through his torso in a fierce, upward movement. The man's intestines spilled from the jagged hole. His eyes rolled up, his face a frozen tapestry of pain and fear.

Gloria turned for the exit, unable to watch any longer, unable to accept what she was seeing. The exit remained unblocked, unguarded, and she fled, stumbling down another corridor, dazed and overwhelmed. She had escaped—but to what? There was nowhere to go. Hell was everywhere.

A tiny exhausted voice echoed from a cave just ahead of Gloria. "No! You can't! You can't do this! It's not fair!" The voice was familiar, though to Gloria it sounded broken and defeated. Just like her own voice.

The one thing Gloria took comfort in was knowing that she had saved her daughter, had sacrificed herself for Angela and the baby. Though Angela turned out to be something Gloria hadn't expected . . . but it didn't matter. Gloria would have given her life a thousand times to spare her child this agony.

Yet that voice, the child's voice pleading, the one now screaming, was unnervingly familiar. And Gloria knew that there were no real bargains in Hell, that she had traded her life and sacrificed her soul to damnation for nothing at all.

"Oh, God . . . Angela." A mother knew her child's voice, especially if that child was in pain. Gloria could have picked that sound from a chorus of thousands of crying children.

The crack of a whip followed the helpless little whimper. Then came shrill screams. Gloria ran toward it, inside a cave a few yards ahead.

Her daughter dangled from the ceiling by her arms nearly twenty feet off the ground. Angela's wrists were chained together, and she was suspended from some type of pulley

81

system. The end of the chain was held by a fat, hideous creature. The thing's body was covered in the same type of gildings that had covered the body of her demon, but this one was half the size. Human size, not an arch demon. Not one of the fallen angels. Whatever this thing was now, it had obviously once been a man.

A razor-barbed leash was gripped tightly in his other hand, and he was whipping Angela to shreds as she dangled helplessly nearly two stories off the ground. Her legs were spread wide by chains shackled to each ankle and affixed to bolts on opposite walls. Beneath her was a pyramid shaped sculpture lined up perfectly between Angela's legs. The tip of the pyramid was tacky with bits of meat and gore.

"Oh no. No." Gloria knew exactly what was about to happen. She looked over at the hideous little demon holding the other end of the chain . . . just as he let go.

"No!" Angela wailed as she plummeted from the ceiling onto the tip of the pyramid.

The sound was like that of a machete cleaving through a watermelon. Sharp and wet. The point of the pyramid gouged up into Angela's vagina, pulverizing the soft pink labia, cracking the pelvic bone and jarring both hipbones out of their sockets. The pyramid point split her sex wide open, drove deep into her womb. A river of blood rushed from the vicious gash, which now extended up to her bellybutton.

Angela's eyes went wide. She opened her mouth as if to scream but blood sprayed from between her lips in a wide arc. All expression drained from the girl's face, and her head drooped towards her chest. If this were anywhere else, Gloria would have thought the girl was dead. But she knew better. They had already died once to get here. Death was a luxury they were now denied.

The little fat demon turned toward Gloria. It grinned broadly, and licked its yellowing rows of fanged teeth with a thick purple tongue that looked like some type of mollusk. Gloria recognized him. Same red ring of hair and ridiculously comical moustache. Same shark-toothed grin. Same black soulless eyes. Even with all the hideous scars and horns and piercings, she still knew him.

"Fucking Vlad," she said through gritted teeth. There, in Hell, torturing her daughter. Now Gloria knew what this had been about. He'd procured Gloria for that big hideous demon she'd left behind in the cave, and in exchange he got to have Angela. Gloria started toward him. He slowly hoisted Angela back up into the air, her body dislodging from the pyramid with a hideous sticky ripping sound that made Gloria's stomach lurch. Blood cascaded from between Angela's thighs as she ascended once more towards the ceiling.

"My little girl. What have you done to my little girl?"

Her daughter's head wobbled listlessly on her limp neck. Pain had destroyed her mind. She looked like a lifeless marionette, and her suffering wasn't over. It would never be over as long as she was in Vlad's hands.

The skin on Gloria's neck bristled. From behind her, something was coming, fast. Something large, something pissed.

Lumbering down the corridor, filling up the entire passageway with its bulk, was *her* demon. She cried out, and moved back away from the cave where her daughter had been hoisted into the air to be dropped again onto the point of the pyramid. She threw herself against the wall of the tunnel, afraid to move, nowhere left to go. All she wanted was to melt into the stone, to disappear from this room. All she wanted was to not have to face that demon again.

She searched, hysterical now, for a place to hide.

There was nothing.

The demon reached out and casually snatched her up, wrapping one gnarled, taloned hand into her nest of filthy, greasy hair. It yanked her from the wall, pulled her down onto all fours. The beast headed back toward the cave, dragging Gloria behind. She tried to fight its grip but it was like trying to pry open the jaws of life. She beat at its unyielding flesh with her tiny fists until her own knuckles bruised and bled.

"No! No! Let me go! Oh God, please just let me go! Don't hurt me! I can't take anymore. I can't. I can't!"

The demon ignored her. It didn't scold or threaten—it said nothing. It barely appeared angry. There was no need to threaten. Gloria knew exactly what she was in store for. Her knees chafed and tore as she was dragged back to the cave, kicking and screaming the entire way.

***

Gloria was back in the cage. Her demon had not punished her yet, had simply shoved her back into her prison and collapsed onto his rotting bed of human hair and flesh. There was no hurry. He had all of forever to make her pay for trying to escape, for being a sinner, for being born. Soon he was fast asleep and Gloria was alone again with her thoughts.

Tears dripped from her face and splattered onto the floor of the cage, sizzling and turning to steam. Gloria wanted to be strong but this was all so hideous, so terrible, so unfair. She had fucked a lot, used the body God had given her not as a temple but as a toilet, a receptacle for semen, drugs, and alcohol. She'd been a whore, a sinner, weak, gluttonous, lustful, proud. She'd taken the Lord's name in vain, committed adultery. She'd done every terrible thing she could possibly do to herself. She'd given blowjobs to horses, donkeys, and pigs. Let them fuck her in the ass and ejaculate inside of her. But there were much more terrible sins. Sins that seemed much more befitting the type of punishment she was being subjected to.

She hadn't murdered anyone or stolen from them. She'd never raped or molested anyone. She had defiled herself but she'd hurt no one else. How could she deserve to spend eternity being raped, tortured, and mutilated? What kind of God would allow such a thing? Gloria moaned and wept herself to sleep.

When she woke, the demon was staring into her cage.

"God, no! No! Don't hurt me! God, please don't let him hurt me!"

"Stop saying that! There is no God! Not for you and not for me! He has abandoned us both."

The sound of the demon's voice startled Gloria. It was the first time he had spoken since she'd been in his possession, and despite the harshness of his words and the powerful volume, an obvious attempt to sound menacing, his voice was like music.

That's why the arch demons never speak . . . they still have the voices of angels.

"Why do you say that?" It was a stupid question, but Gloria wanted to hear him speak again. Something about his voice gave her hope. A creature with a voice that beautiful had to have some good in it. Hidden beneath those adornments of tattoos and piercings and scars, beneath the hideous body art, those brands, burns, and surgical modifications, there had to be some sympathy and compassion. Some divinity.

"Answer me. *Please.* Why did you say that? Why did you say that God—"

The demon reached in and clamped a hand over her mouth. His claws pierced her cheeks. Gloria tried to scream but her cries were muffled by the demon's filthy gore-streaked paw. His gnarled talons fished for her tongue through the holes it had gouged in her cheeks. When he caught it, he ripped it out of her mouth, yanking away the flesh from her cheeks and lips and the lower half of her jaw.

Knowing that it would grow back did nothing to alleviate the horror of seeing her face dismantled.

Her screams were a gargling hiss like the whine of a leaking gas pipe as he dragged her from the cage and tossed her against the cave wall. Her arms and legs were clamped into iron shackles. Gloria knew what this meant. He only chained her up when he was planning something particularly vile.

"Never try to run away again." His beautiful voice was no longer a comfort.

He picked up the tiny whip that he'd held earlier. The one with the thin chains ending in rat skulls. The demon began to twirl its wrists, and the rat skulls whirled faster and faster until they were a blur as they rained down on her chest. Within seconds her breasts looked like ground beef. When he began brutalizing her sex with it, bludgeoning and flaying her cunt with the punishing rat skulls, Gloria dry-heaved. Her stomach cramped from the terrible pain. Her abdominal muscles contracted so hard that they nearly touched her spine, but nothing came up from her empty stomach. Blood spewed from her eviscerated face.

The demon stalked off and came back with one of the candles from the wall and a scalpel made of sharpened bone. Then he knelt between Gloria's thighs and began to cut. It was the worst pain Gloria had ever felt . . . right up until he brought the candle flame to her clitoris.

***

Gloria had begun counting seconds. There was no sunrise and no sunset. No clocks. No way of measuring the passing of each moment. So she counted seconds to keep track of time. Sixty seconds was a minute and sixty minutes an hour, so she figured she could track each and every hour, each passing day, by counting seconds. She wanted to know just how long she was in Hell.

She began counting the day she'd discovered Angela. Three hundred and forty-five thousand, six hundred seconds had passed. Nearly a year. She hadn't kept track of how many times she'd been tortured, raped, beaten, and mutilated, though it seemed to happen every two or three hours. The demon would accost her after each of his naps.

Gloria had spent a lot of time thinking about the demon. Wondering about his voice. He hadn't spoken to her since the day she'd run away—and she hadn't tried to run away since. But she remembered that sweet lyrical voice like a cool breeze whispering through trees. Like birdsong and church bells. She was sure that underneath it all, he was still an angel. And there was something else that made her wonder: she'd seen him alter himself. Seen parts of his flesh whither away and die to be replaced by new flesh that he'd grafted onto his body. She thought that his flesh was stolen, that those animal tusks and horns and fangs, those claws, his entire hideous body, was just a mask worn by the soul. That would explain why he slept so much.

Since the day Gloria had begun counting, she hadn't slept. Not an hour, not a second. Her soul seemed to not require it. The need for sleep had been a weakness of the flesh.

But the demon slept. *Because it was flesh*. An unnatural marriage of spirit and flesh. The very thing the angels had

86

envied in humans. One of the very reasons they had revolted in the first place and were cast into the lake of fire. Gloria was convinced that beneath that hideous facade of tortured meat was still the soul of an angel. She had to believe it was true. It was her only hope.

For months now, Gloria had been trying to figure out a way to kill the demon. Murdering the thing was the only way she'd be able to escape, the only way to get out of there and find her daughter.

She'd heard rumors about a way out of Hell, a tunnel that led back to earth. Had heard the demons talking about it. There was a way out. If it existed she would find it, but first she had to get away—and that meant her demon had to be destroyed. She wasn't going to try to escape, only to have him drag her back and torture her again.

The problem with killing the demon was that nothing here seemed to die. *She* couldn't die, and that demon had been here centuries longer than she had. How could she kill something that was immortal?

Gloria watched the thing sleep as she sat in her cage. She stared at the decorative scars that zigzagged along its body. The animal parts stitched onto its flesh. Its skin was a tapestry of pain. But what if she could remove it all? If she could get him to see what he once was . . . what he truly is. But how?

She looked around the room at the torture devices, the whips, brands, scalpels, knives, canes. Any of them sufficient to remove flesh, but all would take too long. The demon would disarm her and have her chained against the wall, mutilating her vagina before she could do any damage. She needed something that could remove its flesh all at once.

Then it came to her: the lake of fire!

But how could she get him into it?

***

"Talk to me . . ." she whispered, reaching through the scorching bars of her cage. Her fingers caressed the top of the demon's head, sank into the apertures and brushed along the jutting horned protuberances. The touch repulsed her, made her quiver, but still she stroked him. If he felt her touch, he didn't acknowledge it.

"Please talk to me. I need to hear your voice."

The demon swung its arm, splintering her wrist. She cried out and withdrew her hand. Still she persisted, risking excruciating punishment.

"I've obeyed you since that day . . . when you brought me back. You've tortured me and I never tried to leave you. Can't you show me any kindness at all? Please! I beg you—I need you to talk to me."

The demon lifted its head, slowly, and looked up at Gloria. It parted its bloated, misshapen lips, and for a moment, she thought it was going to speak. Its response was a low, warning growl.

"Do you even know why I'm here?" she whispered. "Do you know what I did to deserve this endless pain, this eternity in Hell?"

It turned away, clearly not interested in her plea.

"No more talking," was all it said before collapsing onto its bed.

Still, those words had been enough. The lyrical quality of its voice calmed her, entranced her, like raindrops hitting a windowpane. She closed her eyes and pretended she was back on earth, in her bed, snuggling beneath the comforter drawn up to her nose.

The sensation of being watched was strong, and when she opened her eyes, the demon was staring at her.

She puffed out her cheeks, mentally gearing up for what she knew was inevitable. Its torment had become predictable over the months; there were just so many ways she could be beaten or raped or flayed skinless. Just so many ways her vagina could be shredded, her throat torn open. The torture had become strangely commonplace, and as much as she hated it, she had learned not to dread it. Complacency had replaced dread. She was resigned to her fate and knew the more she fought it, the worse it would be. So she'd stopped fighting, and instead steeled herself against the pain.

The demon reached inside—the cage doors were never locked—and yanked her out. No reason for them to be locked. No reason to attempt escape. And the demon knew this. She was sure she was being tested and didn't want to anger the demon, because as bad as the torture was, it could be that much worse.

It threw her down on the bed of rotting human flesh and knelt above her, its knees planted on the outsides of her calves, its massive cock aimed at her face like an accusing finger.

She turned her head and waited for the attack. Instead, it leaned down until she felt its stinking, steaming breath on her face, and it licked her with a tongue like sharkskin, tearing up the skin between her mouth and cheekbone.

"This no longer bothers you," he said. "Why is that?"

"It bothers me," she gasped.

The demon shook its head. "No . . ."

It bit the tip of her nose off and spat it out. Her head throbbed from the pain, and blood gushed from the wound, but she didn't move. She was terrified at what the demon might be thinking. At what it might be planning.

The barbed choker around her neck, the ring adorned with her aborted fetuses, began to pulse, the metal heating, scalding her skin. Still she remained motionless, waiting for the attack to end. Waiting for it to begin.

The demon reached up and unlocked the ring, dropping it onto her stomach.

"Suffering is the reason for being. Suffering is your life force. Without agony, there is no redemption."

"Haven't I suffered enough?" she cried. "Doesn't this ever end?"

The demon shook its head. "Not my decision."

"Then *whose?* Who decided I deserve this?"

The demon shackled her wrists to the wall, and then stood back. "Your children," it said. "They would have been your children."

Lying across her stomach was the ring of fetuses, hanging like aberrant charms on a bracelet. They were distorted versions of would-be children, contorted visions of damaged or missing limbs, of malformed heads and tiny jutting ribcages. One by one the four unborn offspring squirmed and struggled until they were free of the ring. They crawled in different directions, leaving behind slimy sludge trails of amniotic fluid and streaks of blood-specked gore. Two reached her breasts and latched onto the nipples, tiny briery teeth slicing into the tender skin.

"Wait," Gloria cried. "Wait! This isn't fair!"

The demon crossed its arms over its chest.

The third fetus slithered down her stomach and over her crotch and burrowed its way into her cunt. It squirmed inside her, the heteroclitic creature now searching for its return to the womb.

Gloria shrieked, lifted her legs, tried to push the fetus out, to expel it from her body as she had so many years ago. The demon whipped her legs with a razor-studded whip until the skin flew off in bloody chunks. Gloria stopped trying to abort the fetus.

The ones suckling at her breasts had given up trying to draw milk and settled on blood instead. They'd chewed their way through her nipples and were now consuming the flesh around the areolas.

The creature inside her cunt turned around, a breech birth correcting itself. It left behind slimy residue and bits of rotting flesh as it worked its way outward. Its tiny fingers clawed the walls of her vagina, and its tiny feet kicked her cervix. Its misshapen head jutted from the opening of her cunt, malformed fingers clinging to the labia minora. It slid backwards and pulled itself out again, repeating this move. Then it turned, slithered around inside the gaping maw of her sex, and its barbed gums slurped her clit.

The fourth aborted suckling slid across her thigh and plopped with a wet sucking sound onto the ground. It reached her perineum and bit into the tender flesh, chewing a hole above her asshole. She felt its tongue and teeth working the new hole, ripping at it until it was large enough for it to wriggle into. Moments later it was crawling around her bowels, digging and chewing its way into her intestines.

Gloria moaned, beyond words, beyond crying. Her eyes rolled back and she fought against the agony, both physical and emotional. The demon's attacks had been nothing. The past year had been nothing.

"Please!" she cried, finally able to find her voice. "Make them stop!"

But the demon ignored her plaintive cries. Of course she knew she would be ignored. Begging had been a last-ditch effort.

One of the monstrosities that had been devouring her tit oozed across her chest, deformed digits clawing flesh for purchase. A thick, foul secretion filled her nose and mouth as the fetus rested on her face. She shook her head, tried to dispel it. It slid its insignificant protuberance of a penis into her mouth, its balls like raisins resting against her lips. It spasmed and jerked, fucking her mouth. Claw-like fingers dug into her cheeks. The fetus's head rested against her damaged nose, the tip missing from when the demon had bitten it off. It seemed to like the scent and taste of her blood and chewed into the hole while its dick raped her mouth.

Slowly, the fetuses chewed their way across and through her body, consuming first her internal organs, her breast, her face, her cunt, working their way through the rest until she was nothing but a pile of bloody bones.

***

When she woke, she was again whole. It was the first time she'd slept in over a year, but she'd had no choice. There had been nothing left of her, and she'd needed to regenerate.

She glanced down at the demon, who returned her look. It stretched its arms over its head, as if it had just woken from a deep sleep. It probably had.

"Now what?" she muttered. "What else is in store for me?"

"Don't ask questions you don't want the answers to."

"I want to know."

The demon stared at her for quite a few seconds, which made Gloria uneasy. It was usually at times like these that the demon dispensed its worst punishments—after it had time to be reflective.

"I've grown tired of you." The demon's lyrical voice was soothing.

"What does that mean?"

"I'm giving you to another demon."

Gloria's heart pounded. Despite her torment, she'd grown used to this demon. The thought of facing a new one was terrifying. A new demon might be even worse.

"Or maybe I'll just toss you into the lake of fire and let you burn there for the rest of eternity."

"But why?" she cried. "I've done everything you've asked! I haven't tried to escape. Why would you want to get rid of me?"

"Enough talking! Just shut your mouth."

"You don't know why I'm here. Do you?"

"It doesn't matter why you're here. You *are* here. That's all that matters."

"Vlad sold me out. That's why I'm here—because that bastard gave me to you. I don't belong here!"

"Stop talking!"

Gloria twisted and contorted until she was at the edge of the cage, her fingers wrapped around metal bars searing the flesh from her fingers. "Listen to me," she begged. "What if I really don't belong here? What if I've paid for my sins a thousand times over? Does that matter at all to you?"

"You're in *HELL*," the demon bellowed. "Nothing matters here!"

And for the first time since Gloria had been cast into damnation, the demon stormed out, clearly unnerved by what Gloria had said.

***

The demon returned a short time later and dragged Gloria out of the cage, chained her to the wall. It retrieved several of its favorite instruments of torture: the razor-studded whip, the phallic club mottled with barbed wire, the cat o' nine tails made of thick chain.

"I'll do whatever you want," Gloria said, "but please don't send me away. Please."

The demon raised the whip and drew back its arm, its massive, bulging muscles flexing. Gloria winced, preparing for the pain. The moment seemed frozen in time. The agony of waiting for the attack was almost worse than the attack itself.

The demon dropped its arm. Gloria exhaled, relieved just for the moment, waiting for the inevitable pain.

"You weren't lying," it whispered.

"What?" she gasped, almost tripping over the word. Had she heard correctly?

"You don't belong here." The demon turned away, clearly thinking, clearly struggling with a decision. It turned back to her. "But that doesn't matter. I have to do this. I have no choice."

"Yes you do! You don't belong here either."

"There is no hope for me, Gloria. And there is no hope for you." With that, the demon raised the whip and flayed the skin from her torso. It switched weapons shortly after. Even through her pain, Gloria sensed the demon was only going through motions. The usual joy it took from destroying her flesh was absent.

As she lay on the floor a writhing, hemorrhaging pulp, she tried to speak. Words did not come easily from her crushed jaw and lacerated tongue. Blood gushed from her mouth in a steady stream. The demon smashed her skull with the club until the side of her head caved in, until green-gray bits of brain and bone decorated the weapon like a coat of paint.

This time the demon didn't throw her back in the cage. She was left on the floor, free of the chains, and slowly her body regenerated.

A few hours later, she was able to speak again, but the demon was asleep on its bed.

"Can you hear me?" she asked. There was no answer. But she recognized when he was sleeping—recognized after all this time the signs: the change in the rhythm of its breathing; the pattern to the rise and fall of its massive chest; the disturbed twitching when it had one of its frequent nightmares. The demon lay still, but without signs of sleep.

"I think you can hear me. And maybe you'll listen this time." She waited a moment before continuing, afraid that the demon would be angry and would lash out. Instead, it remained silent.

"I've done awful things in my life. I've sold my flesh, I've experimented with every drug imaginable. I've caused heartache and grief. I've done so many things I regret . . . but I wasn't an evil person. The only reason I'm here is because Vlad sold me out. I'm here because I committed suicide—but the only reason I did was to save my grandchild. It was either kill her, or kill myself. I know you probably don't believe me . . . there's no reason you should. But it's the truth. I'm trapped here for all eternity but I shouldn't be."

The demon's head stirred, but it didn't turn to face her.

"My daughter Angela's here as well. And I don't know why. I don't know if she was murdered, or tricked, or what. I can't imagine what that child might have done to end up in this place." Tears streamed down cheeks that hadn't completely regenerated. "You don't belong here either . . . do you?"

"It's not that simple," the demon said, its back to her. "I've been condemned. There is no hope for me."

"The animal parts you graft onto your body, the tattoos and markings . . . what would happen if you stopped? What would happen if you refused?"

The demon sat up and faced her. It looked heartbroken, she thought. Sorrowful. "I was tricked as well. I followed the wrong path. It's too late for me."

"I've seen beyond your exterior. It's not too late. You can save yourself."

"'It is better to rule in Hell than to serve in Heaven'."

"Do you rule?"

The demon turned its head, almost in shame. "I can't reveal myself. I would be destroyed. No place in Heaven, no place in Hell. Banished to nothing."

"It would mean the end of your torment."

The demon cradled its head in its hands, as if in anguish. "Stop!"

94

"Please let me die, then," she bluffed. "Please banish me to nothing. There's no place in Heaven or Hell for me either."

"You don't know what you ask! You don't know what it's like."

"Do you?"

"Trust me when I tell you, you'd rather spend an eternity here."

Gloria crept over to the demon, and gingerly touched its cheek. She waited for it to lash out, to break her arm or jaw or neck. Instead, it lay still. "You don't want this," she sighed, tickling his face with her breath. "You're torn. You want to be redeemed."

The demon looked up at her, tenderness in its horrible eyes.

"I imagine what you looked like, with gossamer wings and beautiful features. I imagine what you once were. But I can't imagine why you accepted this. It seems cowardly, and you're no coward."

The demon sat up, grabbed her upper arm tightly in its clawed hand. Blood tricked from beneath its fingers. "You say too much!"

"I'm sorry! I didn't mean—"

The demon dragged her down the corridor, her bare feet scraping on the small stones, her knees ripped skinless when she tripped. They moved quickly, and she was too terrified to question his intentions.

They reached the vast cavern that Gloria had stumbled into a year earlier. It was unchanged, still packed with shrieking, tortured souls dissolving into a boiling stew of white-hot effluence, equal parts molten earth and liquefied human flesh. A bubbling cauldron of misery and anguish, where the guilty and condemned melted into a noxious steaming sludge, its banks overflowing with the damned.

"Why are we here?"

"Redemption."

Gloria panicked. She had hoped to convince the demon to jump in alone, but now it appeared that he intended to take her with him.

95

Perched on a cliff overlooking the endless river of burning sinners, he clutched her wrists tightly. There was longing in his eyes.

Gloria hoped she could save herself. "You want to be an angel again, don't you?" she babbled. "You want to return to what you once were. You want to be forgiven."

She wasn't sure he'd heard her. He did not so much as turn in the direction of her voice. Just stared into the lake of fire.

"He used to love you once. I'll bet He still does. He loves what you were, when you were an extension of His will. When you were beautiful. How can He love you now? This isn't what you were meant to be. This isn't what God made you."

This time the demon responded with a wince, as if her words had wounded him. He looked down at his scarred and mutilated claws, then back across the burning river.

"I bet you're still beautiful. Deep down. Underneath all of that tainted flesh, you're still an angel of the Lord."

"I know what you're trying to do," he said, shaking his head. "I'm not a fool. My decision to return here wasn't impulsive—your words aren't that convincing, Gloria."

She gasped, swallowed the lump in her throat. "I wasn't—"

"All I ever wanted was to be loved by Him. As He loves humanity. I want to know that union of flesh and spirit that He gave you but denied us . . ." He spread his vast arms and looked himself over. His flesh was a tapestry of pain and rage. " . . . and for that I have become a monster."

"It wasn't your fault. This isn't what you want—you can be beautiful again."

"Yes," the demon whispered. He began to claw the flesh from his body, slowly at first, digging deep into the muscle and wrenching it free from the bone, and then with greater and greater vigor. The demons below stopped what they were doing and stared up as he raked away the hideous facade of meat and bone in long bloody strips. Beneath those layers of muscle and fat, glimpses of pure unblemished spirit began to shine through. A spirit more radiant than that of any human, like the soft morning sun shimmering off a placid lake.

The other demons began charging toward the cliff.

"No!" They sang out with voices all as sweet and beautiful as windchimes, contrasting with the menagerie of hideous features that shaped their grotesque bodies. Gloria stepped away from the demon. Chunks of flesh fell at her feet as he continued to dissect himself. Blood sprayed from countless lacerations. The demon stared across the lake, as if transfixed, even as he tore out handfuls of flesh and cast them aside, now even snapping bone and pulling it out through the skin to pile at his feet.

The other demons were scaling the cliff, still crying out in chorus. They had almost reached him when the demon that had tortured Gloria for months without relent cast himself into the lake of fire.

Part III

"... Punishment hardens and numbs, it produces concentration, it sharpens the consciousness of alienation, it strengthens the power of resistance ..."
      —Friedrich Nietzsche, *The Genealogy of Morals*

"... Straight is the gate, and narrow is the way, which leadeth unto life, and few there be that find it ..."
      —Mathew 7:14, *Holy Bible*

Gloria was consumed with a stillness at her core as the demon/angel sank into the burning river. She felt nothing for him. Neither the exaltation of revenge nor the sorrow of loss. She had no feelings to spare, ill or otherwise. Her emotions were now focused on her daughter.

The cliff was crowded with demons. Gloria could almost feel the anticipation of the others as they watched the ancient demon slip further into the depths of the lake of fire, his flesh burned away, revealing the beautiful angel beneath. Skin a pale iridescent blue like moonlight. Eyes the color of liquid night, dark pools reflecting everything like tiny mirrors. Limbs long and lithe floating on the volcanic current as the flesh dissolved in large liquefying chunks. The demon/angel's melodious screams were terrifying as the last of its hell-born flesh melted away.

The demons crowded in closer to watch the spectacle, ignoring Gloria. The demon/angel sank into the flames, and the other demons sucked in nervous breaths. Their excitement and fear charged the air like static electricity.

Gloria suddenly realized what the other demons were waiting so eagerly for. Not to see the angel unveiled, but to see if the fire would kill him; to see if he could die, if the flames would consume him.

They wanted to know if they could die as well.

Gloria looked into one hopeful face after another as they stared expectantly into the lake of fire. There was a desperation etched on their infernal features. Clearly, they hated it here, too. These torturers were every bit as captive as their victims.

The reborn angel pulled himself out of the lake of fire and stretched his still-burning wings, and the demons' hopeful faces fell in disappointment, twisted in rage. There went their last hope for release from this infernal torment. It had been better to not know and to still harbor hope for this agony's end. But now they knew there was no way out. The revelation that not even death was possible. They charged down from the cliff and overwhelmed the angel.

Their claws tore his wings, ripped them from their moorings in his back. They gouged out his eyes. Flesh exposed, revealed to the bone. His screams filled the cavern with an anguished wail that shook the walls and wrenched tears from Gloria's eyes.

Gloria's last sight of the angel, her demon, was of him being dragged off to the caves. They cursed at him, spit on him, urinated on him. He was an angel but, like her, he was still in Hell. No longer a demon, now only a victim, one more sinner to be punished. A former demon who had abandoned the others, had become a pariah. His sightless eye sockets roamed the cavern; his elegant angelic fingers pawed the air in terror. For a moment those sunless pits seemed to focus on her. His mouth formed her name. Then he was gone and all that remained were his screams echoing throughout the cavern.

Not all of the demons had left the cavern. Some milled about, looking frightened and confused by the loss of one of their own. Then, one by one, they turned toward Gloria.

***

She was not running for her life. She would have stopped by now and accepted her fate if that's all it had been. Gloria was running for salvation, and for that of her daughter. Running from an eternity of rape, torture, and mutilation. But the demons were catching up. Their thunderous tread pounded the ground behind her. Their fetid breath steamed on the back of her neck. She imagined what they would do to her if they caught her, so she ran faster. In Hell she was spirit, and they were flesh. Gloria knew she could outrun them.

Gloria's abused and exhausted soul took flight through the winding catacombs, hurtling like a leaf in a hurricane. The ruckus from the demons' pursuit slowly faded as the weight of their flesh slowed them. Soon Gloria couldn't hear them anymore, couldn't feel them breathing down her neck. When she finally turned and looked, she was alone.

She slowed, and stumbled along through the dark corridors, unsure of where to turn, no clue where her daughter might be. No idea how to find the cave where she'd seen her daughter tortured more than a year ago at the hands of Bill Vlad, and there were countless thousands of caves to search. It didn't matter. Gloria had forever if that's what it would take.

She lifted a torch off the tunnel wall and walked in the direction of the loudest screams. Gloria winced as the sounds of metal striking flesh, blood splattering against stone, shrieks of purest agony, and cries for mercy grew more intense.

The winding catacombs presented danger. Any demon she passed would know she'd escaped, and any one of them might decide to reclaim her. But there was no turning back.

Gloria peered inside one cave. A spear-like dildo was being rammed into the asshole of a rather flabby, sweaty man. He was doubled over, his head and arms locked into a wooden frame, his ass exposed and jutting upward. The head of the dildo was a spiked battering-ram. The demon put his shoulder behind it and forced the long phallus in to the hilt. Blood mingled with a large portion of his internal organs exploded from the man's mouth. The man turned towards Gloria with wounded eyes glazed in agony and screamed, blood sprayed from his lips onto the cave floor. Gloria recognized him.

He was older than when she'd last seen him, but there was no mistaking that acne scarred face and long oily hair. It was Colin, one of the geeks who'd enticed her into having sex with farm animals for money and had gotten rich doing it. She wondered if the spear punching into his anus was as long as the giraffe cock he'd wanted her to take. It was definitely a hell of a lot longer than the donkey's dick.

"Serves you right you son-of-a-bitch." Gloria hissed.

The demon's smile seemed to extend around to the back of his head, like a snake unhinging its jaw to swallow a rodent. He withdrew the battering-ram dildo from Colin's prolapsed rectum and slammed it in again. Colin's flesh split with a wrenching squelch.

Gloria turned her head and crept quietly past.

Each cave possessed a sight more hideous than the last, but Gloria had no choice but to check them all. She had to find Angela.

It seemed that hours—perhaps even days—passed. Time meant nothing here. Her mind reeled from the hundreds of atrocities she'd witnessed. Gloria stumbled into another large cavern.

Other lost souls, like her, were huddled at the mouth of a long tunnel. Gloria's heart stuttered. Her knees wobbled. A smile crawled tentatively onto her face, which had not known happiness in ages, as she staggered toward the tunnel, reaching out desperately, like a drowning man grasping for a lifejacket.

Light was coming from the tunnel. Sunlight.

Nearly a dozen others were huddled at the mouth of the tunnel, but they didn't look as ecstatic as she expected. In fact, they looked even more miserable and terrified than the tortured souls she'd left behind.

"I can't do it. I didn't know it would be like this," a woman sobbed. She appeared to be young enough to be Gloria's daughter—except for her eyes. They were ancient. Something in those eyes told Gloria that the woman had been dead for a long time, suffering ceaselessly for years upon years. She may have been a child when she died, but not anymore. Her childhood had ended here years ago, perhaps even decades or centuries.

"But isn't this the way out?" Gloria asked, perplexed.

The girl didn't look her way. She muttered to herself, hugged her knees to her chest and rocked back and forth.

"Yes. The way out." This voice belonged to an aged soul, one whose astral body looked as if he had been nearly a hundred years old when he died. His eyes looked even older

101

than the girl's. Who knew how long he'd been in Hell.

"Then why aren't you going through? Why don't you all leave? Why stay here?"

"Because *God* is in there. That passageway takes you right past Heaven. He'll see us if we try to leave. I can't face Him. Not after all the things I've done—after all that's been done to me. I can't face Him. I can't do it."

"But how can that be? Heaven is above and we've got to be in the center of the earth somewhere?"

"Heaven and hell are everywhere and nowhere." The old man answered with a defeated shrug of the shoulders.

Gloria looked at the dozens of broken souls that littered the cavern, then glanced back at the tunnel. She thought about the sins that weighed on her own soul, and the atrocities she'd been subjected to since her death. She looked at her spirit body, which was still tacky with dirt, demon feces, blood, and semen. Her every sin appeared as yet another stain on her tarnished soul. Even after centuries buried beneath that mountain of stolen flesh, the angel had looked less disheveled than she did when he emerged from the lake of fire—and he probably had a better chance at redemption.

"I look like a whore," Gloria mumbled. But it was worse than that. It wasn't just her appearance. She *was* a whore. And God would know it. He would see it and He would reject her and send her back to inferno.

But there was no way she was going to let that fear overcome her. Not after all she'd been through. "I'm going in," Gloria said, but her feet wouldn't move. She was suddenly more afraid of that cave than any of the tortures of Hell, afraid of being rejected by the one being who was always supposed to love her no matter what. Rejected by the only one whose love truly mattered, besides her daughter.

Gloria peered into the sunlit tunnel and felt a tug at her soul. It was calling to her.

"I'm going in there," she said aloud. "But not without my daughter."

Gloria turned away from the tunnel . . . toward the catacombs . . . back into Hell to find Angela.

***

No weapons. Nothing to protect her. And the demons were everywhere. She didn't know how long she could continue to outrun them. Twice already she'd nearly been caught. One torturer had reached out from a cave in back of her as she'd stood watching a man being locked into an Iron Maiden. She'd felt the claws dig into her arms and ran as fast as she could, jerking her arms free of his grasp. If his talons had not been as sharp, if they hadn't shred through her like a hand parting a spiderweb but had been able to dig in and hold on, she would have been captured right then.

Later, she'd almost made the same mistake, pausing a second too long to watch a boy who appeared no older than seventeen, have the skin slowly sliced off of him by a demon whose own ill-kept costume of human and animal skin appeared to be decomposing. The demon was cutting long rectangles onto the boy's skin and then grabbing the very edge of it and wrenching the epidermis free with a pair of ordinary pliers. Gloria was transfixed by that wet ripping sound as the skin was torn away in long blood red strips. She almost didn't hear the demon's coming up behind her. Then she was almost trapped as she ran right into another trio of monsters coming in the opposite direction. Only the element of surprise and their sluggish fleshy bodies had allowed her to race past them. But there was no way her luck could hold out for much longer. Not in the hundreds of tunnels she had to venture through, the hundreds upon hundreds of tortured souls she had to pass, the countless demons that lie ahead in those dark catacombs. She had to find Angela quickly before she was caught.

"Glooooooria . . ." the wind through the undercroft seemed to sigh, carrying her name as if in a funereal march. The sound led her further into Hell, lulled her into the caves. Songs of torment, of endless pain, compelling nonetheless because of their dulcet tones. Dragging her farther and farther away from her escape, from the tunnel of light.

"I'm not afraid . . ." she whispered, though her mouth was dry, and she trembled. The surface of the cave wall was cold and tacky as she ran her hands along its surface to guide her through the darkness. Ahead she found candles housed in human skulls and picked one up, aimed it toward the blackness ahead of her.

Back through the caves, witnessing punishment that she had grown numb against, forms of torture that no longer made her cringe. Focused instead on finding her daughter, not caring what crimes the condemned had committed, what sins they had thrust upon others. Though she suspected that they couldn't all be guilty, couldn't all deserve the fate that awaited them. After all, she was in Hell under unconventional circumstances, and had to figure others were as well. But she couldn't care. Like her, they would have to find their own salvation. Their own way out of Hell.

What disturbed her, despite her efforts not to care, were the children. Not that she came across many, but when she did . . . and now, a small boy, perhaps nine—though she imagined that was just the look of his astral body; not knowing how long he had been in Hell. Like the girl at the tunnel, his eyes were ancient; dark and terrible, a child who had seen too much.

He was alone in the cave, alone except for the endless swarms of insects crawling on his body. He sat in a chair, his arms and legs tied down by barbed wire, and Gloria could tell by the bloody welts that he had been fighting against his restraints.

The child glanced at her as she peered into the cave. "Help me," he sobbed, spitting out the cockroaches that skittered into his mouth.

She moaned, rushed over to him, stomped bugs that surrounded and attacked him. Thousands of cockroaches, waterbugs, red ants, chiggers, brown recluse spiders, dung beetles, hornets and wasps—endless species of bugs swarming and flying and attacking the boy, burrowing into his flesh, biting and stinging relentlessly, crawling up his nose and into his mouth and ears.

The boy jerked his head, struggled against his restraints, squeezed his eyes and mouth shut. Gloria swiped madly at the bugs, squashing some beneath her bare feet, brushing them from his face. She knew she had to get him out of that chair, that her assault on the insects wasn't making a difference. They just kept coming.

She had no weapon. She looked frantically around the room for a tool to cut the wire and found nothing.

The boy kept his mouth shut, and his screams were muffled. She raced back over to him and pulled at the barbed wire, trying not to hurt him further. The jagged edges dug into her skin, but she ignored the pain; she would heal again. She managed to loosen the restraints around his arms, and he began to flail, slapping the bugs away from his face and upper body. The barbs bore into her flesh as she tried to free his legs.

She yanked him free of the chair and dragged him across the floor, toward the exit. The bugs followed, streaming across the dirt like a tsunami, and she pulled the boy out of the cave and into the corridor, fleeing with his wrist clasped tightly in her hand. The insects chased, noisily chittering, hissing, spitting, their thousands of tiny insect legs sounding like horses stampeding on the packed dirt floor.

They ran until Gloria could no longer hear the insects' pursuit, until their terrifying screams died out. She rested against a wall and rubbed her hands over her face, trembling.

"Are you all right?" she managed to ask, and the boy nodded. The light was faint in the tunnel, but she could make out the movement of his head. "Why were you being punished?" She couldn't begin to imagine what such a young child could have done to deserve to be in Hell, but whatever it was she didn't care. Even if God didn't give a shit, didn't believe in the innocence of children, she did. Condemning a child to Hell was beyond her comprehension.

The boy shrugged.

"Don't you know?"

He shrugged again. "Thanks for setting me free. Those goddamned bugs were getting on my nerves."

It felt as though those bugs were swarming again. Her flesh crawled and itched at the chilling tone of his voice. "Did I just make a mistake?"

"I dunno—did you?" He grinned, but his eyes remained cold, dark.

She started to move away from him, to head down the corridor, but he followed.

"Where are you going?"

"I-I'm looking for someone." He kept up with her as she backed away. "I have to go now."

"Don't go." His fingers sank into the flesh above her wrist. Gloria jerked her arm, tried to pull away, but his grip was remarkably strong. He slammed her into the wall, bashed her head against the stone.

She crumpled to her knees, her head clutched in her hands. Blood triclked between her fingers. "Why are you doing this?" she gasped, trying to look up at him.

"Because this is what I am. Did you think I was in Hell by accident?"

Then he was upon her, sharp fingernails scoring her flesh, small teeth biting her breasts and face. Her reaction was not to fight but to escape, and she tried to crawl away, to climb out from beneath him. He was a child, after all—and no matter what he did to her, she found it impossible to hurt him. But soon the attack became more severe, and from his blood-smeared mouth fell parts of her body. Her lacerated nipple dangled from her breast by a grisly string of flesh.

Gloria raised her knee and slammed it hard into the boy's stomach, finally slowing him. He grunted and tumbled over, wrapping his arms around his midsection. She dragged herself away on hands and knees, blood pouring from her screaming lacerations. The boy reached toward her, unrelenting in his attack despite his obvious pain.

"Get OFF!" she screamed, kicking out, her heel connecting with his face. His nose splintered beneath her foot and he squealed, fell onto his back, his small hands covering his face.

"Help . . ." he sobbed, his voice small, wounded, and for a moment Gloria forgot what kind of monster he had been, for a moment wanted to help. But he lowered his hands and grinned, his tongue darting, licking the blood that dripped from his nose.

"Like hell I will," she said, kicking him in the head again, sending him reeling across the ground. She couldn't have him chasing after her; he'd already slowed her too much as it was.

She retrieved a candle from a few feet away. She struggled to her feet, using the wall for support, and headed around a corner. "Where are you, Angela?" she muttered, palming blood and dirt from her cheeks. Endless caves ahead, moans and screams coming from all of them, but none of the voices belonged to her daughter.

The candle sputtered. Not much life left in it, and she'd again be plunged into darkness. Wandering around Hell was like being lost in a topiary maze—many false starts, corridors that led to solid walls. She'd often had to backtrack, and at the same time tried not to lose her way. She still needed to remember how to return to the tunnel of light.

The candle flame died. Gloria cursed, dropped it to the ground. The individual caves were lit, but now she wouldn't be able to see if her corridor resulted in a dead-end. Her fingers slid along the stone surface of the wall and she crept along. She sensed someone—some *thing*—ahead, could hear its shallow breath, phlegmy and raspy. Turn back? Turn back to what? This was Hell. She wasn't exactly safe no matter what direction she took.

"Gloria," the thing in the darkness said, and she froze, sucked in a useless breath. "It's about time you joined us. I was just starting to miss you."

"Who are you?" she gasped, and she felt a hand take hers, a clammy hand, but a human one nevertheless.

A moment later she was inside a cave, face-to-face with Vlad.

***

"What happened to you?" he said, tongue racing over his bloated lips, corners of his mouth upturned in a jackal-grin. He reached out and flicked her damaged nipple, and she flinched, backing away until she was up against a wall.

"What do you want, Vlad?" she asked, trembling.

He laughed. "Let's not be coy." He turned partially and stretched his arm out dramatically, as if showcasing the room. "Let's make a deal. Shall we?"

Across the cave, Angela lay out on a rack, splayed arms and legs stretched unnaturally, almost at the separating point of limbs to joints. Bite marks and burns covered her flesh. Torture devices were displayed on a table beside the rack.

Vlad grabbed Gloria's hair and shoved her toward Angela. He pushed her again, and shoved her to her knees.

In front of the table, he fondled the various devices until he selected one, and lifted it to show Gloria. "This is my favorite," he said.

It was a speculum, but three times the normal size, its metal sides layered with razor blades and barbed wire. A knife-life protrusion jutted from its head.

"Angela seems fond of it as well." He pushed it into the girl's cunt, and she threw back her head, unable to move her stretched limbs. She sobbed, begged him to stop.

"No!" Gloria screamed. Still on her knees. She reached out, grasped handfuls of air. "Please stop," she cried.

Vlad fucked the girl with the speculum, chunks of her flesh flying with streams of blood.

"Goddamn you!" Gloria screamed, jumping up and rushing toward Vlad. She threw herself on top of him and knocked him away from Angela.

They landed in a pile a foot away, Gloria pounding her fists into his face. But Vlad laughed, and punched her hard across her mouth. She went flying and landed on her back.

"You're no match for me, you stupid cunt," he said, standing, returning to Angela.

Gloria lay on the floor, moaning, weeping quietly. He was right—how could she ever expect to fight him? He outweighed her by a hundred pounds, and he was a massive little troll. She'd always been intimidated by him, and it seemed as if he had been controlling her life forever. Now he was even controlling her death—and worse, controlling her daughter.

He was raping Angela again with that hideous contraption, and Gloria sat on the floor and watched. Watched the assault on her only child. Watched as the disgusting little man did as he pleased.

She couldn't watch any more.

108

Maybe Vlad didn't know what Gloria had endured, on earth and in Hell. Maybe he didn't know what she was capable of. But she knew. And she wondered how she could have let this fat little bastard intimidate her for as long as he had.

She climbed to her feet and approached the table. Quite an assortment to choose from . . . she wanted something powerful, something with substance when hefted. The mace's handle was thick seared wood, and a blackened steel ball embedded with six-inch spikes topped it. She lifted the medieval weapon high overhead and swung it at him.

He ducked, but it still clipped his shoulder, and sent him reeling across the floor.

"You stupid bitch!" he yelled, climbing to his feet.

"Stay out of my way, you fuck! All I want is Angela."

He slowly approached, eyeing the mace. His face was contorted with rage. "You think you had it bad before? *Do you?*" Spit flew off his lips. "That was nothing. Nothing!"

He extended his hand, and Gloria froze, positive that he had some powers, that he would use them on her. She'd seen him appear in her apartment through locked doors, had witnessed the creatures he'd brought back from Hell. Surely he had some ability, favors bestowed by Hell.

The mace slipped in her hand, but she held on to its shaft.

Vlad rushed the table and retrieved a razor-studded belt. He swung it at her and it tore into her cheek, gouging out chunks of flesh.

She hefted the mace in both hands and swung. It tore his ear off, sent it flying across the room. Blood gushed from the gaping wound, and Vlad slammed his hand against his head.

He looked up at her, stunned. His mouth dropped open and he took his hand away, examined the river of blood pouring through his fingers. "No!" he screamed. "you promised! You promised me immortality!"

Gloria looked around, wondering who he was talking to, expecting to see someone else in the cave. But they were alone. Whoever he was yelling at, they weren't in the room.

Vlad was overcome with a fit of rage and attacked Gloria with the belt, swinging wildly, the razors shredding her skin, flaying her. The last blow gouged out her eyeball, and she threw up her hands, trying to flee his assault. She used the table as a shield, pushed it on top of him when he charged after her again.

Lifting the mace one last time, she brought it crashing down on Vlad's head. The spikes imbedded in his skull, splitting it open, blood and brains oozing from the gaping holes. Vlad spasmed and shuddered, his feet kicking out, vomit trickling out of his mouth.

Gloria dropped the mace. "Do *you* heal, you motherfucking troll?" She rushed over to Angela and untied the girl from the rack. Angela screamed as her limbs were loosened, as her arms and legs popped back into their joints.

"Can you walk?"

"I don't know." Angela's words were hesitant, her voice weak. "I'll try."

Gloria wrapped her arms around her daughter's waist and lowered her to the floor. Angela stood on wobbly legs, but they supported her weight.

Angela looked up at her mother. "Why'd you come for me?"

"That's a silly question."

Angela leaned against the rack and rested. "No it's not. After what I did—why would you come and rescue me?"

"Because you're my daughter, and I love you. We're getting out of this place."

Angela shook her head. "And go where? There is nowhere else. I belong here. In Hell. I deserve to be here. And so do you. I don't love you—I don't even know you."

"You don't belong here, baby. Nobody deserves this. I don't care what you've done. Nobody deserves an eternity of this. We'll leave together, and maybe someday you'll love me. But for now—we have to leave!" She grabbed he daughter's hands and pulled her from the rack, and ran with her toward the cave exit.

Back toward the sunlight.

***

There were horrible sounds coming from up ahead, from the direction of the tunnel home. Sounds of pain, violence, of tearing flesh, splintering bone, shrieks of terror. Gloria knew there was something different about these screams. They were not the normal tortured cries that echoed ceaselessly from every direction. They were more urgent, more like the sounds of battle.

Gloria gripped her daughter's arm tighter and continued running in the direction of the tunnel. The noise increased as they advanced, sounding like a massacre in the darkness. Angela clung desperately to her mother, as if the battle-scarred woman could provide any real protection. Her daughter's fear vibrated through Gloria's skin; the girl's resolve crumbled with each step.

"Are you sure this is the way? It sounds like people are being killed up there."

"This is the way. And we can't die remember? Nothing here dies."

"I'm scared. That sounds so horrible. You hear those screams? Mom, I don't think we should go this way. Something's going on up there."

"We have no choice. This is the way out. I don't care what's up there. If it's standing between us and freedom from this place, then we're going right through it!"

Gloria gritted her teeth and continued forward, staring straight ahead, unblinking, practically dragging her daughter behind her.

"I'm not going!" Angela dug her heels in and locked her legs.

"Yes you are!" Gloria jerked the young girl right off her feet and dragged her across the hard dirt floor.

"I'm scared! Don't make me go!"

Gloria whirled on the frightened little girl. "Do you want to stay here? You like being raped and tortured by these . . . these things? Is this how you want to spend eternity? In unending pain? Well, I won't let you. You don't deserve this. And neither do I."

She snatched the girl up onto her feet and they walked the last half a mile toward the tunnel of light.

"Do you hear that?" Angela said.

"What?"

"The screams. They stopped."

"I can still hear people screaming," Gloria said, never slowing, still charging forward through the darkness toward the light.

"Not the normal screams, Mom. The bad ones. They've stopped."

Gloria paused for a second and listened. "You're right. It's quiet up there."

"What do you think it means?"

"It means we're getting the fuck out of here!"

Seconds later they burst out of the long passageway and entered a huge cavern spattered with blood. The floor was a wet crimson blanket.

"What happened here? Where'd all this blood come from?"

Gloria was quiet for a long time, and when she spoke, it was introspective, more to herself than to Angela. "It's from the others, the ones that were afraid to go in. The demons must have come for them . . . that's why there weren't more of them. The demons must know about this place. We have to get out of here before they come back!"

"But why were they afraid to go in? What were they afraid of?"

"Judgment," Gloria replied solemnly. Then, without hesitation, she plunged into the tunnel with her daughter in tow.

***

After so many months in darkness, the light was almost blinding. Gloria squinted against its harsh glare.

A fork divided the road ahead, but Gloria had been expecting it. Ever since she first discovered the tunnels, she knew she'd have a choice to make. One corridor led to Heaven, the other to earth. She turned left and continued to run, dragging her reluctant daughter by the wrist. Gloria's body grew heavier as flesh returned to spirit, covered her frame.

They'd been running for miles when Angela screamed.

"Oh my god! *What am I?*" The girl shrieked, fell to the ground sobbing.

Gloria looked at her fallen daughter, then looked at her own newly formed body.

Their legs were fused into one long, sallow, cylindrical tube. Their arms were a nest of tentacles that sprang from the centers of their oily serpentine bodies. Their movements were reduced to a crawl, a peristaltic slither, their eel-like bodies rolling and undulating across the cave floor. The only things that remained even remotely human were their faces, and they were quickly changing.

They were turning into the same species of worm that had tried to fuck Gloria to death in that hot tub, what seemed like a century ago. That's where Vlad had acquired the hideous larval creatures. They were escaped souls from hell. That explained the human voices she'd heard in their screams when she'd torn them apart. She had not just imagined it after all.

Gloria began to weep exhausted tears. Their escape had seemed too easy, and now she understood why. This was their choice. They could return to earth . . . return to life . . . but not as humans. *As worms.* Or they could attempt to reach Heaven and face God's judgment. Karma is a bitch.

"We have to go back!" Angela shrieked, scowling at her revolting, pasty gray body.

"Wait, honey. Think about this."

"What the fuck is there to think about? I can't live like this!" Angela's features were melding into her flesh, nose dissolving into a pulpish mash. "What was in that other tunnel? The one we passed?"

Gloria opened her mouth then thought better of it and closed it again. Angela caught it.

"What? You know, don't you? What's in there? What's in that other tunnel?"

"It's better you don't know."

Angela laughed, a cruel, harsh sound that wounded Gloria

113

like the lash of a whip. "Are you fucking kidding me? You're still trying to protect me? Look at me! I'm a fucking *worm*! I've been raped by demons, by a fat slimy con man, by my own father! I've been tortured worse than anyone could ever imagine. And now I've been reincarnated as a fucking king-sized maggot! And you want to protect me? Fuck you! What the hell is in that other tunnel, Mother?"

Gloria gave up. "God."

"What?"

"That tunnel we ran past is a doorway to Heaven."

"Then what the fuck are we doing here? I never wanted to go back to the world anyway. It never was any better than Hell, and I definitely don't want to go back as a giant earthworm. Why didn't we just go into that other tunnel to begin with?"

"Because . . . what if He doesn't want us?"

"What do you mean?"

"I mean what if He sends us back to Hell? What if He takes one look at us and decides that we were right where we ought to be?"

"He . . . He wouldn't. You said it yourself—nobody belongs here. He couldn't send us back!"

Gloria thought about the boy she'd rescued from the insects. Remembering how he'd attacked her. "Nobody's in Hell by accident. You don't think He knows we're here? Maybe He just doesn't care about us. Maybe He put us here himself. It's all part of His plan or something."

"No! Bullshit! He has to love us. That's what all the churches say. God is love. If there's a Hell, there has to be a Heaven. There has to be love!" Angela's eyes filled with tears. That at least meant she was still partially human. Even if she did look like fishbait.

"But what if He doesn't? What if this is all there is?"

"No! I can't believe that. I won't accept that! You can stay here as a goddamned slug or go back to the world or whatever. But I'm going to Heaven." Angela shimmied back down the tunnel, her slug-like body oozing along the ground.

Gloria paused for a moment. From the end of the passageway, she could almost see the afternoon sun high in the sky. She turned and followed her daughter.

Gloria and her daughter crawled back through the tunnel in silence. Their bodies slowly began to lose substance, reverting back to the familiar look of their human souls. Still, they said nothing to each other. Gloria was locked in her own world of fear and excitement. It was not every day that you went to meet your maker.

They reached the spot where the road had forked and Gloria paused. "We could always go back." She sighed in resignation.

"Back to Hell? What—are you on crack? Did you see what happened to the others? Those demons ripped them apart! I'm not going the fuck back there. I'm going to Heaven. Are you with me?" Angela turned without hesitation and entered the light.

Gloria followed on shaky legs that felt like those of a child on her way to her parents' room to receive some unknown punishment.

This new tunnel was much brighter than the first. Not sunshine but something else . . . like starlight, radiating a light like a supernova.

They had walked a few hundred yards when the tunnel disappeared. A field of green surrounded them.

"What is this?" Angela whispered, smiling at her mother. "Is this Heaven?"

"I don't think so. It wouldn't be this easy."

They walked across the field. The sky was solid light. No clouds. No sun. Just endless white. Off in the distance, a figure moved toward them. It didn't take long for Gloria to recognize her.

"Who's that?" Angela asked.

"It's your grandmother. Hello, Mother."

The woman hugged Gloria, who stiffened at the embrace. It had been a long time since anyone had touched her in a way other than to cause pain. And her mother had never been this affectionate.

"Hello, Gloria, Angela. You've both come quite a long way."

"Mother . . . what are you doing here?"

"I was sent to meet you."

"Oh, really?" Gloria muttered. "God too busy? What else is new?"

"God's been with you, Gloria. You just haven't let Him into your heart."

"That's bullshit, Mother. God abandoned me a long time ago."

"So where's Heaven? How do we get in?" Angela asked, skipping the niceties.

"It's right here. But only one of you may enter."

"What? What do you mean?" Gloria shook her head. She and Angela looked at each other with expressions of absolute shock. "That's not fair. How can that be?"

"I'm sorry, but that's the way it is."

She shivered as she imagined going back to earth to live as a human-sized maggot, but it was better than having Angela go through it. "You go," Gloria replied, her shoulders slumped in defeat. "I'll go back to earth."

"Thanks, Mom! Well, let's go!" Angela said, stepping forward and grinning from ear to ear.

"I'm afraid the choice isn't yours, child. It's His."

"What do you mean?" Angela asked.

"I mean only one of you has redeemed herself. Only one has improved as a person during her time in Hell, proved to be worthy of paradise. You, my daughter. You may enter Heaven."

Gloria was speechless. She looked at her mother's smiling face, a face that hadn't smiled at her like that since before Gloria had left home to suck cock and lick pussy on camera for a living. Then she looked at her daughter's horrified grimace as the girl's face fell to pieces.

"No! Mommy, you can't leave me here! You can't! Take me with you. You have to take me with you!"

"But why? What did she ever do to deserve to go to Hell?" Gloria cried.

"_Honor thy Mother and thy Father._ She betrayed you. Tricked you and led you to Hell."

"But that's not right! Why should she be expected to honor

parents like me and Ryan? If I wasn't such a bad mother, none of this would have happened!"

"It's not your fault. We all have free will, and she chose her path. Now she has to live with it . . . for eternity."

"Mom, please. Don't leave me. Please take me with you," Angela begged.

"The choice isn't hers." The old woman scowled bitterly at her granddaughter.

"That's where you're wrong, Mother. The choice *is* mine." Both women looked at Gloria.

"What kind of God would separate a mother from her daughter? How can there be a Heaven when those we love are suffering in Hell and on earth?"

"Mom. *No.*"

"Just like you said, Mother. We all have free will. The choice is mine and I've made my decision. I will not abandon my daughter again."

"She was ready to leave you behind. Ready to abandon you when she thought she was allowed into Heaven, Gloria. You want to sacrifice everything for someone like that?"

Gloria nodded. "I'm not leaving her."

The older woman shook her head.

Angela turned toward her mother with eyes filled with tears. "You'd give up paradise for me?" Her face was a riot of pain, sorrow, and confusion.

"I love you, Angela. There is no paradise. Not if it means leaving you behind to suffer."

"You know what this means?" The old woman asked, staring at her daughter and granddaughter as if they were both two pitiful fools.

"Yes. I know." Gloria took her daughter's arm and turned away from Heaven, back toward the entrance to Hell. Somehow, the tunnel didn't look as dark as it had before.

CHAPTER
II

Part IV

"Hell begins on the day when God grants us a clear vision of all that we might have achieved, of all the gifts which we have wasted, of all that we might have done which we did not do"
—Gian Carlo Minotti

The journey back to inferno seemed to take much longer. Gloria and her daughter stumbled along as if in a daze, now stripped of all hope. The tunnel felt even more claustrophobic now. The darkness grew as heaven receded into the distance.

Even with the light of Heaven shining against their backs, casting frightening shadows against the hot, unctuous cave walls, it was as if they were walking through the dripping bowels of some impossibly large beast. Smells of rancid blood and putrescent flesh assailed their senses. Screams echoed through the dank corridors and bounced off cave walls. Even the heat was more oppressive than Gloria remembered.

Eternity, Gloria thought bitterly. *We have to spend eternity here.* She thought it best not to share her terror with her daughter—although she couldn't imagine why not. What was she protecting Angela from? The kid wasn't stupid.

Gloria tried to keep the tears from spilling, wanted to be strong for her daughter. But the realization of what she'd done overpowered her. She'd turned her back on Heaven. *Heaven.* Had turned her back on God. Now what? *Really*, she thought. *What the hell is next?* She almost laughed at the absurdity.

Though she didn't regret her decision. She'd chosen her daughter over Paradise and was proud she'd found the strength. Now she just needed to somehow live with her decision. And to find a way for her and her daughter to survive damnation.

"Mom? I know I'm the reason you're here. You could've left me behind to rot. I don't know why you didn't, but, um . . . thanks."

"I did it for us." And that was the truth. She had done it for herself as much as for Angela. But something felt off . . . and she tried to ignore the memory of Angela's performance

121

on Earth, how easily she'd tricked her mother. She wanted to believe in Angela. Gloria would die—*had* died—for her daughter, and it had been a selfless act, in part anyway. Part of it was Gloria's personal redemption. Remorse for having chosen her addiction over her child so many years earlier. Gloria realized and accepted this. But whatever her true reasons, she had chosen to be with Angela, to sacrifice her own happiness for her child's.

But she wondered what Angela was thinking. Gloria had experienced far too much misery in her life to take much of anything at face value, even when it involved her daughter. Was the girl truly overwhelmed with love and remorse, sincerely grateful? The skeptic in Gloria had a rough time wrapping around that bit of reality. She tended to believe Angela had one goal in mind: herself.

"Besides," Gloria said. "I have to wonder what kind of God allows the existence of a place like this. And what kind of a god allows the conditions to exist on earth that brought us here."

Gloria shook her head, grabbed Angela's shoulder, and they stopped walking. "Whatever I am," she said, with a bit of urgency, as if these words were vitally important, that Angela would need to hear them to survive. "Whatever *you* are. Whatever decisions we've made—He's ultimately responsible because He made it all. Do you understand?"

Angela shrugged and seemed distracted, bored with her mother's words. She tried to pull away but Gloria held tight.

"If a car doesn't run properly, you don't punish the car, right? You punish the maker. Hell is just where God sends his mistakes so He doesn't have to be reminded of His own failures. We've been swept under the rug. It isn't fair, baby. And I want no part of a God like that. It's better to stay in Hell. At least we know what we're up against here."

"Do we? Do you really think they've done their worst to us?"

Angela was still terrified and uncertain. She looked utterly depressed and defeated. This last rejection had destroyed her. It would be up to Gloria to rebuild her.

Gloria's indignation gave her strength, turned her sorrow to rage. She felt better having focus for her anger, even if it was toward someone as untouchable as God. At least it kept her from turning her rage inward and hating herself. She could understand the desire to project your own failures outward and blame others. She understood why God felt it easier to blame man's free will for the evil in the world, rather than on His own flawed design. She was doing the same thing by blaming Him. It was the only way she could live with the horror, and she supposed that if she were God, looking at the myriad atrocities on earth, she would do anything to avoid taking responsibility for it, maybe even punish her own creations for their faults.

"I don't want to be tortured again!" Angela cried. "What the fuck are we supposed to do now?"

She didn't have an answer. Not yet. But there had to be a way. Had to. Gloria didn't want to be tortured again either, but how long could they avoid it? This was Hell, and there was no way they would be allowed to simply exist in peace. They would have to fight or find some way to escape. Heaven was not an option, but neither was returning to Earth as a ridiculous giant slug. Perhaps there was a purgatory after all, despite all mention of Purgatory having been expunged from *The Bible*. Maybe it had never existed. But if Heaven and Hell existed, then maybe there was a possibility. Maybe another corridor somewhere. Gloria didn't know, but she was sure that if it did exist, someone in Hell would know where to find it. Just like they'd known about this tunnel. There was still so much to consider.

"I promise, I'll never let anyone hurt you again."

"Don't make promises you can't keep, *Mother*."

Gloria winced. The bitterness in Angela's voice wounded her.

As they made their way back into Hell, with the light from Heaven fading in the distance behind them, they saw others walking up through the tunnel in the opposite direction. Each shared physical traits that clearly marked them as related. Mother, father, and three children. Their scarred and filthy faces were filled with the same mixture of fear and enthusiasm

123

that had no doubt been on Gloria and Angela's faces when they first made their way toward Paradise. Seeing Gloria and her daughter returning, looking dejected, seemed to diminish the family's already waning enthusiasm.

"D-did you see him?" the father asked, reaching out for Gloria like a starving man reaching for table scraps.

Gloria brushed him away. She hadn't forgotten what had happened to her the last time she'd felt sympathy for one of her fellow citizens of damnation. Now she trusted no one.

"No," she said. "He wouldn't see us. Good luck to you though." Gloria kept walking, hugging her daughter tight. Angela clung to her mother's side, staring nervously at the family.

The man's eyes widened in fear as he watched Gloria and her daughter head back toward inferno. "He wouldn't see you? Why? What did they tell you?"

"They said we're damned," Gloria said. "We're all damned. That's why we're here. This is just another method of torture, as far as I'm concerned. Just another way to give us hope so it can be crushed again. We're going back where we belong, back to the only place that will have us."

They wandered away, and the man and his family stood in the dimly lit tunnel, clearly petrified to move forward.

The light of Heaven was almost a memory as Gloria and Angela walked deeper into the gloom.

Gloria stopped suddenly and her daughter looked up at her quizzically.

"What's wrong, Mom?"

"Why are they here?" Gloria glanced back. "How could an entire family wind up in Hell?"

Gloria yelled into the tunnel. "Hey! Hey, wait!" She jogged back and found them waiting. "What did you do?"

"What?" The puzzled man studied Gloria's face.

"How did you get here? Why is your entire family here?"

"We died together in a plane crash."

Gloria was almost frantic. Everyone was looking at her like she'd lost her mind, but insanity was so common in this place that her anxiety seemed almost pedestrian.

"But why did you all end up here? Why didn't you go to Heaven? You all couldn't have been bad people. At least the children—"

The father stared at the ground, refused to meet Gloria's eyes. "Because we were atheists. We didn't believe in God. We denied Him."

"So you were sent here? Your entire family? But that's not right. How could He do this?"

"We didn't believe."

"No! That's not right. Kids can't be blamed for—"

"We have to go. Maybe He'll take us now. After all, we can't possibly deny His existence now, right?"

"But . . . how long have you been here?"

"I don't know."

"What year did you die?"

"Nineteen forty-three."

Gloria's mouth dropped open. They'd been suffering in damnation for over sixty years just for not believing? It was so cruel she couldn't get her mind around it.

"We really need to get going. I don't want the demons to catch us. Not when we're so close."

Gloria and Angela watched the man and his family walk off into the light. She held her daughter as they walked back toward Hell, more determined than ever to find a way out. They wouldn't spend eternity there.

It wasn't fair. None of it was fair.

***

By the time they fully exited the tunnel, a group had gathered at its entrance. She recognized their frightened, apprehensive looks and knew that seeing her and her daughter walk out did nothing to embolden them.

"Did you see Him?"

"What was He like?"

"Why didn't He take you?"

"She must be a murderer or Satanist or something."

"Why didn't He take you?"

125

"I'll bet she murdered babies back on earth."

"She must have been a child molester or something."

"Maybe she committed suicide. They say that's an unforgivable sin."

"Why didn't He let you stay?"

Gloria had to fight her way through the small angry mob, trying to protect her daughter from their questions. Terrified, confused faces, all wanting answers, none wanting answers.

The crowd turned vicious. They tore at Gloria's hair. Someone slapped her. Someone else punched her in the stomach. Angela screamed as they attacked her, too. They were knocked to the ground and the crowd moved in to kick and stomp them. Angela's screams grew louder and Gloria crawled over, using her own body to protect Angela's.

Gloria took the brunt of the attack, her ribs bruised, head bloody from the assault.

"Why are they so mad?" Angela screamed. "Why are they hurting us?"

Gloria tried to respond but a boot smashed down on her mouth, shattering her teeth. She coughed and spit blood as she was stomped again. Her eye was squashed and sunk down into her skull. They pummeled her with rocks plucked from the cave floor. It felt as though every bone in her body was being mashed to bits.

Gloria screamed, the pain in her ruined face and head unbearable, but she knew that screaming was a huge mistake.

Then, the sound of thunder as demons poured down the corridor and into the chamber. More than a dozen filed in, their skin a gruesome tapestry of scarified flesh decorated with animal horns and teeth, metal and bone, grafted into their skulls, torsos, and limbs like the demon that had held Gloria captive. Fallen angels self-modified into hideous monsters. They each stood more than seven feet tall, stooping with their backs scraping the cave ceiling. Their mouths were filled with jagged shards of metal, bone, and stone filed to sharp points. A profusion of fangs and tusks, glinting in the flickering torchlight was embedded in their gums in no discernable order, the insane artistry of some demented orthodontist. They grinned and snarled, gazing with sadistic, undisguised lust and cruelty upon the frightened humans, their intentions etched into their twisted flesh as plainly as the scars and tattoos that adorned them. Quickly they fanned out to block both exits, cutting off all avenue of retreat. The trapped humans began to cry and pray and beg. Some of them simply laid on the ground, curled into fetal positions, shivering with fear, waiting for the blows to fall, for the pain to begin.

Massive clubs and axes swung with lethal ferocity at the fleeing humans, mowing them down like blades of grass, hacking everyone to pieces. Some of the demons simply scooped up the fleeing souls and shredded them with their teeth and claws, literally chewing them up and spitting them out. Still others took the opportunity to satiate their savage lusts, raping and sodomizing anyone they could get their hands on even as they eviscerated and dismembered them.

Gloria had never seen such wholesale slaughter. She doubled over, dry heaving, unable to regurgitate with an empty stomach. The screams were deafening. She clamped her hands over her ears, trying to block out the din, then added her own screams to the chorus.

Body parts flew in every direction as the demons tore the mob apart. Bits and pieces hit Gloria in the face and smashed against the cave walls. Gloria tried to crawl away from the carnage, dragging her hysterical daughter with her. Their only hope was that the demons wouldn't notice them escaping, would be too caught up in their apparent glee at attacking the humans who were still mobile.

They hid in a nearby hole carved into the cave wall, barely able to conceal themselves in the small opening. They dragged the remains of other human on top of them, hiding beneath severed limbs and organs. So far the demons hadn't seemed to notice. Gloria glanced over as a demon beheaded the last human. Not that that would pose a problem for any of them—they would all regenerate, and knowing the demons' behavior the way she did, they would wait patiently so they could attack the humans all over again.

The demons were laughing. Standing over the body parts

and laughing, pointing at chunks of human meat strewn throughout the cave, still hideously alive. Unable to die despite the grievous injuries they'd suffered. They watched the undulating limbs, heads, and torsos, the beating hearts and expanding and contracting lungs that had been ripped from ruptured chests with ghoulish glee. Taking delight in stomping them into pulp, relishing the sounds of cracking bone and squishing meat and organs.

Some were still furiously copulating with the dismembered bodies, forcing the hideously wounded souls to submit to intercourse and anal penetration, forcing them to perform fellatio, raping their headless necks, eviscerated stomachs and eyeless skulls along with any other orifice they could find or create. Lubricating their malformed phalluses with the blood of one before sodomizing another in an orgy of violence that seemed to go on forever.

"Watch," one said, its bulbous head topped with a profusion of horns, antlers, and tusks, wobbling as it laughed. It picked up a woman's head, her eyes blinking furiously, her tongue trying to work despite her head no longer being attached to her vocal cords. The demon snatched various body parts from around the cave and pressed them together, like trying to fit the wrong pieces into a puzzle. But the limbs began to reattach and regenerate as piece by piece was added, until the demon had created its own type of human.

The human-thing stood on mismatched legs, its male torso supporting its female head. The other demons followed suit and created their own human hybrids.

The small human mob that had attacked Gloria and Angela were herded out of the cave, some crawling on distorted limbs, others trying to walk on arms that had been assembled where legs should have been. One had had his head reattached backwards and screamed hysterically when he realized it was permanent.

"We're okay," Gloria whispered through her shattered mouth, her arms tight around Angela's shoulders. Her face was already beginning to regenerate.

Her daughter's eyes were squeezed shut.

"It's okay to look. They're gone." Gloria made sure to keep her voice as quiet as possible.

Angela looked at her mother and shook her head. "You look horrible. What did they do to you?"

"I'll be fine."

"I'm so scared."

"Me too."

"That could have been us!"

Gloria nodded. "I know," she whispered. "But you have to be quiet. Very quiet."

Angela nodded. "Serves them right. For what they did to us. They deserved that!"

"No one deserves that, Angela."

Angela scowled. "They were disgusting. Horrible and disgusting."

Gloria cradled her daughter's head against her shoulder. "Try to relax. Get some sleep."

The need to sleep—along with every other bodily function—no longer existed, yet like breathing or gasping for breath when pain became too much to bear, the overwhelming desire to curl up in a warm cozy bed, bundled beneath a comforter was something Gloria yearned for. As it was, she would accept curling against a rock and shutting her eyes, hoping dreams would take her far from this place. But there never were dreams, never the solace of escape. Only nightmares, asleep and awake.

When Gloria opened her eyes, Angela was staring at her. "How can you sleep?"

"I told you, I—"

"But it's not real! And you're putting us in danger. How can you be so selfish?"

Gloria excused the remark as teenage angst. And stupidity. And a young lifetime of living with a degenerate father.

"What would you like us to do then?"

Angela scowled, huffing her indignation.

"Picnic, perhaps? Take a walk along the shore?"

"You know what I mean, *Mother*."

Gloria always wondered why her daughter didn't finish

that with *fucker*. "All we can do is hope to survive. We have no place else to go. Not yet anyway."

"There has to be someplace. You said so yourself."

"Where else do you have in mind? I'm open to suggestions."

"You're the mother. You're supposed to know these things." She sobbed, wrapping her arms around her knees, hugging herself for comfort.

There were moments—moments of weakness where Gloria knew she didn't belong here, knew she could escape, could desert her daughter and escape into Heaven if she desired. And it was tempting . . . she'd even convinced herself that once there, she might be able to plead with them, convince them to allow Angela in as well. All she'd have to do is leave Angela behind. Angela, the girl who had betrayed her in life, had subjected her mother to an eternity in Hell.

Gloria hadn't exactly been a saint on earth. She'd done what she'd needed to do to survive. But she didn't deserve this, and Heaven seemed ready to forgive her transgressions, including sacrificing herself for Angela's baby, which had amounted to committing suicide, despite the selflessness of the act.

"Can we go now?" Angela whined. "Find some food or something."

"You're not hungry."

"Yes I am!"

"When's the last time you ate?"

The girl shrugged, scowled, turned away. "I had a cheese-burger."

"Months ago. You don't need to eat. These bodies aren't even real, not real flesh anyway, despite being able to touch and feel. There's no *need* to eat. Do you understand?"

"Whatever." She studied grubby fingernails that would never come clean enough. "But I *want* to eat. Just like you and your stupid naps. You can't be tired. We don't get tired here."

"Fair enough. What would you like to eat? Grubs? Maggots? Rats? I haven't seen much else."

"Why are you doing this to me?" the girl whined.

"Because you're being ridiculous. We can't waste time on nonsense. We've got to get out of this place." She laughed in

130

spite of her fear.

"What's so funny?"

"Nothing. Reminds me of a song by The Animals. You know?" Gloria sang quietly, "We gotta get out of this place, if it's the last thing we ever do."

Angela rolled her eyes. "Never heard of it. Must be one of your Golden Moldies."

"Yeah, well, not a big surprise. That group was way before your time."

"Do you think we ever will? Get out, I mean."

"We have to. Right? We have to. It's not like we have a choice. I'm not spending an eternity in this—" She almost said *hellhole.* "—place."

"What will it take?" Angela asked, in a rather strange way, Gloria thought. A little introspective, as if the question had been for herself and not her mother.

Gloria grabbed Angela's hand. "Come on."

"Where?"

"I have no idea. But we should keep moving. Things have been way too quiet. Our luck's bound to run out, especially the farther we travel into Hell."

They passed demons and humans along the way but managed to evade capture and not attract attention. Gloria knew it wouldn't last. There were just too many sadistic creatures roaming around, and she shuddered, afraid to imagine what they might encounter next.

Or how they'd survive.

But there had to be a way out of Hell. Had to be.

Angela abruptly stopped walking and yanked Gloria back half a foot. "Why are we going this way?"

Gloria thought for a moment and half shrugged. "Not too many choices."

"Yeah, but we were safe where we were. Right? So why leave?"

"We weren't safe."

"Well not exactly, but compared to the rest of the place? It's only going to get worse the further in we go. Why don't we go back?"

"Because there was nothing there, Angela. No freedom. No escape."

"And you think going back into Hell is a way to escape? That makes no sense!"

"You have to trust me."

"No, I don't! I think you're nuts. I think maybe you enjoy being fucked over and over again by those things."

"Don't be stupid. Of course I don't!"

"Bullshit. Why else go back? You didn't go into Heaven and why would *anyone* want to go into Hell?"

"Angela—"

"No!" She yanked away from her mother's grasp. "I'll bet it's your fault I turned into that slug thing. I'll bet if I went by myself they would've let me in."

Angela stepped back, as if repulsed by having to share space with her mother. "Tell me, *Mother*, what kind of deal did you make? How did you sacrifice me? You've done it before, so I don't know why this surprises me. You gave me up because you loved drugs and *fucking* more than you loved me. So what did you do this time?"

"Lower your voice. We're too close."

"Fuck you!" Angela screamed. "Fuck you fuck you fuck you!" The girl smirked.

"Jesus," Gloria muttered, cringing at the sound of heavy footfalls echoing in the corridor.

"Protect me from *that*, you lying bitch."

"What are you?" Gloria snapped. "Bipolar?"

From around the sharp corner three demons emerged.

"Uh oh," Angela whispered, but Gloria was sure she saw the girl grin.

The first demon wielded a club studded with railroad ties. He swung it at Gloria's head and she ducked, barely escaping the swing, and it smashed into the wall instead, now embedded in the rock. The demon cursed her and the club, and struggled to pull it free.

"Run!" Gloria screamed, but the second demon lunged for Angela, grabbing hold of her calves. Rows of hooks jutted from the creature's arms, a fishing accident gone strangely

132

awry, and he dragged his forearms down the length of Angela's legs, destroying the skin, chunks of bloody pulp sticking to the hooks. Angela landed on her stomach, the wind knocked out of her, and she pawed the earth trying to escape.

The third demon opened its mouth and leaned into Gloria. She hadn't been ready for the attack, had been watching Angela, trying to figure out how to save her daughter. Inside the demon's mouth was a second mouth like a crocodile's snout, and beyond that a third mouth like an eel, all three filled with row upon row of jagged razor-like teeth.

Gloria shrieked and cowered as those endless rows of teeth swallowed her head up to her neck, hot puddles of sizzling, acid-like saliva cauterizing her skin. The last thing she remembered was the crunching, the chewing through her flesh and bone as her head was severed from her shoulders.

***

Gloria woke to the fleeting memory of the man with his head on backwards, terrified for a moment until she was able to determine after a quick check that she was again in one piece, all of her parts in their correct place and none that did not belong to her.

Lying on the ground, naked again, as if these monsters had nothing better to do than steal the filthy rags she'd managed to scrounge. Never mind the smell—despite a lack of bodily fluids, the body retained the memory of past odors. So sweat and exertion generated a musky, earthy, offensive aroma. And death itself? Besides the smells of dirt and embalming fluids, Gloria's body emitted an offensive reek of decay. She wondered if it was something she would ever get used to.

"Angela?" No sign of her daughter. "Angela!"

The shape huddled in the corner, curled into a fetal position and facing the wall was most definitely not her daughter, although Gloria had no idea who it might be. And she didn't care.

Until he rolled over to face her.

"Oh my God," she sputtered. "Dad?"

133

He pushed himself into a standing position, pitching forward a bit on wobbly legs. His face was grossly scarred, and bones in his arms and legs had healed badly.

"Gloria. Dear sweet Gloria."

She threw herself into his arms and sobbed, holding him again, pure joy. She thought she'd never again feel his touch, enjoy the warmth of his scratchy chin against her cheek. It had been so long. An eternity.

"My god. Dad." He'd died so long ago. Long before her porn and addictions.

"But why are you here?" he asked, stroking her hair.

"Long story."

"It has to be a mistake."

"Yes," she said. "In a way. Not that I'd led a good life. I did . . . things. I'm not proud of what I did with my life."

"I know," he said, fingers now entwined in her hair. "I've seen."

"You have?" She tried to gently pull away but his fingers were snarled, and he didn't seem to be letting go.

"Sure. They show us lots of interesting things in Hell."

Gloria nodded, tried again to pull away. She felt uncomfortable now but figured it was just the usual. Almost everything in Hell felt uncomfortable.

"Oh, Dad," she said, trying to enjoy his embrace. It had been so long since she'd seen him, and even longer since she'd had any normal physical contact with anyone other than Angela—and even Angela was stiff, restrained most of the time.

Still. . . .

"Why are *you* here?" she whispered, trying again to pull away. Again unable. Starting to panic just the slightest.

He leaned in closer, until their naked bodies were pressed together, until she felt his hot breath in her ear.

"You weren't the first," he whispered. "But you were the best."

"What?"

"Let's not waste time with the psychobabble," he said, then laughed, spittle flying into her hair.

She shoved him, tried to anyway, but he held tight, possessing some bizarre strength he couldn't possible have held in life.

"Let go," she whined, reduced to tears, reduced to feeling once again like a small child, unable to protect herself. "Please," she begged. "Don't."

He forced her to her knees and followed with her, one hand holding her wrists above her head, his other hand roaming, fingers toying with her pussy. His tongue lapped at her breast, teeth razing over the nipple.

She tried to fight him off, begged him to stop.

He was too strong.

"Tell me you want me," he groaned. "Like you used to. Say 'fuck me, Daddy!' Say it."

"No! You never molested me!" She threw back her head, bucked her legs. "Get off!"

"I plan to," he laughed. He planted his knees between her legs and forced hers apart.

"Don't do this," she sobbed.

His huge cock was studded with barbs that shredded her flesh as he penetrated. She was used to agony, used to demons fucking her with their ridiculously oversized phalluses, but she'd never been so emotionally assaulted. Even rape by her aborted fetuses had been somehow impersonal—faceless, nameless little creatures. But this—this was her father, and she had no memories of what he'd claimed he'd done to her. *You weren't the first but you were the best.* She only remembered a gentle, loving man who had died way too early in her young life.

The thing crushing her pounded away, fucked her hard while biting chunks from her breast, chewing at the soft tissue until he'd bitten the nipple off. The hand not restraining hers squeezed and yanked on the other breast as if trying to tear it from her body.

He jerked as he came, spastic shuddering, legs and ass quivering. When he pulled out, his barbed cock shredded a fresh layer of skin from her pussy.

Gloria lay on the ground even after he released her, even

135

after he climbed from her trembling body. She knew the wounds would heal. She didn't know how easily she would be able to recover mentally from this assault.

She crawled onto her knees, wincing in pain. The monster standing before her stroked his cock, and it was already growing hard again in his hands.

"You're not my father," she said, suddenly realizing he couldn't be. "My father was good. He-he wouldn't be here. You're not my father!" Gloria was crying, body hitching and jerking as it spasmed with sorrow. This was the worst thing she could imagine. Somehow she had never expected anything this reprehensible, never expected it to go this low. It sounded ridiculous, but she had somehow expected that even in the inferno there would be some standard of decency, some line they would not cross. Incest? Child molestation? If these were not off limits then nothing was. She felt more terrified now than she had in all her time in hell.

"Of course I'm your father," he said, licking his lips. "Don't you recognize me?"

Gloria scrambled away from him on her hands and knees, blood pouring from between her thighs like an open faucet. This couldn't be her father. No one would do this to their own child, not even in hell. But even as she said it she knew that it was a lie. On earth there were fathers and mothers who used and sexually abused their own children, children far more innocent than Gloria had ever been.

"If-if you were my father—stuck in Hell like I am—you wouldn't be rewarded. You wouldn't be down here fucking whoever you wanted to. You'd be getting fucked. You'd be getting raped and tortured and mutilated like me! You wouldn't be allowed to fuck me. They wouldn't let you feel any pleasure!"

"I've been here a long time, pet. I've paid my dues. I'm a demon now, a minion. It's my job to bring misery to others. This is my occupation now, fucking damned whores like you."

"Bullshit."

'Believe what you want," he said, stroking his engorged cock, avoiding the barbs. "Whatever makes you feel better. If it helps you cope."

He grinned. "Now come to Poppa."

"Get away from me," she yelled, angry, afraid, repulsed by the slobbering thing in front of her. Whatever it was, father/demon, it was hideous.

"Get the fuck away from me!" She kicked out at him as he reached for her. Her naked foot collided with his chest and knocked him back.

But he wasn't giving up that easily. "I said come here." He grabbed her shoulders and knocked her to the ground. He ignored her punches and kicks and crying and pleading and easily shoved his cock inside her again, digging deeper, pounding fiercely.

She couldn't fight him. More than human, he was a demon, and he possessed a demon's strength.

"Fine," she snapped. "You come *here*, you crazy cock-sucker!" She wrapped her legs around his, pulling him in even deeper. The pain was staggering, brought stars to her eyes, his barbed cock carving her pussy into raw pulp. But she wouldn't give up, wouldn't give in.

"What are you doing?" he gasped, still raping her but more slowly now, trying to pull away from her.

"Doing?" she moaned. "I'm . . . fuh-fucking *you!*"

He rammed her hard, going deeper, deeper still, until her stomach was one big cramp, until she wanted to vomit.

But she wouldn't give up. "Yes!" she cried. "Harder! Come on, is that all you got? Fuck me harder!"

"Shut up!" he roared, and punched her in the mouth.

"You suck at this," she taunted. "Even the lowliest drug dealers could get me off."

His fists moved so quickly she couldn't see them, couldn't tell where one would land next. Her face was a bloody, bruised mess. He pulled out of her and continued the assault, punching and kicking until she thought she was going to black out.

In a rage he yelled, his bellow shaking the chamber walls.

Then he discorporated. His body dissolved into an advanced decay, liquefying into an ichorous flesh pudding that oozed out of her mutilated sex and into the cracks of the

137

cave floor. That overpowering stench of death exuded from her once more as the demon's putrescence continued to leak from her bleeding sex.

Gloria lay on the ground for the longest time, until she was again able to get to her feet, able to at least try to limp away, knowing she would heal, and wanting to get moving before some other loathsome thing claimed her for further abuse.

She staggered through the cave entrance, her legs trembling, blood cascading down her thighs, her nerves singing out in anguish. She found her discarded rags.

None of this is real! Nothing could be this terrible. Even in Hell there has to be mercy!

She had found mercy in her demon, the one who had claimed her when she first came to Hell. He had pitied her or loved her—or whatever passed for love in this necropolis of pain and woe—and had sacrificed himself to reclaim the beauty he'd once had as an angel of God. He had shown her mercy and that had allowed her to escape and find her daughter and the pathway to Heaven.

But hope and faith are human weaknesses.

Weaknesses that Hell viciously and casually exploits.

Gloria wondered if her entire flight from Hell had been preplanned, orchestrated to cause her even more pain.

And what about Angela? Why isn't she here? Could she be part of it too?

Finding her daughter in the endless corridors of Hell had seemed like a miraculous stroke of good luck. Now it seemed too miraculous, too coincidental. Countless millions of souls must inhabit these caves. . . . Yet somehow she'd managed to find the one thing in all of creation that she gave a fuck about? Stumbled across her in the dark? It wasn't possible. It had to have been a trick. Maybe that wasn't even her daughter, just as that grotesque thing that claimed to be her father couldn't have been. Maybe Angela had been some incarnation sent to confuse her, to trick her, to guarantee that she would renounce her one chance at redemption and turn her back on God.

Gloria staggered through the dark corridors, her mind reeling, trying to put everything into some coherent framework. Her thoughts dashed about and tripped through her head in riotous disorder. And then a new question, one that her father had sparked in her mind. *Is there a way to become one of them? One of the torturers instead of the tortured?* Of all the multifarious torments of inferno this constant state of confusion was by far the worst.

The further she made her way through the inner corridors of Hell the more the smells of blood and flesh intensified. Horrific screams of incalculable anguish echoed from every direction. She had become so used to the constant cries of torment that she failed to notice the increase in volume and duration until it was all around her, making her head feel as if it would split as the piercing cries lanced her skull. It sounded like thousands, perhaps even hundreds of thousands, being tortured at once. As if someone had filled a stadium with the damned and was now burning the whole thing down.

Gloria rounded the corner and her legs collapsed from under her. Her senses screamed in denial, retreating from the overload of terrifying imagery.

The Lake of Fire was apparently a mere artery of this infinite ocean upon whose banks she now stood. Thousands of miles of twisted flesh and bone seethed and undulated like a living thing, a vast creature that screamed out in pain from its every pore. Waves of liquefied meat crashed against the beach, spilling their shrieking contents onto the rocky earth before the next wave rolled in to drag them back into the sea. No horror she'd ever been subjected to in Hell or elsewhere compared to the sheer magnitude of this abomination.

This was the true heart of Hell.

There was no flame. No lava. The entire ocean was composed of boiling blood and fat and tears. Bodies in varying degrees of degeneration and regeneration crowded every inch of it. Most of them were screaming and praying and cursing, but it was the silent ones that Gloria found the most disturbing, the ones staring out at nothing, with minds empty of everything except their own unending agony.

It was no different from the lake she'd seen her demon captive throw himself into, the ocean only shocking due to its sheer enormity. An endless sea of boiling humanity larger than all the oceans of the world combined. The concept of eight billion souls burning in Hell was one that the human mind simply could not fathom, too large for the finite human mind to encapsulate. Seeing it was more than her mind could bear.

Gloria tumbled to the cave floor, staring up at an endless sky of blue and brown and green, swirling like a vast kaleidoscope above that boiling ocean of flesh. It was not a sky of clouds and stars but a revolving world hovering miles above Hell. It looked like pictures she'd seen of the earth from space and it rained an unending torrent of bodies into the cauldron of flesh and blood beneath it, as if Earth were defecating its human waste. A relentless deluge of the damned flooded the sky, hurtling toward Hell a thousand souls a second.

Angels with skin like untouched snow, with eyes like starlit night, hairless and sexless with wings three times the length of a human body swooped down among them, dodging in between the cascade of hurtling bodies, catching some before they plunged into the sea and carting them away. Tears spilled from Gloria's eyes as she watched, wishing they would take her away as well, but there had never been an angel for her. No one to lift her up and fly her away from the horrors of the world. The only angel she'd ever known had been the demon who'd tortured and imprisoned her when she'd first arrived. Briefly she wondered what had become of him. What terrors he was being subjected to now that he walked damnation, undisguised, as a living example of God's fickle mercy.

She remembered him as she'd seen him last. Those midnight eyes that somehow still cast light, that seemed to swirl with every color of the rainbow and burned like exploding stars, skin like morning light, unmarred despite eons imprisoned in that tomb of disfigured flesh. He had been beautiful, the most beautiful creature she'd ever seen. Now he was being tortured because of her. She tried not to think about him being cut and burned and sodomized and whipped, his wings torn from their sockets over and over again as they regenerated. Being defecated on and pissed on as she had been at his hands. All the things they would do to him to shame and

140

degrade him, to vent their rage and frustration at being trapped in inferno.

Gloria tried to push these thoughts out of her mind, to concentrate on finding Angela. Angela was her priority. Still, her thoughts kept drifting back to her beautiful angel. She wanted to see him again.

Perhaps he could help her escape. Even take her to Heaven with him. Surely he has suffered enough. God would have to take him back. God has to have mercy for one of his own.

But Gloria wasn't so sure. She looked back out over the Ocean of Fire, watching as more bodies fell into its scalding waters, trying to count how many the angels rescued. It was maybe one in a thousand. The odds weren't good. She looked down at the souls boiling in that sea of liquefied flesh and wondered if God had any mercy at all.

Then her mind shut down.

She dreamt of her life before Hell. Even in her current surroundings her life still seemed like a nightmare. She remembered the height of her porn career. The fame. The money. The sex. The drugs. At the time it had seemed like paradise. She had thought she had everything she could ever want. Now it all seemed like one great tragedy. She awoke screaming, the remnants of her last dream fading from her mind too slowly. The image of Vlad's fat leering face still fresh in her mind, and the taste of worm semen haunting her tongue. She sat staring at the Ocean of Fire for a long moment, her will diminishing more and more the longer she watched the ceaseless influx of the damned. It took all her remaining resolve to peel her eyes away from it and turn her mind back to her task. *Find Angela. Find a way out of Hell.*

She rose slowly and turned to the nearest tunnel, walking toward whatever fate awaited her. Now even more determined to find Angela and her angel. In one or both of them she was sure her salvation would be found.

Before she'd taken more than a few steps, she spotted the old man she'd met in the tunnel, the father who'd been trying to rescue his family from Hell. He was alone now, and his face had fallen, as if all the vitality had been leeched from his soul. He stared longingly out across the Ocean of Fire as tears ran the maze of wrinkles and worry lines down his face. Gloria recognized the expression: defeat, resignation. He was walking toward the boiling ocean in a trance. Gloria was certain that he was seconds from throwing himself in.

"Hey!" Gloria called out, getting no response. Her voice was swallowed in the ceaseless din of tortured souls screaming out for a release that would never come.

She walked toward him and called out again, now so close she could have spit on him. Still, he gave no indication that he'd heard her. Odd behavior for a longtime citizen of Hell, she thought, where constant wariness and vigilance was the only defense against victimization.

Gloria reached out and grabbed his shoulder. He glanced at her with a look devoid of all recognition.

"It's me. I met you in the tunnel. You were trying to get to Heaven with your family. What happened?"

His eyes focused on hers and his mind slowly returned from wherever dark place it had been. "They made it. God took them back. But He wouldn't take me."

"Why?"

"Because I was the one who convinced my wife to turn her back on Him. I was the one who decided our children would be raised as atheists. I was the one who damned them. It was my fault. I'm the one who should be punished."

His eyes swam away from hers and his face once again began to take up that vacuous expression.

"Then why did He send them here in the first place?"

"What?" His eyes focused on hers again.

"If it was your fault, if you were the cause of their sins, then why did He send them to Hell at all? Why make them suffer for more than half a century in this place for something you did?"

The old man stared at her for a long moment and then laughed. "You're new here."

"What the fuck does that have to do with—"

"I've sat on this beach many times, for decades. Do you know what I see?"

142

"What?" Gloria stood beside him and looked out at the ocean.

"Chaos. There's no order here. There's no order any-where—here or in Heaven."

"What do you mean?"

"Those angels out there—how do you think they know which souls to rescue from those that fall? How do you think they identify the sinners from the saved?"

"I don't know. God tells them or something?"

The old man laughed again. "They don't."

"Don't what?"

"They don't know. They don't pick out the good ones. It's random. I've seen the worst of sinners whisked away to heaven, men I knew and recognized, famous men. I have heard of serial killers and mass-murderers in Heaven. Now how does that make you feel? That's supposed to be the grand example of God's mercy, that a sinner can get into Heaven. I'm sure they have to repent their sins or some such bullshit before they're allowed in, but who wouldn't to escape this? And I have seen many an honest man wind up here instead. It's all random."

"But that can't be!"

"And why not? He's the Almighty. In His mind He owes us nothing, no explanation, *nothing*. And we owe Him everything. We have to accept that it all makes sense from his infinite perspective. I have seen hundreds sit on these banks trying to make sense of it, trying to understand God's logic. Why they're in Hell when the worst thing they'd ever done was worship the wrong God or have premarital sex or cheat on their wives. Then they see some famous criminal whisked off to paradise. They wander down that tunnel, thinking that surely their sins will be forgiven. If Albert DeSalvo can get into Heaven after strangling all those women . . . but they come walking back down that tunnel more confused and disheartened than ever when they're rejected."

"That doesn't make sense!" Gloria could feel herself starting to panic. Of all the lies and curses and insults and threats hurled her way since coming to Hell, this was by far the most horrible thing she'd heard.

"Why do you think that tunnel's there? In case a truly honest soul winds up here? There are thousands, millions of honest souls here. But some do make it out. If they can find it. And if they have the guts to try. Most just figure they must have done something to deserve damnation. Who can't look over the vast experiences of an entire lifetime and find at least one sin for which they believe they should be damned? So they just stay here forever with the child-molesters and murderers. The afterlife is just like life. Lightning bolts strike churches as often as bars and strip joints on earth. Good befalls the bad and bad befalls the good. Why would you think things would be different here when the same god invented it all?"

The old man shook his head and turned his back on the flaming sea of flesh and spirit. He looked long into Gloria eyes then dropped his head and began to shuffle away, casting one last longing gaze back at the Ocean of Fire and at the sky above.

"Maybe God does have a plan," he said. "Maybe it all makes sense to him and our limited, finite minds are just too weak to grasp it all. Or maybe it's all just as senseless and random as it appears and we are all just deluding ourselves."

Gloria licked her lips, letting his words sink in. What he said was insane. Yet she believed him. She'd seen enough to know his ridiculous words rang true. "So now what? Where do we go from here?"

"I'd kill myself if I could. But we're already dead so I guess that idea's pointless. What are your plans?"

"I have to find my daughter and . . . someone else."

"You're going to just wander around Hell by yourself? You'll never find her."

She shrugged. "Probably not. But I have to try. You could help if you wanted. You seem to know the deal around here."

He shrugged. "I could. There's not much of this place I haven't seen. But why would I? I told you. It's all pointless. Even your love for your daughter means nothing here."

Gloria sighed and shook her head. "I know."

"But you have to try. Don't you?"

144

"It's all I've got."

"Then you've got nothing." He looked once more out over the boiling sea of screaming souls. "But I'll help you. What else is there for an old fool to do?"

***

Again unmolested during their trek . . . Gloria suspected it was more than coincidence, more than good luck. Synchronicity held no court in Hell. If they were being allowed safe passage, there had to be a reason.

The caves and corridors she'd chosen to explore were random. Dan, the old man, offered no suggestions, never tried to sway her in one particular direction, so her suspicions of him—particularly his eagerness to help—were most likely unfounded, she started to believe.

The corridor before them was unlike any she had previously encountered. The walls, although adorned like all others with sconces fashioned from human body parts, were well-lit, almost . . . cheery. Dried blood decorated the walls in a myriad pattern, brown and burgundy splotches in a dadaist pattern. Few skulls littered the ground.

"Maybe we should turn back," Gloria whispered, chills tickling her spine for some unexplained reason. If anything, this quiet hallway should bring her peace, but it was doing the opposite.

"Why?" He pointed down the hall, as if that gesture explained what was on his mind.

She didn't have an answer because she was running on instinct. A gut feeling was telling her this was too easy, that something wasn't quite right. "It's too quiet."

"Maybe we got lucky."

"In all the decades you've been here, how 'lucky' have you ever been?"

He nodded. "I see your point."

"No," she said, more to herself, "this isn't luck. This is something else."

"Fate?"

What an odd response. She waited for the other shoe to drop. "Fate? You think we follow some sort of force? That we have some kind of controlled destiny?"

"Without a doubt. Why should anything be different in Hell?"

"Because *everything* is different in Hell!" She'd spoken more loudly than she'd intended and lowered her voice. "That's absurd. You're going on the assumption that I believe in fate to begin with. You're telling me everything happens for a reason, right?"

He nodded again. "Pretty much."

"What about the Ocean of Fire? That's basically a crapshoot, isn't it? Where the righteous end up facing the same torture as the damned. How is that fate?"

Dan chuckled and scratched his chin. "Chaos theory."

"What?"

"It's a relatively new concept on earth but a very old one here. The greater the chaos the greater and more immediate the resultant order. God wants to intensify mayhem in Hell and on earth so that all of it will resolve itself into order. His order. The perfect civilization on earth, the perfect system of justice and punishment in Hell? Neither of those would equal the perfection that will come out of this madness. That's your Judgement Day. All this insanity collapsing in on itself, imploding into perfect sublime oblivion. God said 'Let there be light' and has regretted it ever since. Who do you really believe rules Hell?"

Gloria rested against the wall, trying to avoid the severed arm sconce. "Satan?"

Dan laughed and shook his head. "Satan is a paper tiger."

"A what?"

Dan ignored her question and grabbed a torch from the wall. "It gets dark farther down. We'll need this." He took a few steps down the corridor but Gloria refused to follow.

"You know exactly where we're going. Don't you? When you talked of fate or destiny . . . you knew all along where you were leading me."

He glanced back at her and didn't answer for several

seconds. "I'm just supposed to make sure you get there."

"Get where?"

"You'll see."

"No," she snapped, "I won't. I'm not going any farther."

"They want to meet you."

"*They* who?"

"I'm not allowed to say."

"This is bullshit."

"Please. Just come with me."

"Why not just capture me out there? Why bring me to them? Why all of this?"

"They never venture into Inferno. It's beneath them. They may rule here, but they don't soil their hands or feet. There are many corridors of Hell and some of them can be quite comfortable, even seductive. That's were they live, the place where all sins are indulged. It's another blasphemy against Heaven, a mockery of God's laws. But not all sins are painful, only their consequences. They instructed me to bring you to them."

"Why?"

"I'm sure they'll tell you."

"I'm going back."

"Suit yourself. But all roads lead to the same place. Some just take a little longer."

"I'll take my chances." She turned away from Dan and took a step in the direction they had come from.

But the passageway was gone, replaced by a solid wall of rock.

"Fuck," she mumbled, not entirely surprised by the sudden appearance of a wall. She turned back toward Dan. "You were saying?" She pointed down the corridor, indicating he should lead.

"Told you."

"Yeah, thanks. That helps."

They walked a short distance in silence, Gloria wondering where everyone was. After all, Hell was notoriously overcrowded. So why were no creatures roaming in this section?

147

She broke the silence. "What happened to your family? I find it hard to believe God let them all in after all."

He shrugged. "The Lord works in mysterious ways."

"So now what? You just stay here and work for them?"

"I've worked for them a long time. How do you think I was able to keep my family together? That was the tradeoff. I bring them new souls and I get to keep my family. Just like your buddy Vlad. Though his rewards for service to them were not quite so noble. All he wanted was power."

"So what do they want me for? I'm already in Hell. Why would they reward you for bringing me to them here? I can't be worth shit to them now."

"You'd be surprised." Dan smirked.

As they walked, the corridor darkened, became almost impenetrable. The light from the torch provided minimal help. Gloria couldn't see her own hand when she held it in front of her face. She cursed herself for not grabbing a torch as well.

"In case anyone ventures this far, there are safeguards to keep people out. We're about to cross a chasm. One that's virtually endless. Watch your step. You go first."

"No, that's not a good idea."

"Go first so I can catch you if you stumble."

He reached out and found her waist, and she knew that if he wanted to he could easily push her into this bottomless pit. But why would he? She figured he wouldn't bring her all this way just to shove her into a hole.

They stood on a narrow crossbeam. On either side, the ground disappeared. Dan held his torch out but the blackness was too thick to see more than a couple of feet.

They walked slowly across the beam, Gloria shuffling her feet, afraid to take a real step.

Dan paused.

"Why did we stop?"

"Listen."

Gloria heard nothing. "Listen for what?"

"Shhh. Can you hear them?"

"What? I don't hear—"

"Come with me," a voice in the darkness said. There

was something androgynous about it, like a woman trying to imitate a man's voice or vice versa.

Someone touched her, and Gloria jerked back. Someone slapped her across the face and she rocked back on her heels, almost stumbling off the beam.

Hands grabbed her and pulled her forward onto solid ground. There was something bizarre about the touch, cool and slippery like latex.

"Fuck off," she said, shrugging away from that cool, smooth grasp. She still could see nothing. The darkness was absolute. Dan and his torch were gone.

A hand touched her back and it had an almost hypnotic effect. That touch somehow comforted her, though she still couldn't see who it was attached to. It was so smooth, so soft. So unlike everything else she'd experienced in Hell. The invisible contact, so delicate and unexpected, was somehow erotic and sent a pleasing tingle through Gloria's body. She imagined what it would feel like to have those smooth fingers caressing her everywhere. It had been so long since she'd been lovingly touched by another living creature. All she knew was hurt and degradation. She wondered if pleasure here was as raw and intense as the pain. She tried to shrug off the feelings but they overwhelmed her, and she couldn't control them.

The hand on her back pushed her forward. She stumbled along a few steps, the sensation of that touch still vibrating along her spine. Gloria was no longer concerned with where this invisible creature—which she assumed was a female, out of intuition and not sight—was taking her.

She began to obsess over that touch, imagined those silken fingertips stroking her everywhere.

She stumbled forward, again felt those slippery smooth fingers on her back urging her on. This time the hands lingered, sliding down her spine to her waist before pushing her forward. Gloria's body tensed, imagining those fingers traveling further, down over her ass and up between her thighs. Her legs began to tremble and a moist throbbing began at her root. She turned to look but could see nothing in the impenetrable gloom.

"Who are you?" Gloria asked.

"No one."

"Tell me."

"Keep walking."

She stopped abruptly. "Then kiss me."

Gloria didn't know why she'd said that. Didn't know why she was suddenly overwhelmed with the desire to fuck this creature. After so long without it, her body now cried out with the desire for contact, for love. She needed desperately to be held, caressed, made love to. But more than that she wanted to cum. Orgasm wasn't something she'd given much thought to since coming to Hell, but feeling that erotic tingle radiate through her at this woman's touch had awakened those long dormant desires. Besides, she felt entranced, hypnotized, and she wasn't sure the words coming out of her mouth were even hers. But she didn't care right now. She didn't fight the feelings.

"Please," Gloria urged. "Fuck me."

There was a long pause. Gloria breathed heavily, despite the lack of true lungs or oxygen to feed them. Her breasts rose and fell, heaving with each agitated breath as she waited for those incredibly soft hands to touch her again. She quivered with anticipation but nothing happened. No movement at all in the darkness.

"You still there?" Gloria finally asked.

"I'm here."

"Then come to me."

"Why?" The voice grew softer, more lyrical, almost childlike.

"Because I want to touch you. I want you to touch me. I need to feel you."

"You'll hurt me."

Gloria was surprised by this. Was it afraid of her, or was it teasing her? "I won't hurt you if you don't hurt me."

"How do you know I won't?"

"I don't. You might tear me to pieces. I don't know who or what you are. But you can't be any worse than the things I've already survived."

"There's always worse and you always survive. No one dies here. We wish we could sometimes, but we can't. No one touches here except to cause hurt."

"We can change that. We can be the first lovers in Hell."

"We wouldn't be the first. There are plenty of those and they all hurt each other."

"I won't hurt you." Gloria reached out into the darkness. She didn't know how near the woman was and she was surprised when her hands encountered that same slippery soft skin, only now she found two enormous breasts. She caressed them, bent down to suck the large nipples. A milky substance like sweet cream dripped from the woman's nipples onto Gloria's tongue. It seemed like forever since Gloria had tasted anything sweet. She sucked harder, greedily gobbling up the nectar.

The woman moaned and suddenly those silky smooth hands were roaming Gloria's body. She still couldn't see the woman, but what she felt was incredible.

There were so many hands on her, too many, but Gloria didn't care. She counted six in all, with that same delicate smoothness. Gloria figured they belonged to the same woman. She'd seen such body modifications before. It was no longer shocking. What was shocking was the realization that the tender kisses and caresses, the fingers expertly titillating her every erogenous area belonged to a demon.

Gloria tensed, waiting for the pain, waiting to be stabbed or whipped or cut or burned. But then she felt the softest lips she'd ever felt kiss their way down her neck to her cleavage and begin to suckle Gloria's breasts and her fear melted into ecstasy. They fell to the cave floor, licking and sucking. Gloria was only mildly surprised to find both a penis and a vagina between the woman's legs. It was another common body modification. She lapped at the woman's engorged clitoris and sucked her swollen cock until the demoness came in a torrent of that same sweet cream that flowed from her nipples. Gloria gobbled up every drop of the woman's juices, unable to recall when she'd ever been so happy to swallow cum without getting paid for it.

The demon's tongue parted the folds of Gloria's vagina and began to flick across her clitoris, which had swollen to the size of a grape. Gloria's orgasms were almost immediate, urgent, powerful, racking her body like a thousand volts of electricity. Her back arched so violently she thought her spine would break. Then she came again and again, one orgasm tumbling down over another, their relentless intensity threatening her sanity as the demon's tongue slid deep inside her, fucking her with a tongue as long as a man's penis.

The demoness withdrew her tongue from Gloria's dripping wet vagina and slid it along the crack of her ass, circling her puckered rectum before slipping it deep inside her. Gloria squealed and came again as the woman fucked her in the ass with that long slippery tongue. Her every muscle tensed, the tendons and sinews locked, vibrating with the force of the orgasm, feeling as if she were having a violent seizure. Gloria was an expert on sex and no orgasm had ever felt this way. Pleasure in Hell was every bit as intense an experience as pain.

They lay there on the floor in the dark, sucking and licking each other, hands caressing every inch of Gloria's body, stroking her face, breasts, ass, even as those incredible lips and that salacious tongue wound its way up inside her. Gloria's face buried in the demoness' vagina, trying to force her own tongue as deep into her as possible while jacking her off with one hand and sliding two fingers in and out of her asshole. Gloria had never before felt so inadequate. The pleasure she was giving to this demoness could in no way compare to the pleasure she was receiving, and Gloria felt almost guilty. She cried out and collapsed into tears as orgasms continued to tear through her like machine gun fire.

Her body was sore and spent when the demoness finally withdrew. Gloria didn't want to move. She wanted to lie there, holding her incredible demon lover forever.

"You're a demon."

"Yes."

"Then why aren't you torturing me?"

"How do you know I'm not?"

Gloria could hear the smile in the demoness' voice. "That

felt amazing. I haven't felt anything like that in so long. I mean, I've never felt anything like it."

"There is every imaginable sin here. Not all of them are painful, just like on earth, but they all have their consequences."

"I'm willing to pay it, whatever it is. Just stay here with me forever. I can take anything if I have you with me."

"Still the addict after all this time. I can't believe *He* almost took you back. You haven't learned shit. We have to go. They're waiting."

Gloria winced at the demon's harsh words. "Who's waiting? Why do we have to go anywhere? Why can't we just stay here like this forever?"

The demon's soft hands caressed Gloria's cheek. "Don't be silly. We can't stay here. My Masters are waiting for us. Your Masters are waiting."

"Masters?"

"*The* Masters."

The demoness pulled Gloria up from the cave floor with surprising ease. She was so gentle it was hard to remember that she was a demon capable of snapping Gloria in two if she desired.

Gloria stumbled along in the darkness for what seemed like hours. She was almost thankful for the darkness. It gave her an excuse to hold her lover's hand, to wrap her arms around her waist as they scrambled over rocks or tiptoed on the edge of some precipice. Gloria was thankful for one other reason as well—she still didn't know what the demoness looked like and didn't want to spoil the illusion. Every demon she'd seen so far had been dizzyingly, nauseatingly grotesque. She didn't want to know if her new lover was as monstrous as the rest of them.

The demoness had no problem navigating the tunnels. She led Gloria along with the ease of one who had traveled these passages many times before, and with her eyes better adapted to this eternal night than day, the darkness seemed no obstacle to her at all.

Gloria spotted the first faint flicker of light at the end of the passageway and a knot twisted in her gut. In minutes they'd be there and she'd finally get to see the face of her demon lover. She rubbed her fingers over the back of the woman's hand, feeling the strange slippery soft skin, wondering just how hideous something that felt so incredibly wonderful could look.

As they approached, Gloria was finally able to make out the woman's silhouette. All six arms sprouted from her shoulders rather than up and down her torso as she would have expected. It made her look like some willowy tree. She was completely bald as Gloria already knew from running her hands over the woman's silky smooth scalp. Her legs were as thick and muscular as a bodybuilder's. Her hips were thick and full, child-bearing hips, with a large and perfectly round muscular ass. Her shoulders were muscular as well and the arms that sprouted from them were of two sizes. The main two were heavily muscled with bulging biceps and triceps while the remaining four were long, thin and delicate, ending in graceful, elegant hands.

Nothing Gloria could see so far disturbed her. She found the odd structure of the woman's body quite amazing, beautiful in an artistic sense, but she was only looking at her from the back and still in darkness that obscured her features. She could not yet even make out the color of the woman's skin, although it appeared extremely dark.

A few steps more and Gloria could finally make out the woman's complexion. It appeared black but there were colors swirling inside it like oil in sunlight. A rainbow of reds, oranges, greens, blues and pinks shimmered across her ebon flesh as Gloria stared at her back, watching as the increasing light illuminated more and more of the demoness' remarkable body. Her skin looked just as it had felt, like something born at the bottom of the ocean.

They stepped into a hall filled with light. Gloria was temporarily blinded. When she opened her eyes the very first thing she did was study her demoness, now in full light, who had turned to face her. She was aware there were others in the room, but she didn't care. She was not the least bit afraid of who they were and what they might do to her. All she wanted was to see her lover's face. Her watery eyes began to focus and

Gloria could feel her useless heart banging away in her chest, pumping nothing, merely reacting to her increased anxiety the same way it had when she was alive. Gradually the demoness' features swam into view. Gloria gasped.

Her huge eyes completely dominated her face like the eyes of some predatory insect, like a praying mantis or a hornet. They were as black as her skin and swirled with that same kaleidoscopic rainbow, fanned by long thin lashes like the plumage of some great bird. Her lips were obscenely large as well, bee-stung lips like the ones fashion models and porno stars paid thousands of dollars for. Her ears and nose were almost too small. They disappeared on her head, overshadowed by her other more prominent features. Her teeth were perfectly straight, brilliantly white, and sharp as hypodermic needles. She had two tongues that slithered around in her mouth like serpents. One was longer than the other, nearly ten inches long as Gloria had estimated when she'd felt it wriggling its way up inside her. The other was only slightly longer than normal.

Gloria dropped her eyes from the woman's face to her voluptuous breasts, which were that same liquid obsidian, capped with purplish nipples. Between her muscular thighs sprouted an erect penis bobbing above a large pink vagina with labia like rose pedals. The demoness smiled, razor teeth glistening with a sheen of saliva, and reached out her many arms.

Gloria swooned into her embrace. "You're so beautiful."

The demoness broke free and turned Gloria to face the other demons filling the brightly lit cavern. They were all beautiful in that same bizarre and terrifying way. Their pigments were dark and oily, deep purples and reds like burgundy wine. Others were that same slick liquid black as the demoness. Many were hermaphrodites as well. One had a nest of half a dozen penises varying in size from a foot and a half to a modest six inches, seething between his thin bowed legs. Another had a line of vaginas starting from between her thighs up between her breast to her mouth which had labia and a clitoris in place of lips, though the tongue remained. Still, another had vaginas on either side of his head beneath his finely chiseled cheekbones and two penises jutting out from between his thighs like gun turrets. There were demons with rows of perfectly shaped breasts descending their torsos like udders. Many of them had additional limbs and some had multiple heads. They were all beautiful somehow, despite their bizarre deformities.

"These are your Masters, Gloria. They are the true hierarchy of Hell. Greet them."

The demons moved forward as one, surrounding Gloria in a tight circle. Lust bristled in their collective gaze, boiling in the air, shimmering in the space between them like summer heat reflecting off hot asphalt. For the first time since coming to Hell, Gloria did not feel the least bit afraid. Hands, lips and tongues began to explore every inch of her with the same skilled and delicate touch as her beautiful demoness. She felt the swollen organ of one demon part her buttocks and slide effortlessly into her anus, followed by two more cocks. She could feel all three of them crowded inside of her, throbbing against each other. Then they began to slide in and out at different speeds and rhythms, sending a riot of sensations through her nervous system. Two or three other penises inserted themselves into her vagina and began thrusting deep inside of her, some quickly and forcefully, some slowly and luxuriously. Two more parted her lips and slid into her throat until she was completely filled.

Those smooth satiny hands were all over her, and tongues and lips licked and sucked her everywhere. She came again and again as they came inside her. She was pushed past ecstasy to a place where pleasure was all there was, the only sensation she knew. She could feel nothing except her own relentless orgasms.

Days seemed to pass before they released her. Gloria collapsed on the floor of the cavern, too exhausted to move.

"You were delicious. You chose well, Madria."

The beautiful demoness bowed toward the speaker and smiled proudly.

Madria, Gloria thought, holding on to the sound of that name as if it were a keepsake. She hadn't thought to ask the demoness her name. Gloria turned to look at the demon who'd spoken her lover's name. He was tall and lean with bluish black skin streaked with fiery veins of red. Huge tusks sprouted from his head and six rows of human teeth ran down the center of his skull. The only sexual modifications Gloria could see were his small nipple-less breasts and a vagina in his abdomen just above his thick penis. His face was remarkably human except for that bizarre coloration.

"Are you . . . Satan?"

They all laughed.

"Satan? There is no such person. Well, there is. But he's not what you think. He's not a demon like us, just like he was never really an angel."

"Then what is he?"

"None of your concern."

"Who are you?"

"I am Mephisto. I am your master."

"But, why am I here? Just to fuck you all?"

"Oh, no. We have much greater plans for you. There's an entire world out there we want you to fuck. We're sending you back to earth."

"You-you're sending me back? How?" Gloria was immediately fearful. The news that she would soon be returning to earth brought no joy, only suspicion. Nothing in Hell happened without a price. This was a place of punishment, not generosity or mercy. She imagined herself back on earth as one of those hideous worms.

"I-I'll just stay here." She turned to look for Madria. "I'll stay here with her."

"This is not a choice. You're not free here. You must know that by now, if you've learned nothing else. Humans are our possessions, our toys. We break them. We fix them. And we break them again. We do whatever we want with them."

"But I don't want to be one of those horrible worms. Why can't I stay here with you?" Gloria sobbed, nearly in a panic

The demon laughed. "You're not going back as a worm. That's only for those who escape. You will not be escaping Hell, you'll be bringing it with you. You will still be our property even while you walk among the living. Your soul will remain tethered to Hell. You are going to be a recruiter, just like your dear friend Vlad. But first we have to return you to your body. You cannot go back as a disembodied soul."

Two humans walked in carrying what looked like a body wrapped in a filthy sheet. They dropped it on the floor at Gloria's feet and walked away without a word.

The sheet fell open and Gloria found herself staring at her own decaying body. There were tears in her skin from where the flesh had ruptured like a blister from the gases that had built up inside it as it decayed. She could see the huge bags of silicone through the rents in her breasts. The skin was green and moldy and had begun to shrivel up and slip away from the muscles. The eyes had collapsed and fallen back into the skull. She was surprised she even recognized herself.

"Is that me?"

"Who else would it be."

"Where did you get it?"

"From the earth. Welcome home, Gloria."

"You want me to get back in there? I'd scare the shit out of anyone I see!"

"Don't worry. We'll fix you up. After you rejoin it."

"But why can't you fix my body before you put me back in?"

"Because that wouldn't be Hell, now would it?" The demon smirked, and the others laughed.

Gloria turned to look for Madria. This was all so terrible, so wrong. The beautiful demoness was behind her. She placed a hand lovingly on Gloria's shoulder and batted those long luxurious lashes. Gloria stared into Madria's midnight eyes, at her own tiny reflection mirrored in those pools of liquid night, and felt her unease lessening. She didn't know why she was getting so attached to this demon. She was certain that the woman held no true affection for her. She was little more than a pet or a toy, as Mephisto had said. Still, she felt a closeness to Madria that she didn't feel toward the others. It was almost as if she knew her, had known her for years.

"Are you ready?" Mephisto didn't wait for her to answer. He picked Gloria up and slammed her down into the rotting corpse that lay on the floor between them.

"No! Oh God! Help!"

One of the first things she'd learned in Hell was that uttering God's name was blasphemy. But she didn't care. She was overwhelmed by the horror of her own putrefying flesh. Her senses screamed out, revolting against this rotting meat casket she suddenly found herself entombed in. She was suffocating. Her heart and lungs were useless and she felt as if she were dying all over again. Then she felt hands working inside of her, ripping out organs and replacing them with other parts. Her heart suddenly began to beat but it was not her heart. This one was different, more powerful. It beat with a thundering pulse that vibrated through her bones. She screamed as she felt layer after layer of skin being grated from her body. Every nerve-ending shrieked in bone-jarring anguish as she was unmade and remade in her new form. Her eyes, her breasts, her mouth, even her vagina was reworked or replaced.

She felt nothing like herself when she finally rose from the cave floor. Her nerves were still on fire from the crude surgery, but the pain was fading quickly. Her new muscles surged with power like dynamos. She could feel an unseen energy vibrating in her sinews.

"You've spent your entire life as a victim. Now you're going to get a taste of what it feels like to be the victimizer. Go. Enjoy yourself. Bring us souls!" Mephisto laughed and the other demons joined in.

"But what do I do? How do I bring you souls?"

"You'll figure it out. Now go!"

"Where?"

He pointed. "There. I believe you already know the way."

"But what—"

It was the tunnel. The same one she'd walked through with her daughter so long ago. She had no idea where Angela was now. She wasn't even sure she still cared. Nothing mattered to her now. Nothing could be worse than what she was leaving behind.

She stumbled toward the tunnel, taking one look back before disappearing.

159

Part V

"If you are going through hell, keep going."
—*Winston Churchill*

Heaven's light looked gray in the distance, a mocking reminder of Gloria's sacrifice. She wondered if she was somehow again being punished, and if the demons knew that God had accepted her.

Of course they had to know. What was it Madria had said? She couldn't believe He'd almost accepted Gloria. *Would He still?*

She glanced down at her new form, skin glistening like the skin of the Masters, muscles rippling beneath the surface, alive when she should not be, on her way back to earth to bring the Masters more souls. The very fact that she was alive again, going back to earth, was a defiance of God's will. He had condemned her to death and to Hell and now she was alive again. The Masters were sealing her fate, making sure she would never be forgiven now.

Her new body was fast and tireless. In no time she had reached the fork in the tunnels. One way led to Heaven's gate. The other led back to life. Gloria stopped and looked into both tunnels. She wanted to run back to earth but wondered where Angela was, if she was okay. But she knew now there was no way she could ever save her daughter in this place. Besides, she reasoned, it had been insanity for her to risk her own salvation for the sake of the ungrateful child. She wondered if she'd still be forgiven if she went back to heaven now, in her demon form, with *their* blood running through her veins, *their* organs beating in her chest, most of the flesh and blood God had given her still rotting in Hell. Would He accept her like this?

Did she care anymore?

Part of her wanted so badly to try, wanted the misery and confusion to end but she was terrified of being denied. She'd turned her back on *Him* when He'd offered her salvation.

Gloria turned and headed back into the tunnel, once again turning her back on Heaven and God. She was not ready yet.

The tunnel narrowed as she made her way through. She had gone far past the point at which she and Angela had become worms. Now she was crawling along on her belly, scrambling her way through the ever narrowing tunnel. Claustrophobia began to set in as the space grew progressively tight and became unbearably hot and moist. Soon she was completely submerged in some viscous fluid, holding her breath and trying not to panic. The walls surrounding her felt more like flesh than stone; she could smell blood and mucus and bile, hear a heartbeat and feel it pulsing around her. When she pushed hard enough the walls of the tunnel expanded. Gloria started to suffocate again. She suddenly realized where she was.

Her fingers prodded the lining of her casing, and she scraped its sides, trying to dig out a hole, to escape. Panic set in as she began pushing hard against the flesh that surrounded her, punching and clawing at it until it gave, until she began to see light through the rents she tore in her tomb of meat and bone. Something began cutting its way to her from the outside, widening the gash she'd ripped in the living flesh around her. Another pair of hands reached in and grabbed hers, helping to pull her free.

With their help she ripped her way completely out of the body she'd been trapped inside and spilled onto the floor in a gush of blood and amniotic fluids.

She looked up and wiped the gore from her eyes. Black candles flickered around her in the near darkness. Beneath her was an altar, and behind her was a huge crucifix made of gold and silver, with Jesus' crucified body pointing toward the floor. A giant pentagram covered the entire surface of the altar.

Figures in black robes chanting in Latin surrounded her. Gloria rose to her feet. The men who had helped to free her bowed as they backed away. Their arms and chests were stained crimson from the blood of whatever vessel had born her.

The body of a young girl lay torn open from her clavicle to her vagina, internal organs spilled around her corpse, her

161

face twisted into a grimace of anguish. Her hands and feet had been bound by barbed wire, and it had shredded her skin down to the bone, no doubt as she'd tried to struggle to free herself while Gloria tore her way out of the young girl's flesh. The "vessel" had been no more than fifteen years old. Young enough to be Gloria's daughter.

"Who did this?" Gloria pointed back at the dead girl.

One of the hooded men who'd helped pull her out slowly stepped forward. "I did, uh . . . your unholiness. . . . I am the high-priest of the Order of—"

Gloria reached for him, meaning to grab him, shake him, slap him across the face—whatever helped her express her outrage, her anger. But she didn't know her own strength. She punched her fist into his stomach and drew back a handful of organs, pulling them slowly from his body, staring into the man's eyes as his soul fled. And Gloria knew where it was going.

She lifted her other hand to support him, to keep him from falling but the talons sliced into his neck, arterial blood spurting. Gloria disemboweled him, her hellish claws digging deep into his entrails, tearing out much of his liver and lungs. The man's hood fell off, revealing an unlined, hairless face, and braces when he opened his mouth a final time to scream, already dead, his body just going through the motions.

Gloria dropped his lifeless body and stepped back in horror as she realized that this "high priest" was little more than a kid himself. He was no older than the girl on the altar.

"Oh my god, she murdered Jerry!" Another worshipper fell to his knees, sobbing, finally scrambling away from Gloria.

"She's going to kill us!" someone else screamed.

But then a voice boomed from the back of the church. "Silence! What the fuck is wrong with you kids? I thought you fools wanted to go to hell? Well here it is! You should be happy for your friend. He has gone on to glory."

Gloria instantly recognized the voice. He wore a pinstriped sharkskin suit and looked like he was auditioning for a bad '80s mobster movie. He still had that reptilian grin and those beady black eyes, that pasty white skin, that ring of flaming red hair circling his bald head. Murdering him had done nothing to improve his looks.

Gloria nodded, not exactly surprised at his sudden re-appearance in her life. Just like a bad penny. "Vlad."

"Welcome back, Gloria. You look lovely, dear! Very becoming in your new skin." He walked toward her from the back of the church. "You ready to start your new arrangement? The Masters sent me here to watch over you. You know, make sure you don't fuck up your part of the bargain."

"And if I won't do it?"

Bill Vlad pulled out an oversized cigar and bit off the end. He was still grinning as he held it between his teeth and lit it, inhaling deeply, blowing the smoke into Gloria's face as he approached her.

"If you don't do what you're told, what you've been recreated to do, you'll never see Angela again." His smile widened until it seemed to swallow the entire room. "But I will. I'll see her every day for eternity."

Gloria looked away. The very sight of the man disgusted her, made her want to peel the man's face right off of his skull. She thought about Angela suffering in that Stygian pit. She remembered how the girl had tricked her into killing herself. How she'd given up her last chance at Heaven for her, and how Angela had then rejected her again even after her sacrifice.

"Why should I care? The girl hates me. She set me up. All she's ever done is fuck up my life and make a fool out of me. I've already given up too much for her. Fuck her. I've got to think about myself for a change."

"Oh, I will. I'll fuck her in ways you can't even imagine. Ways your brief stay in Hell still could not allow you to comprehend. I'll cut off her head and fuck her throat and she'll feel every minute of it because she can't die. She can't ever die, but she can suffer. And I know you, Gloria. I know you better than you know yourself. You could never allow that to happen, not even now. You believe Angela really does love you, the same way you believe your filthy cum-sucking ass will someday get into Heaven. You're hopeless and pathetic and you will do whatever the fuck I tell you to."

Gloria raised one of her taloned hands, preparing to rip the con-man in two.

"Oh, please do. I love the pain. You can't kill me. I'm a demon—just like you now."

"I'm not a demon."

"Oh, really. You think you could have ripped that kid's guts out if you weren't? I guess you did that sort of thing all the time when you were alive. Look at yourself."

Gloria knew what she looked like. But what they had done to her physically didn't matter. She wasn't a demon! Couldn't be.

She stretched out her arms and looked at her hands which now ended in long hooked claws. Her skin was an inky bluish black, with spidery red veins and capillaries visible just below the surface. Her breasts were larger than they'd been in life, and now there was no silicone beneath them. It was all hell-spawned flesh.

Vlad held up a mirror and Gloria snatched it from his hands. She trembled as she raised it to her face. Her hair was long and platinum blonde as it had been in life. Her lips were full, and behind them were row upon row of fangs. The most startling transformation were her eyes. They looked just like Madria's, dark oily pools swirling with color, all pupil, no whites at all.

"You are one sexy demon bitch. They're going to fucking worship you!" Vlad practically danced around as he spoke. "I'm going to form a whole religion around you. The Masters will have more souls than they know what to do with, and we'll live in Hell like royalty! Just look at how these poor sacks of shit adore you."

Gloria looked around the room at the hooded figures. Some were on their knees, heads pressed to the floor in supplication. Others had removed their hoods and were staring at her in adoration.

"These stupid bastards will do whatever the fuck you tell them to. And there are thousand more like them. Probably millions."

"So?"

164

Vlad drew deeply on the cigar. For effect, she assumed. Gloria was less than impressed. "I don't think I like your tone," he said.

Gloria tried to meet his eyes but her nerve wavered. She was powerful, more powerful than she'd ever dreamt of being, but beneath it all, she was still Gloria and it was hard not to still think of herself as a victim after all she'd been through.

The reptilian sneer on Vlad's face was replaced with a stony expression, clearly some sort of warning. Vlad had a strange habit of playing good cop/bad cop all by himself.

"Don't think for a second I can't take this all away from you," he said, leaning closer to her, blowing smelly cigar smoke in her face. "With the snap of my fingers—" He eyed her carefully, as if weighing options, as if wondering how far to push her.

Gloria turned away, dropping her head to stare at the floor, still terribly uncomfortable in her new form, hoping he wouldn't push too far. This was all so confusing. She wasn't sure what she was capable of, or what Vlad was capable of now that he'd been reborn. He had only been human before and he had fucked her life up eight ways to Sunday. Now he was immortal and still driven by the same perversions, the same need to control, to corrupt, to pervert and degrade. As much as she wanted to tear his heart out of his flabby chest she didn't want to find out what depravity he was capable of now. She didn't want to find out that she was still a victim after all. It was better to wait until she had time to fully assess her powers.

Vlad was still staring at her as Gloria flexed, marveling at her new body, the phenomenal strength in her demonic muscles and sinews. Out of the corner of her eye she could see Vlad licking his fat lips, lusting after her, stroking the pudgy organ in his tight pants. Even now, her sexuality, the fact that everyone wanted to fuck her, was still her greatest asset. For once, she told herself, she'd have to find a way to use it rather than be used by it.

Gloria kept her head turned away in disgust. She needed to find out her limitations soon but she knew better than to ask Vlad. He was a master of lies and deception and would twist any weakness she showed to his own advantage. Even after ripping that kid apart with her bare hands Gloria was still feeling strangely fragile. Better to just follow Vlad's lead … for now.

"You're still quite the human, aren't you?" Vlad said, tongue playing with the unlit end of his cigar. "You're a fucking *demon*, girl. Don't you know what that means?"

"That I could crush you?" she said, still testing him.

Vlad threw back his head and laughed. "Noooo . . ." he crooned in an annoying singsong way. "Not even close. But you could crush them." He raised his hand and swept it from one shoulder to the other, indicating the small cowering crowd at the altar.

"But why would—"

"No, no, not *them*, not literally. They represent the mindless sheep who *will* follow you. The ones who don't? *They're* the ones you'll crush."

"You really are a sadistic little bastard."

"No, Gloria, I'm an opportunistic little bastard. But you. You'd better learn to get over that nasty humanitarian streak of yours if you want to survive." He puffed hard on the cigar, which had since extinguished. "No! Scratch that. Not survive—conquer! If you want to rule here, you'd better get your head out of your ass."

Rule?

There was something odd about Vlad's little plan. Since when did Vlad care about conquering? He was just a weak manipulative little man, a bootlicker, a con-man. He wasn't the type to be a leader. That wasn't his thing. He was a bottom-feeder and an opportunist, a schemer and a planner who always made certain to stay out of the line of fire. That's why he needed her. He wasn't the type to lead a battle. He was a vulture that scavenged off the remains of dead warriors and kings. He would put her up front to take the slings and arrows while he sat back pulling the strings and reaping the rewards. *But who was pulling his strings? The Masters? And why her? She wasn't exactly a warlord either. What was he up to?*

166

"And the Masters?" she asked, having a difficult time taking her eyes off her own glistening skin. So much to take in. so much to experience and admire.

"What about them?"

"We're supposed to be collecting souls to bring back. How does ruling the planet fit in?"

"You ask too many questions."

I hit a nerve? she thought. A self-satisfied smirk exploded onto her face.

Gloria hated to admit it but she felt good in her new body. She loved it. Even knowing that she was here, on earth, in this form, at the whim of devils, she felt in control for the first time in a long time. She felt like she was once again a young desirable woman at the height of her sexual attractiveness, the same sexuality and power she'd felt when she'd first entered the sex industry. Like she could have any man she wanted, any *thing* she wanted. It was a feeling she'd almost forgotten. This body, this cloak of demon flesh was a vast improvement from the drug, disease and age-ravaged body she'd been encumbered with during her last years of life. She raised a taloned hand to push back her hair, an old habit but one that could now cause serious damage. Her claws raked her skin, got tangled in her hair and didn't remotely have the impact she would have liked.

Vlad chomped down on the unlit cigar and grinned. "Maybe you think I'm fucking around here."

"I don't care. I just want to get this over with and get the hell out of here."

"That so?" He sounded truly curious, but she suspected he was full of shit. "And where were you planning to go?"

"Back to Hell. To . . . I thought, to be with them." Her voice wavered and grew quieter with each word. "To, um, be one of them."

"Ah. I see. Is that what you thought?" He shook his head. "I can't figure out if you're stupid, or just naïve. You're pathetic either way."

"Just leave me alone! I'm not interested in anything you have to say." She shoved her way past him, strutting along

167

rows of highly polished pews, across a tiled mosaic floor where her taloned feet clicked a symphony of her passage.

"I thought you might feel that way," he said quietly, too quietly, so unlike his usual boisterous way, and Gloria stopped abruptly, turning back to look toward the altar.

"For whatever reason, you give a damn about these mind-less siphons. Good for me, since there are just so many of them around. And I'd be willing to bet that fucking up just one of them, maybe the youngest here, will *really* fuck with your head. Hmmm? What do you think? Have *I* hit a nerve?"

She turned completely to face him. For a moment she considered bluffing, pretending she didn't care about their fate but something about his choice of words: *Have I hit a nerve?* They were her exact words, the ones she'd thought. *Can this freak read my mind?* If so, there was no point in bluffing. He'd know she was faking. But why did she care? Hell, she was a demon! Why was she still cursed with compassion for the same fucked up species that drove her to drugs, porn and prostitution? Why did she still give a fuck?

Gloria knew she wasn't prepared to witness any more innocent deaths should he call her bluff. She'd been to hell and the idea of sending anyone else there was one she couldn't accept. Vlad had nothing to lose. He'd never had much humanity. He'd always been a predator, a parasite, but she had everything to lose. Even beneath the layers of infernal flesh, she still had *her* humanity.

Vlad stuffed the remnants of his cigar into his shirt pocket, very slowly, exhaling grandly as he moved closer to the altar. "I don't like the way you're behaving," he said, as if addressing a child. "I need to believe you'll obey me.

"So," he said, stepping quickly back onto the altar now, faster than she had ever seen him move, "every time you disobey, they'll suffer for it."

He grabbed the first worshipper within reach and clamped his hands around the throat of the hooded figure.

Gloria had almost forgotten they were there, they'd been so quiet. She took maybe two steps toward the altar before Vlad shouted for her to stop.

168

She stopped.

"That's better." He pulled back the hood and revealed the face of a terrified girl, maybe all of 17, her long dark hair spilling over her shoulders.

"Please," the girl begged, scratching at Vlad's hands. "I don't want to die!"

Vlad turned his head back to face Gloria. "She doesn't want to die. What a surprise." He turned back to the girl. "Not even for your demoness? You aren't willing to sacrifice for your master?"

"Please!" the girl cried, beating her fists against Vlad's two-fisted grip around her throat. "Can't . . . breathe . . .!"

Gloria tried to force herself not to care. She tried to think of all the hell, literal and figurative, people had put her through over the years. She tried hard not to see herself and her daughter in the face of the terrified young girl.

She failed. "Let her go, Vlad!" Gloria moved another couple of steps toward the altar.

Vlad roared, squeezing harder, choking the life out of the wide-eyed girl. The crunching of her neck bones ricocheted off the church's stone walls. He dropped her lifeless body at his feet.

Gloria leapt across the altar, connecting with Vlad, knocking him onto his back. She pummeled him with her fists, raked her claws across his face and neck, tried to tear his head from his shoulders. Blood spurted with each slash, great gouges of skin hanging from his cheeks, one eye dislodged from its socket and hanging by a fleshy thread.

He lay there silently, trying to block her attack, his arms folded across his face. She continued the assault until he lay still, until she had no strength left to continue. With great effort she crawled away from his still body, amazed it had been so easy, that he had simply taken the beating.

He raised his badly beaten head and sat up. "Feel better?" he said, though speaking was difficult with his lower lip torn from his mouth. Despite the attack he grinned, revealing bloody nubs where teeth had been. His nose was mashed flat and was closer to his ear than the center of his face.

169

She knew she couldn't kill him—couldn't kill any demon—but she hadn't expected him to recover so quickly. This was going to be hard, she reasoned. Maybe impossible.

"You love to learn the hard way. You always have." His face began to change, to regenerate. Gone was the damage Gloria had caused: his lip healed, the deep furrowing lines plumped up. But worst was what he was changing into. Vlad barely resembled a human now. His forehead and chin elongated, almost to points, and his skin took on a marbled, cheese-grater quality. He stuck out a ridiculously long, reptilian tongue, split down the center, and flicked it at her. His body continued to grow and change before her eyes, toughening, growing muscular and glistening and *hard*.

She was looking at his true demon form.

He charged, grabbing Gloria by the throat and lifting her off the floor with one hand. She pounded against him but he backhanded her, and carried her quickly across the altar, slamming her into a stone pillar. The pillar cracked, great chunks of plaster falling on their heads. He slammed her several more times until Gloria was sure she would black out.

He pulled her back and lifted her above his head, throwing her across the altar. She smashed into a frieze of Jesus' Last Supper, stained glass shattering, fragments spraying the air and littering the floor.

She fell to her knees, chunks of glass jutting from her skin, her face a ruined mess, her head a bloody pulp. After a moment of trying to stand she collapsed to the floor, the effort too great, the pain too intense.

Then the screams began.

Gloria tried to look but every movement was agony. "Please, Vlad," she tried to say but wasn't sure what came out of her mouth.

Something came rolling up the aisle toward her. It bounced off the column and settled a few feet from her side. This one a boy, a teenager, peach fuzz just beginning to show. Rough shreds of skin was all that remained of his neck, and his eyes were huge, the terror of his death trapped for all eternity in the expression of those eyes.

There was commotion all around her, people begging for mercy, screams of terror and pain. Try as she might she couldn't lift her head, couldn't put a face to all that carnage.

Then the room grew silent, save for the steady quiet plinking of something wet dripping off the marble altar.

Gloria fought against the pain and struggled to her feet, her body finally beginning to regenerate, to slowly heal. She scanned the church for signs of life and found none. Body parts were scattered everywhere, and blood coated the altar like a fresh paint job, dripping off the railings, smeared across frescos and friezes and statues of saints. The painting of St. John the Baptist suddenly took on a whole new meaning. Everyone was dead. Her defiance had cost all of their lives and if she knew anything about how the afterlife worked, then they were all now burning in the Ocean of Fire, waiting for some perverted demon to pluck them out of that burning vat of liquefied flesh and molten earth to make them his playthings for the rest of time. No one deserved that.

"You made me ruin my suit. I'm going to take that out of your ass."

Vlad's features relaxed and remolded themselves back into that ridiculous corpulent body with the red hair and handlebar moustache. He was naked and sporting an erection.

He licked his fat, slimy lips and squeezed the head of his cock until a teardrop of black cum dribbled from the tip. Gloria shivered and her stomach rolled in revulsion. She took that as a good sign. There was a time when the thought of sucking his chubby little cock or taking it in either of her other two orifices would not have fazed her in the least. All she would have been worried about was how much money she'd get for doing it and how much heroin or meth that money would buy. She continued staring at Vlad, who was still stroking his rigid organ, milking more of that hellish black cum from the swollen gland, leering obnoxiously and sliding his tongue out from between his lips until it hung down past his chin. Gloria turned away and a chill raced up her spine.

"Come here!"

This is the last time. This is the last time I will let anyone humiliate me, the last time I will let anyone hurt me and victimize me. This is the last time.

Gloria's anus continued to stretch, her viscous black blood leaking down her thighs as Vlad's organ grew inside her, each thrust lacerating tissue fiber and rupturing capillaries.

She had laughed when he'd first pulled the thumb-sized nub from his pants and ordered her to bend over and take it in her ass. She had thought it was a joke. She could have taken four cocks that size at once, even when she'd been human. But then it had begun to swell . . . and once it was inside her it had continued to swell. Lengthening and thickening more and more each time he pounded it into her bowels. His penis was already the size of a chair leg and though Gloria could feel her flesh tear and chafe she marveled at how little pain there was, or rather, how much agony her demon form could endure. The pain was excruciating but not unbearable. She wondered if there was any pain, anything, that this body could not withstand.

She felt her hip joints pop out of their sockets and her pelvic bone crack as Vlad's tumescent organ swelled to the length and thickness of a man's leg. Vlad's animalistic grunts and snarls and the long ropes of saliva drooling from his blubbery lips down her back were far worse than the pain. Vlad's hairy stomach was propped up on her ass, where he'd hoisted it out of the way so that he could worm his oily little cock between her perfectly sculpted asscheeks.

Gloria could hear Vlad's bones popping, his sinews and ligaments stretching and pulling, tearing and snapping, the flesh ripping as Vlad began to reshape himself. Gloria felt Vlad's cock shift inside of her, wriggling up through her intestines as if it had a mind of its own. Blood sprayed from her lips as he thrust again, battering her organs. More saliva dripped onto her back, down her arms and chest as she knelt on all fours, grimacing and crying out as Vlad's megalophallus dug a tunnel up into her lower intestines.

She felt Vlad's tongue like a giant worm slithering over the back of her neck, wrapping around her throat and licking her cheek, leaving a trail of slime as it lapped at the salty tears weeping from the corners of her eyes. Gloria screamed as Vlad's unctuous tongue wormed its way into her mouth. Her cries were choked off as it slid down her throat and began to thrust in and out of her, fucking her mouth even as his cock tore through her rectum. More tears dripped from Gloria's eyes as she felt Vlad shudder and howl, his body jerking and thrashing as he reached orgasm. Sharp gnarled claws raked at her back, exposing her spine. His thick molten seed exploded inside of her, burning her insides like liquid fire.

Vlad withdrew from Gloria's rectum and she collapsed and curled into a fetal position. His cock slithered out of her anus like a serpent, trailing blood, semen and excrement. Gloria kept her eyes closed, not wanting to see whatever it was he had become as he wiped his cock off on her forehead. He shook his rapidly diminishing organ and drops of blood and semen splattered her face in thick pudding-like dollops that left burning trails down her face, corroding her flesh like acid.

"Ummm. I've been wanting to do that for a long, long time," he moaned.

Never again, Gloria thought once more. *Never-a-fucking-gain.*

Her inky eyes swirled with colors as she stared at Vlad, watching his body reshape into its normal nauseating form. Whatever demon he became when angered or aroused looked like some cross between a pig and buffalo, with the teeth and claws of a reptile. She didn't want to see it again. Not until she could figure out how to kill it. There had to be a way. There had to be a way to send his sick perverted ass right back to hell.

"Get dressed, bitch. We've got a world to conquer."

Part VI

"All sins tend to be addictive, and the terminal point of addiction is damnation. "
  —W. H. Auden

Gloria grabbed the boy's head and thrust it deeper between her legs. "If you stop licking my pussy I'll crush your head like an egg."

"I'll never stop. Never, mistress."

"Don't talk with your mouth full."

Gloria tried to forget her own pain as one of her many acolytes knelt between her thighs, sucking and licking her engorged clit as she shuddered with orgasm after orgasm. She had no idea where Vlad got them from but there seemed to be no end to them. They would walk into the lair that Vlad had constructed for her—a gaudy parlor of inverted gold crosses and platinum pentagrams hung on red and black velvet, and silk covered walls—and drop to their knees in awe. She would make them perform acts of worship to prove their devotion to Hell, things she would invent to amuse herself. And without hesitation they would do anything she asked.

And then she would kill them and send their souls straight to Hell.

They came from all walks of life and every corner of the globe. Young, old, white, black, Spanish, Asian, Middle Eastern, Pacific Islanders, from the rich and powerful to the destitute and desperate, they all adored her. Gloria began to enjoy the things they could do for her, the humiliation and pain they willingly endured in her honor.

The 20-something with the washboard abs, blond hair, muscular arms and chest and handsome features whose face was buried in her cunt was the son of a US Congressman. The 37-year-old Saudi Arabian man with the piercing eyes and olive, sun-baked skin, who was kneeling behind her, rimming her asshole with his tongue was an Arab prince from one of the richest oil producing countries in the world. Here they were all equal.

A white-haired man in a blue pinstriped suit walked with his arm draped affectionately, proprietarily around Vlad's shoulders like someone who was used to being the most powerful person in the room. He had an Italian accent and when he smiled it looked almost as deadly as Vlad's shark-toothed grin. He took one look at Gloria and all the color left his face.

"Oh my God! I-I thought you were kidding. What is she? She . . . she's beautiful! I've got to have her. How much do you want for her?"

Vlad chomped on the cigar that seemed to perpetually hang from his lips. "She's not for sale. She's as close to a god as you're ever going to see on earth. You don't own her. She owns you."

"Nobody owns me," the Italian said, indignant, his chest puffing up.

"Then you're in the wrong place." Gloria's voice startled him. It had a deep gravelly quality and echoed as if it had been run through a synthesizer. The white-haired man's jaw hung open as he stared at her, not knowing what to say. Gloria locked eyes with his, and blue lightening flashed in her black eyes. The man took an involuntary step backward, then steeled himself and stepped forward again. He lifted his head defiantly to meet Gloria's gaze.

Gloria clamped onto the congressman's son's head between her thighs and reached back to push the prince's tongue deeper into her ass. The man never took his eyes off Gloria as another orgasm ripped through her.

"I want her." The white-haired man began to undress. He quickly dropped his pants and shrugged out of his silk boxers. He smiled, clearly proud of himself as he unveiled an erection that was nearly ten inches long.

Gloria growled. "Put it away!"

Vlad stepped forward. "Gloria!"

She ignored him and continued to lock eyes with the white-haired Italian man. "I said put it away, or I'll tear it off your fucking body!"

The man wisely decided against arguing with the demon and quickly reached for his pants. His face flushed red. "Okay, fine, I'll put it away."

"Wait. Forget the pants."

"But you said to put it away!" The man was suddenly deflated, his arrogance and self-assurance gone.

"Stick it in there," she said. "In Blond Boy over there." She pointed to the naked ass of the congressman's son.

"I'm no fucking homo!"

"You're either a homo or a corpse!" She raised one taloned hand and flexed her fingers. The Italian turned to look at Vlad, who had stepped away from him and was smiling mischievously, clearly amused. The Italian looked back at Gloria. She smiled, revealing a mouthful of razor sharp teeth.

Blond Boy lifted his head from between Gloria's thighs and screamed as the Italian eased his enormous cock into the man's ass. Gloria pushed Blond Boy's face back into her sopping wet pussy. "Where do you think you're going? You're not done yet."

She turned around to look at Vlad, who was staring back at her with a look of almost scientific curiosity. She watched impassively as the Italian gentleman slammed his cock in and out of Blond Boy with increasing ferocity, staring at Gloria in terror while the boy continued licking Gloria's pussy. Blond Boy grunted with each thrust of the Italian's cock but didn't dare stop licking Gloria's grape-sized clit. The Arab prince continued eagerly eating her asshole like he was licking icing from a cake bowl.

"My star pupil," Vlad crooned, his voice grating on Gloria's nerves, a goddamned gnat buzzing around her ear. He circled her—them—and made ridiculous noises, little chirps and whoops as if encouraging them. As if they needed encouraging.

Not that she minded an audience, but something about Vlad's persistent need to be a fucking voyeur at every turn grated on her nerves. Besides, he was screwing up her concentration, which would ultimately screw up her orgasms. And that in itself was pissing her off.

"Don't you have some virgin to eviscerate?" Gloria snapped at Vlad, pulling away from the lapping tongues and moving flat onto her back on the ornate Persian rug. The Italian finished butt fucking Blond Boy and pulled away, looking embarrassed and out of his depth.

She tried to ignore Vlad. She had more interesting things to attend to. "Gentlemen," she said, "I didn't say we were done."

She sat up and stroked the Italian's cock until it began to stiffen in her hand. She sucked the rim, and her tongue licked the shaft until he was hard enough to be interesting again. "You wanted me? You wanted to fuck me?"

The Italian nodded slowly, cautiously, terrified.

"Well, I've been fucked quite enough by men like you. Men with power. Men who take and never give a fucking thing in return but pain." She leaned in close until her black eyes were peering directly into his. "Well, I do all the fucking here. I give all the pain. But I'll give you one shot, one shot to make everything right, to leave here with your life. If that precious cock of yours can make me cum I'll let you live. But if you don't, I'll hurt you worse than any human being has ever suffered on earth or in Hell. And this is not your decision to make. You either do it or you die. You're in because I say you're in. Now... you may fuck your goddess."

She smiled wide, revealing all of her razor sharp teeth, as much a threat as an expression of joy. Gloria was loving this, exalting in her new power.

Is this what Hell will be like with my new Masters? The power to punish all those men who hurt me and all those who have hurt so many women like me? The power to control them, to destroy them? I could learn to love this.

The Italian moved between her thighs but she pushed him back. "You'll have to be more creative that that. We need room down there."

She gestured at the Saudi prince, but he seemed confused. "What should I do?" he asked, looking from her to the other men.

"Do me," she said. "And you'd better be good or I'll rip

your fucking head off."

He eased between her legs but she shoved him back as well. "What the hell is wrong with you people? Can't you figure this out? A bunch of inexperienced assholes!"

She pushed the prince to his knees and pulled him down, moving him onto his side, and she slid a few inches toward him until he finally caught on. From his sideways angle on the floor he shoved his cock inside her, draping one leg across her thighs. He leaned up on his arm for leverage and his free hand explored her tits, squeezing roughly, overeager, awed.

She looked up at the Italian and gestured, hoping he would finally catch on. She'd hate to have to kill him before he got her off. Finally he seemed to get the message because he sat beside her, his legs splayed in front of him. Slowly he inched toward her, his enormous cock bobbing, until he maneuvered beneath the prince's legs and thrust his enormous hard-on inside her ass.

She threw back her head and relaxed against the floor, arms outstretched over her head. Blond Boy stood above them stroking his cock.

"Don't waste it," she said. "Stick that thing somewhere."

He knew better than to try to get a blowjob from Gloria. The Italian's ass was flush against the floor, so Blond Boy crawled behind the prince, who was lying prone beside Gloria. The prince didn't look too happy but was clearly more afraid to refuse. Blond Boy parted the prince's ass cheeks and probed the man's asshole with spit-slick fingers until he found the leverage he needed, until the man's hole was wet enough to fuck. He shoved his cock inside the prince's virgin ass and the man howled in pain, his face pinched and distorted.

"Harder!" Gloria yelled, and they picked up the pace as if one unit, each man fucking harder, grunting and panting, the thrusting out of rhythm, exciting Gloria even more. The prince's grip on her tit grew tighter with every thrust up his ass until she thought he might rip it from her body, an incredible mixture of pleasure and pain until Gloria began to pulsate with orgasm after orgasm.

Vlad hovered over her head, and she'd forgotten he was even in the room. She was experiencing such incredible waves of pleasure she couldn't have spoken if she'd wanted to. She didn't give a shit anymore if he stayed and watched.

Instead, he dropped a small brown bag on the floor by her head. "A little treat," he said. "For ol' time's sake." Then he disappeared.

Before she even opened the bag she could sense what was inside. Knew the familiar series of rattles, knew the smell of something entirely odorless, would recognize the weight and feel of that fucking little bag the moment she touched it. And god help her, she was salivating.

Cocks were pounding every orifice yet she no longer felt a thing. She'd gone completely numb, resistant to the feelings of her lovers, her fuckers, to their touches, their attempts to bring pleasure.

All she knew was the contents of that bag.

In fact, these motherfuckers were now just an annoyance, in the way of her real pleasure.

"Get off!" she howled, jumping up and moving so lightning fast, so fiercely that her movements severed body parts. The prince backed away screaming, blood gushing from his dickless crotch, his quickly withering penis still dangling from Gloria's snatch. He stared down at his sexless groin and moaned, a long, sorrowful sound, his eyes bulging in disbelief as his hands reached down to staunch the flow of blood.

Gloria rolled her eyes, sickened by the noise pouring out of this moron's mouth and threw back her arm, delivering a blow to his jugular that crushed his windpipe, bits of bone splintering into his throat, spiking out the back of his head. The force of her strike was so powerful his eyeball popped out and flew across the room, leaving a gaping hole in his dead face that dripped aqueous ulcerous liquid and gristly strands of retinal fibers. He dropped to his knees, still clutching his neutered crotch and landed on his face with a sickening crunch as his nose exploded beneath the force of his body, chunks of cartilage shattering his brain.

The Italian's penis had survived but a violent contraction of her rectum had crushed it into a bleeding lump that resembled a tube of liver pate'. He didn't utter a sound. He just stared at the mangled meat between his legs, dripping blood from his urethra onto the floor, his mouth twisted into a silent scream and his eyes bulging and quivering. Still, his presence was distracting her from her goal, the only thing she wanted right now, her one true love. She glanced at the Italian, who stood in a widening puddle of his own blood, piss and shit, the veins and chords in his neck standing out prominently, the scream trapped in his throat. He smelled like a charnel house.

"Come here," she said, but he didn't move. Going to him would be too much of an effort; too much of a distraction from her real passion. But it didn't matter because moments later he was dead, or sure as hell looked like it. She doubted the blood loss had caused it, not this quickly. But it didn't matter anyway. She certainly could not have cared less about his life or his pain. This was the type of man who had used her in her past life. He was the type of man who bought and sold women like her. She had been a victim for so long that a bit of revenge would have felt good. It had felt great ordering him around like her own personal sex toy. Making him scream would have felt even better.

She inched over to the dead Italian and shook him, hoping he was still alive, hoping he was faking. Hoping he could still *feel*. His body toppled over, and she laid him on his back.

Her hand moved to the mangled ruin that had been his dick. Gloria slid one of her sharp talons into his bleeding piss-hole, using the claw to tunnel deeper, coring out his cock like she was seeding an apple, boring down into it until his penis began to rupture and split. He screamed and clasped his hands onto her wrist, trying to pry her claw from inside his cock. Gloria smiled and resumed drilling into the Italian's brutalized member.

An ear piercing howl tore from his lungs as his cock split into bleeding strips and she continued digging up into his guts as he struggled beneath her grip.

"That hurts! Please! Pleeeease! It hurts! It fucking hurrrts!"

"Ahhh, you were faking!" she cried, laughing, shoving several fingers deeper inside him. Shoving one of her long sharp talons deep inside his anus, coring it out as he screamed and convulsed. Blood poured from his rectum like rainwater through a gutter as her claws carved out his asshole and the orifice where his cock once dangled, now resembling a menstruating vagina, until it was little more than a ring of lacerated pink flesh like a half-eaten grapefruit. She clamped his hands behind his head and sat on them.

"Please! God! Oh god, noooo!" he begged, choking, sobbing. "Pleeeeeease!" His screams tapered off into gurgling noises as his mouth filled with blood and his eyes rolled back into his head.

Gloria grinned, loving the sound of his voice, loving his pleads. She finger fucked him while he bucked and thrashed beneath her. Her free hand trailed along his abdomen, claws raking lightly, drawing pink lines along the flesh. She leaned forward until her cunt rested on his face. "Suck my clit," she said. "Get me off."

But he wasn't able to do much with his tongue. He had already begun to convulse in what were probably his death throes, but Gloria wasn't done with him yet.

She lowered herself further until his face was buried, her powerful legs pinning his arms against the floor. He bucked furiously beneath her, trying to breathe. Before he could suffocate and end her fun, Gloria dug deeper into his crotch, her entire fist inside him now. With her other hand she trailed her claws around his belly button, drawing small circles that widened with each turn and eventually began to tunnel inside his stomach, round and round and deeper and deeper, peeling away layer after layer of skin until her hand plunged inside his body, feeling his warm wetness up to her wrist, and deeper now, tunneling further and further inside his body until her hands met inside him.

He spasmed once, his bowels evacuating, and he finally lay still. This time she knew he wasn't faking.

"Selfish fucker," she said, pulling out of his quickly cooling body, bloody chunks of entrails coating her hands. "I didn't even cum."

She sat beside the dead Italian and took in her surroundings.

Across the room the dead prince lay in a ruined heap, a

puddle of blood surrounding his body like a chalk outline. Blond Boy had managed to escape with everything still attached and was hovering in a corner, his arms wrapped around his head. He was shivering and sobbing, saliva and snot dribbling down his face.

But Gloria ignored him for now. She had pressing things to attend to. Her addiction was calling. On hands and knees she scuttled across the floor, dragging the little paper bag along in her bloodied fist. She squatted against the wall, bringing the bag up to her face, her exceptional sense of smell detecting the contents of the bag before she even opened it. She was beyond salivating now. Head pounding, palms sweating, mouth and tongue slick with a coating like moss and decay, remembering those days, remembering it all, remembering the incredible highs, the exhilarating sense of freedom. Remembering what she had been denied, what she had been missing all these years.

She would have that again. Finally, finally! After suffering in Hell, after suffering *through* hell, Gloria would be free, just like old times, just like she used to be, exactly like—

Exactly like she used to be.

She glanced at the Italian, suddenly aware of what she had done, of how much pleasure she had experienced while doing it.

And the room *was* a charnel house: the odors of death, reeking of quickly rotting body parts, of swiftly coagulating thick and pungent blood mixed with excrement, bowels evacuated in terror and demise. Ruined bodies, ended lives. And she in the middle of it, her beautiful ebony skin ruined by the tattoos of misery and tortured deaths. She had truly become a demon after all. She had become something she despised. She had become Vlad.

Inside was an array of pills and powder-filled baggies and balloons, and she could easily identify each one. And each was tempting in its own right, even now, even after she saw what she'd become, or what she was fast becoming. The realization scared the shit out of her because she wanted to be in control. But what was she doing? Fucking around. Obeying Vlad like a mindless drone and going through the motions, pretending to play the part of some demigod demon when she suddenly realized she had no control whatsoever. Why? What exactly had he promised her? W*hat did it even fucking matter* what he had promised?

She squeezed the bag, clutching it against her chest. What did it matter, indeed.

Inside was a buffet of uppers, downers, psychotropics, hallucinogenics, amphetamines and opiates and whatever the hell else Vlad had thrown into the mix. She considered and reconsidered her options, knowing this was her chance to break free, her chance to finally redeem herself, regain control.

She parted the edges of the bag and glanced inside.

"Fuck it," she said right before she plunged her face in, her tongue scooping up half the contents and sucking them back into her throat.

***

It was one of those tragic realities of life that victims inevitably became victimizers, that they find some way to transfer their pain and humiliation onto others. There was no longer any reason to resist. She was beyond addiction now. She existed for no other purpose but to consume, corrupt, indulge. She was now, thoroughly, a creature of Hell.

She didn't care.

She glanced over her shoulder at Blond Boy. "It's your lucky day," she said to the shivering, cowering mess in the corner of the room. Thoughts of eviscerating him fled her mind. He didn't matter. Nothing mattered. Nothing but this incredible feeling of ecstasy flooding her brain.

Blond Boy slowly looked up, his eyes squinting, his body trembling and covered with the splattered blood and gore of the dead. "Wha-ut?" he asked, his voice barely above a whisper.

"Get out!" she screamed, feeling guilty for what she'd done but wanting so badly to do it again, to feel that power. Resisting the urge because of a sudden overwhelming feeling of empathy but knowing the feeling might not last. He would be wise to get the hell out while he still could.

Blond Boy wasted no time scurrying to his feet, fleeing the room without bothering to retrieve the clothes that were in a heap somewhere in the room.

***

Vlad had been busy preparing the room for her. An ornate glass and gold hookah filled with opium and marijuana was within arm's distance. She settled in against a stack of throw pillows and took a hit off the ever-lit hookah. Then she scooped a long claw into a bowl filled with heroin and brought it to her nose, snorting the drug now dusted with dried flecks of blood and small intestine. Until now she had managed to avoid the drugs, believing they would be the final unraveling, the catalyst to the ultimate depths of perversion she had tried to avoid. Sex was one thing—hell, sex was something warm and familiar and indulgent, another high, another of her many addictions—but drugs were something else. Something beyond the chemical high, beyond the ephemeral psychedelic feeling of want, of need, of the pinnacle of understanding. Drugs were a life force, a purpose, a sense of being unmatched by an army of mindless, suffering parasites that surrounded her when all she wanted was to actually *feel something*. Drugs gave her that. Drugs gave her a sense of purpose. Drugs made her forget everything she never wanted to remember in the first place. Like her stupid bitch of a daughter.

***

Above the basement chamber Vlad had turned into a gaudy sanctuary for Gloria's worship and worshippers was the rest of a church, St. Bernadette's, one of the oldest on Manhattan's lower East side. Closed down for years now because of ruin: a crumbling back wall; the stations of the cross—imported from Paris in the late 1800s—defiled, destroyed; a carved marble and Caen stone altar built by a Benedictine monk cracked and ruined by man and weather and apparent neglect. But it proved the perfect refuge for Gloria's followers, a place

184

for squatters to worship undisturbed, forsaken by the very neighborhood that once fought to keep the doors open. But the city abandoned it, and Gloria's legion now called it home.

Those who hadn't been killed by Gloria believed they were safe, untouchable, that she had for some reason spared them, making them more loyal. They brought her new recruits daily, extending their own longevity that much more. They adored her—this demon, this goddess, the beacon of light who would deliver them from the mundane, who would deliver them to the depths of Hell and beyond.

And she was an incredible fuck, and quite generous with sexual pursuits. She was insatiable, she was perfection. She was their god.

Gloria, stoned out of her mind, wandered the basement hallways, searching for something elusive, something she had been thinking about just moments before but was no longer accessible in her mind. That didn't matter. She figured if she wandered around long enough it would come back to her. She marveled at how closely this corridor resembled Hell, with its dank, steamy atmosphere and dark, almost tarry walls. Vlad outdid himself this time, though she found it a bit depressing, found herself somehow longing for the familiarity of Hell. These surroundings, this body, being back on solid ground . . . it was all somehow unsettling. She felt lost, without meaning and purpose. The drugs helped fill that void, but even that was lacking. The mindless, suffering, unwashed masses waiting for her upstairs had become tedious, more like work than pleasure. Gloria would never admit to an existential angst, not in this form, not in this reality. She knew she didn't really exist, didn't belong anywhere no matter what Vlad told her, so what was there to be existential about? Or angst-ridden for that matter?

Her followers were forbidden from entering the basement unless invited. Gloria climbed the stairs and entered the narthex, waiting in the shadows. The crowd was restless, aimlessly wandering around the church or huddled together in makeshift beds on the pews.

No one noticed Gloria when she first approached. In their presence, she felt omni-conscious of her inhumanity, the strength, the lethal power rippling beneath her glistening black skin. For several minutes she stood silently in the back of the church, observing the nonchalant arrogance in the room. How stupid of them to be so cavalier, as if no one in the outside world would object to what they were doing. They were lucky not to have been assailed by the pious overzealous fools who fear and despise those who oppose the Christian church. This was more than careless; this was painfully foolish.

Finally someone noticed her, before she spoke. A gasp, then a cry, followed by a chorus of moans and exaltations, people scrambling to their feet in a flurry of bows and genuflections. Gloria shook her head, clicked her finger-claws along the wood of the back pew. The room grew silent as they waited for Gloria to speak.

"What are you doing?" she asked quietly, unsure yet how she wanted to proceed. The bloodlust was gone for now; she felt calm, at peace, but she also knew that once the effects of the drugs wore off, so would her serenity.

No one answered. They looked at one another, pained, puzzled expressions on their faces.

"I asked you a question!" she felt dizzy, unfocused, the drugs were clouding her thoughts making her feel suddenly vulnerable, afraid, and that . . . was making her mean, like a wounded animal.

No one volunteered to respond. They hung their heads and stood in stunned silence.

Finally, a young man stepped forward from his hiding place behind a great marble pillar. He held his trembling hands out to her, his black monk's robe too big for his small frame, the hood obscuring much of the curly black hair on his head. "Muh-mistress? We, we were waiting for you."

Gloria licked her lips and stopped scratching the wood. "And what were you waiting for? What did you expect would happen?"

He shrugged, and his dark skin had gone ashy. His hands shook more than ever. "I don't know, Mistress," he whispered. "Wuh-we were waiting for you to tell us what to do . . ."

Gloria stepped closer to the young man, and he squeezed

186

his eyes shut. A single tear fell. "Why are you crying?" she demanded.

"I'm afraid," he whispered, looking like he wanted to crawl inside the pillar. "You're so . . . so mighty. So powerful. I don't nuh-know what you might . . ." He didn't finish the thought.

She stepped before him now, and using a claw pushed the hood back. Her hand caressed his head, and his lips trembled at the touch, his body shaking. "You're wise to fear me," she told him, then turned to the rest of the followers. "You would be wise to fear me! I could . . . I could . . . I could kill all of you!" she exclaimed as she almost staggered into their midst as the room swirled, her mind reeling from the stew of narcotics surging through her blood.

She felt like she was losing herself. Her own voice, her words, felt alien, as if they were coming from someone else. This arrogance and grandiosity wasn't her. It was the drugs. This was how she sounded when she was high. This demon had been inside her long before her flesh wore its reflection on the outside.

Almost at once the rest of the followers fell to their knees.

Gloria smirked. This wasn't what she wanted. A flock of mindless toadies doing her bidding with no real purpose? What was the point? Why were they even here?

"Get up!" she cried, suddenly furious, the drugs taking her mood from one extreme to the next. She didn't know what she wanted, what she needed. She wished there was one person in this room who possessed a backbone.

Most stood. A few seemed frozen with fear, groveling and cowering from their places hidden in the pews. A few feet away a huddled lump lay on the floor, trying to shove his or her body beneath the bench. Gloria grabbed whatever part she could reach and dragged the body out into the open. She flipped the cloaked mass over and a terrified pair of eyes glanced back from beneath the hood.

"Did you not hear me tell you to get up?" she asked quietly. She blinked her long luxurious lashes repeatedly, trying to focus.

The girl nodded, and pulled herself into a fetal position.

Gloria reached down and used her claws to shred the cloak, exposing the terrified girl hidden beneath the material. She began to giggle uncontrollably as her mind swam in a narcotic fugue. "You're a moron," she told the girl, and ignored her for the moment while she turned to the rest of the crowd.

"Do you even know why you're here?" she asked, looking from face to face, scanning the room.

No one answered.

"Answer me!" she bellowed as she staggered once again and barely avoided toppling over. Still, the room remained silent.

"You're not . . . you're not s'posed to come up here," the black kid behind her said. Gloria was impressed. Moments earlier the kid was ready to piss his pants. "It's too . . . too dangerous up here for you."

"*Dangerous?* Do I look like I'm in danger?" she yelled. "I'm a *demon!*"

He nodded. "I know. But there are people who would like to hurt you. We, we're supposed to . . . to protect . . . you . . ."

"You're supposed to protect me," she said, facing the crowd again, her devil-made might and delirious intoxication fueling her bravado. "You? How? How do you expect to *protect* me?"

They wouldn't look her in the eye, which she found infuriating. They were all cowards. These were her worshippers . . . her protectors? All they wanted was a chance to fuck her. There was no worship here, no respect. Bunch of fucking cowards is what they were.

Gloria reached down and clutched the girl off the floor, holding her up by the throat. She was pretty. So fucking pretty. The girl kicked out, tried desperately to find the ground. Garbled, strangled words tried to slide out of her throat. Gloria reached back and sliced the girl's shirt open, exposing her back, and held her up even higher.

"Does anyone in this fucking room have a backbone?" she cried.

She tossed the girl to the floor like a forgotten toy, then turned and staggered back down to the basement. The bitch had ruined her high.

Part VII

Nathan Weathers was the only son of a United States Congressman. His mother's family were tobacco tycoons. He'd grown up in a mansion attended to by nannies and servants. He'd attended the best private schools. In college he'd begun experimenting with drugs and got hooked on heroin and cocaine, graduated to meth, and spent the last few years in and out of rehab facilities that were more like country clubs.

Then he found religion: experimenting with Buddhism, a brief turn as a Hari Krishna, then studying Scientology before meeting Bill Vlad after his last stint in rehab.

Eventually he wound up at the old church on 9th street, enthralled now by the most amazing creature he'd ever beheld. Living proof of Heaven and Hell. He'd signed over his trust fund to Vlad, along with all of his worldly possessions in exchange for being among the privileged few to meet Gloria face to face in her private chambers. Nathan had never needed or wanted for anything and he had never been so scared in his entire privileged life the way he'd been last night in that basement.

The beautiful ebon-skinned demoness had been like something from his wettest dreams and darkest nightmares. He'd almost suffocated between her thighs; his jaw had locked up and his tongue had chafed from licking her thumb-sized clitoris. When she came he'd nearly drowned in her juices, burning his throat like cheap tequila. Dying with his face between her thighs would have been a blessing to him. What he'd felt for her, from the moment he'd set eyes on her, went beyond adoration or even awe, it was more like love or a spiritual lust. Even when she'd ordered the Italian to fuck Nathan in the ass and he'd felt violated, humiliated and

189

debased, he'd still felt honored, blessed to be in her presence, to do whatever she desired, to die for her if she commanded it. He had been terrified beyond reason yet so powerfully entranced that he couldn't leave, couldn't turn away. Even as she began to eviscerate and dismember the Italian and the Middle Eastern guy, neither the love swelling in his chest nor the erection straining at his core had diminished one iota. He'd found himself rooted to the spot, still enthralled by her beauty, her savagery, her raw power and sexuality, waiting for her to bring him his death, longing to feel her flesh once more even if it was rending and tearing his own. He'd closed his eyes and imagined her claws digging into his entrails, her fangs tearing out his throat and he'd nearly ejaculated. But she'd dismissed him, refused him the salacious annihilation she'd granted her other subjects. He'd been unworthy.

Nathan couldn't look at the other worshippers as he made his way back up the basement steps and into the main chapel. Shame raged on his cheeks, a burning reminder of his unworthiness.

He'd touched a *god*, had made love to her, offered his life—and she'd rejected him. He felt like everyone around him now looked at him differently. Their questions brought tears to his eyes.

"What was it like?"

"Man, I thought for sure she was going to kill you."

"What happened to those other dudes who went down there with you?"

Tears stung Nathan's cheeks as he turned and ran out of the building, still naked, clutching his clothes and shoes to his chest as he dashed down the church steps and into the night. He paused at the corner to dress himself. It was raining, but Nathan appeared not to notice as he made his way through the dark streets, sobbing uncontrollably, stricken with grief and disappointment and shame.

Nathan had been a fuck-up all his life. A disgrace to his father, a burden to his mother, and now he wasn't even worthy of hell—not even good enough to be disemboweled and dismembered by a demon. But this was one thing he wouldn't fuck up. Not this time. This brutal death was the only end that would make sense of his life. It would drive his parents crazy imagining how much he must have suffered, wondering how he could have volunteered for such an end. They would be forever haunted by the look of satisfaction on his face as he lay in his coffin. There was nothing left of his life; he needed this death. But first, he knew he needed to prove his worthiness to Gloria so she would take him to Hell with her.

He passed a pizzeria filled with cops, then a newsstand attended by an old man in a raincoat who was desperately trying to pull his newspapers and magazines in out of the rain. Nathan kept walking. He passed liquor stores, and the few straggling peepshows left in post-Giuliani New York, storefront churches with signs almost indistinguishable from the peepshows except for the "Jesus Saves!" plastered in flashing bright red neon letters instead of "Live Nude Girls!"

He turned the corner onto a dimly lit street lined with prostitutes of various ages. An array of old, young, Black, White, Asian, Puerto Rican, tall, short, slim to morbidly obese strutting in the rain before a line of slowly cruising cars, johns feeding their disease before returning home to their wives and children or their lonely apartments. Most of the streetwalkers wore mini-skirts or Daisy Dukes, some wore sheer catsuits or fishnet body stockings. Some of them wore only a g-string and a halter top, looking pitiful and shivering in the rain. Nathan passed a pregnant whore wearing a bikini and a fluffy pink faux-fur jacket. She looked like she was ready to drop at any moment.

Nathan knew exactly what he needed to do to make himself worthy of Gloria. He would bring her a sacrifice.

The handsome young son of a US congressman walked up to the pregnant whore, pulled out his wallet and removed the last six hundred dollars he had left to his name. "How much for the whole night?"

The whore smiled at him. It would be the last smile of her life. She snatched the money from his hands and shoved it into a tiny sequined purse, then stuffed the purse into her skimpy bra.

"This'll be enough. You can call me Kitty. Where to, handsome? Where's your car? There's a motel around the corner, the owner knows me there." She adjusted her breasts and shifted the purse around in her bra. "Or maybe I should get a cab? We could go to your place."

Her face had once been pretty but was now haggard and pockmarked, her teeth rotted from meth and crack and bad hygiene. Her breasts were bloated leaking milksacks that stained the little pink triangles of fabric that strained against her nipples. Her legs were thick and muscular but jiggled with cottage cheese where her thighs met her gluteus maximus, which was large and round and likewise dimpled with cottage cheese. Her eyes were still a gorgeous ocean blue and her lips were still full and seductive. She even had dimples. Her hair was jet black, long and curly. She had no doubt been quite attractive at one time, before drugs and pimps and johns had leeched away her beauty. She looked like what Sandra Bullock would have looked like as a pregnant crack-whore.

"We should walk," he said. "It's just a few blocks. I live at that old church on 9th."

"A church?" She looked at him suspiciously.

"It used to be. Me and a few friends are renovating it. Going to turn it into lofts or something."

"And these friends—they part of the bargain?" She hadn't started walking yet and was looking around as if planning an escape route.

"Does it matter?"

She snorted. "Hell yeah it matters! I'm fuckin' *with child*, if you hadn't noticed. I ain't in no kind of shape for a gangbang."

He smiled kindly at her. "How nice of you to be concerned for your unborn child." He cleared his throat. "It'll just be me and my lady. Nobody else."

That seemed to relax her. "She wants to fuck a prostitute? Or just watch?"

"Oh, she participates. You'll like her. In fact, I'm sure you'll love her."

"Does she eat pussy? It's been forever since I had another

bitch lick my pussy. Not since I got knocked up."

"I have a feeling she'll eat the hell out of your pussy."

Kitty's smile widened. "And she won't care, me being knocked up?"

"I have a feeling she'll be delighted by it."

"Well fuck, let's go! I feel like I should be payin' you!"

***

Gloria woke from her drug-induced stupor to the sound of screaming. On the edge of the bed was a pregnant whore in a fuzzy pink jacket. She wore a pink bikini that just barely covered huge lactating breasts perched atop an enormous belly.

The woman was screaming at the top of her lungs and backing away from Gloria's bed. She tripped and landed on her ass but kept scooting away. The blonde boy whose life Gloria had spared the night before was trying to drag the crazy bitch back to the bed.

The whore's screams intensified as Gloria rose from her bed. An excruciating high-pitched shrill oozed from every pore as she tried her best to scramble back up the basement steps, fighting with the blonde boy, kicking and scratching at him with her long fake nails.

Gloria was tempted to kill her just to stop her from screaming. "What's this?" Gloria stepped off her bed, which had been decked out like a throne, encrusted with gold and diamonds and human teeth and bone.

"A sacrifice," he murmured, head cowed. He trembled in Gloria's presence.

The six-foot demoness with skin like moonlight moved quickly toward the two idiots tussling on the floor.

"A sacrifice," he repeated. "She's pregnant." He wrestled the woman onto her back so Gloria could see her bloated, stretch-marked stomach. "I thought you'd be pleased. I brought you two sacrifices, see. You can take the baby too." He was smiling like an ape with a handful of shit.

"Excellent." The voice came from the stairs. Gloria and

the blonde boy turned as Bill Vlad waltzed down the stairs, looking more foppish than Hugh Heffner-esque in his silk smoking jacket while chomping on a fat Cuban cigar. Gloria wondered just what kind of look Vlad was attempting to pull off, and if he ever realized how absurd he actually looked.

"How perfect, Nathan. I'm sure your goddess is pleased with your thoughtful offering. I know I sure as shit am." Vlad smiled that unnerving stretching of the lips that revealed too many teeth. He reached down and rubbed the whore's belly.

The prostitute had stopped screaming and was staring at Gloria, panting rapidly, shivering, making wheezing and moaning sounds as if she was experiencing terror, shock, and withdrawal symptoms all at once.

She reminded Gloria far too much of herself once upon a time. "I don't want it. Get it out of here."

"But Goddess . . ."

Gloria kicked Nathan in the side. He crashed onto his back, grimacing in pain as he held his shattered ribs.

She reached down and grabbed Nathan by the front of his shirt, pulling him partly off the floor. "I said get this whore out of here! Take her back to whatever street corner you got her from and never come back here again!"

Nathan's bottom lip trembled. He supported his busted ribs as he climbed to his feet and turned to leave, struggling to breathe, wondering if he'd punctured a lung. The whore scrambled to her feet with him, clutching his arm as if he were her protector and not the one who'd brought her here to be sacrificed.

Vlad stepped into their path and barred the stairway. "No one's leaving. The goddess will accept your sacrifice."

"No, Vlad," Gloria started but Vlad ignored her, raising his voice to drown out her protests.

"The Goddess knows what it's like to be human. She knows what it's like to be human *in Hell*. And she never wants to go through that again. Right?" Vlad chuckled, shaking his head, his tongue darting in and out of his mouth in an overtly sexual gesture that made Gloria's skin crawl.

"Of course, if she doesn't want to be a goddess anymore

we can always arrange for her to be human again. That way the two of us can spend the rest of eternity in Hell getting reacquainted. How does that sound, lover?" Vlad smiled again and chills raced up Gloria's spine.

She rushed forward, grabbed the whore by the throat and tossed her flat on her back onto the bed. The girl barely struggled, making this easier for Gloria. Vlad had made it rather clear it was either the prostitute or Gloria, and she wasn't about to sacrifice herself for some whore. Not for a lifetime of damnation.

Gloria stoically parted the prostitute's legs, leaning into her to keep her still. The woman struggled a bit but she seemed paralyzed with fear, right up until Gloria began easing one taloned finger, then another and another until she had all five fingers up to the knuckles inside her. Then she began to kick and scream but Gloria held her tight. The whore moaned and squeezed her eyes shut.

"Oh God. Oh heavenly Father. Oh fuck."

Gloria shoved her fist inside, stretching the whore's vagina worse than any john ever had as Gloria pushed through her cervix and into her womb seizing the fetus inside the woman's uterus and dragging it out in an avalanche of blood and amniotic fluid.

The whore writhed and screamed, bleeding all over Gloria's bed. Gloria held the baby up, the umbilical cord still attached and trailing from the agonized mother's bloodied snatch. The fetus wailed like a tortured goat.

Vlad applauded slowly, smiling that lecherous predatory smile. "Wonderful, Gloria. But you're not done yet."

"What? I took the damned sacrifice! I took the sacrifice! I played your demon-god for you," Gloria said, raising her arm to indicate the viscera hanging from her claws, her skin, at the vital tissue shreds and clumps of busted blood vessels that had once been on the *inside* of the whore now scattered on the bedspread. "She's *dead*, Vlad."

"*That's* not." He pointed at the fetus.

"Do what you want with it." She held it up for Vlad to take but he shook his head.

"I don't want it," he said, taking a step back. "I think maybe you need to do something more than snap its little neck."

"But why?" Nathan cried, stepping from the shadows. "I thought you—I thought you'd just . . ."

"Just *what?*" Vlad demanded, moving toward Nathan. "What did you think? That we'd kill the creature's mother and maybe send him to live with Mary fucking Poppins? That this *thing* would have a happy ending? Just what were you thinking?"

Nathan shook his head and his cheeks reddened. "I-I-I-" he stammered. "I wanted to please my goddess. I didn't think that far!"

Vlad snorted. "And now? What did you think you'd accomplish speaking up now?"

Nathan opened his mouth but had nothing to add. He swallowed hard.

"Too bad, kid. I guess you didn't think that far—again." Vlad turned to Gloria. "There's still too much humanity in you. You know that, don't ya?"

She stared at him but knew he was right, knew the empathy she felt for the whore and her progeny would be her undoing. Beneath all of her demonic flesh and might, she was still human, still Gloria. She didn't know if this was a strength or a weakness. Right now, it felt weak.

She was a *god* and shouldn't have to constantly remind herself. She looked at the knotted cords of muscle running down her arms and the sharp talons at the ends of her fingertips, still dripping in blood. There was nothing human left in her besides her conscience, her soul. She was a demon, a goddess, a being far superior to the wretched whore she had been, the victim, far superior to these wretched creatures she still pitied. But she didn't feel love or compassion toward them. They had, after all, never felt any for her. It was for them that she had fucked thousands of men on camera. It was for them that she'd had sex with dogs and pigs and cows and mules and horses. They were the ones watching on the other side of the computer. They were the ones buying that shit. They were the ones who could have helped her and didn't. She had felt compassion for Angela, her own flesh and blood, and had been betrayed, had wound up in Hell. Then she had done it again, given up Heaven for the ungrateful brat. Was she about to be stupid again? Give up godhood for these selfish, ungrateful, corrupt and greedy humans?

Fuck, no.

She felt sorry for the baby, the way one might feel having to put down a favorite pet. They were her pets now. They were her fuck toys. Her cattle. Her sheep. And no matter how small, they were here to do her bidding. Nothing more. If they were in her place, they would have done the same to her. They had murdered her soul and filmed it for all to see. What was the difference?

And just like that, victim became victimizer. Gloria knelt on the bed beside the dead whore and raised her arms over her head, stretching the umbilical cord until it was nothing but a long string. The newborn wailed and kicked uselessly, its tiny bloody body too new to this world.

"I think it misses its mother," she said, bringing it to her face to stare at it. Vlad huffed, as if preparing to deliver another lecture on humanity, when she added, "I think I'll reunite them."

Gloria took a deep breath, preparing to take a step so far outside of her nature, her humanity, there would be no going back. With this act, her humanity would forever be a thing of the past. Part of her wondered if there truly was such a thing as inhuman cruelty. She wondered if there was anything so cruel that humans had not done it many times before. In Hitler's Germany, in Darfur, Rwanda, Europe during the Inquisition? Was there any act so heinous that committing it would make you truly inhuman? Truly monstrous? Truly evil? She was about to find out.

Grabbing the infant around its middle, she shoved it back inside the whore's snatch headfirst, pushing the squealing newborn deep inside its dead mother's cavity.

"Oh, God, no!" Nathan screamed, blood draining from his face, fingernails dragging trackmarks down his cheeks. "Please!" he sobbed, falling to his knees.

Gloria's body quivered, shaken by her own cruelty, but not yet finished. She had not yet gone far enough, not yet gone beyond her own humanity, beyond child soldiers being forced to gang rape women and chop off the limbs of their own parents. She had not yet gone beyond the Nazi death camps, the human experiments, lamps made of human skin and placed on display at museums. She had not yet gone beyond the physical interrogation techniques like burning, skinning, dismembering, dislocating limbs, and mutilating genitalia that were employed by the Christian church to ferret out werewolves and witches. She hadn't gone beyond virgins being stoned and burned alive for sinning against Allah by letting themselves get raped against their will. She hadn't gone beyond women like her being forced to suck off donkeys to feed their heroin addiction or get gang-banged by fifty men and then covered from head to toe with their cum for a couple thousand dollars. What she had done so far was nothing. It was amateur, small-time.

She turned her attention now to Nathan. "You," she said, trying to put the self-confidence in her voice she didn't quite feel yet. Trying to sound the way she imagined a god should. "Come rescue him if it means so much to you."

He looked up at her. "Ruh-really?" He wiped the snot and tears from his face.

"Better hurry. I don't think he can breathe in there."

Nathan swallowed hard again and licked his lips. With one great effort he got up off his knees and hurried to the bed. "Bless you," he said, near hysterics. "You are magnificent. You are truly a goddess."

Gloria watched as he reached inside the whore. The baby had stopped crying by now, but that didn't dissuade his efforts. Gently he pulled the tiny feet until they were protruding from the hole.

"You're too slow!" she said. "Here—let me give you a hand."

And with that, she grabbed Nathan's head and began to push him inside the dead whore's snatch. He screamed and punched blindly, but she held him steady, slowly shoving him inside, his head inside the cavity now. Gloria's tremendous muscles strained as she forced him inside of the whore's bleeding vagina, tearing it wide, cracking the woman's pelvic bone and separating it as Nathan's shoulders followed his head into the dead woman's uterus, then his arms, pinned against his torso. The whore's body was acting like a giant anaconda, seeming to contract and expand to accommodate Nathan's body, tearing and splitting as Gloria forced him further inside. Nathan's muffled screams echoed through the bleeding rents in the prostitute's abdomen. Dripping red muscle fibers and popcorn-colored globs of fat gleamed through the large open wounds, and through those, she could see Nathan's face, no longer screaming, turning blue. Gloria pushed from one end while holding the mother's body still with her other hand, until Nathan was buried up to his hips inside the dead flesh.

The whore's body had split like a cheap suit up the middle, and mother, baby and Nathan began to ooze out through the gaps, a liquefying mess of blood and fecal matter. The whore's legs were almost perpendicular, her body split like a wishbone. The lower half of Nathan's body hung out from between her splayed legs, kicking and twitching a bizarre St Vita's dance that made it look like the whore was still alive and convulsing, trying to give birth to a man-sized baby.

"Did you find him yet?" she said, laughing, crying, breathing hard as if about to come. "Did you find him yet?" she said louder, as if he simply hadn't heard her. She would have been incredibly shocked had Nathan been able to answer. She knelt down and kissed Nathan's lips where his face was visible between the whore's ruptured ribcage. One breast saturated in blood flopped on either side of his face.

She whispered, her lips still touching his, "Still think I'm magnificent?" Tears ran down her cheeks onto his lifeless face.

Vlad looked stunned. He wiped his palm across his face and raised his brows. "Well damn," he muttered. "I think that took care of your little humanity issue."

Gloria climbed off the bed and approached Vlad. She wiped her last tears from her eyes and flicked them away and with them, her last connection to humanity. "We have work to do."

Vlad was obviously aware that a shift had taken place and he fell easily into this new order. Gloria knew that to him, this was just a new opportunity to exploit as soon as he could figure out how. But Gloria was in charge now.

Vlad nodded. "We do. What did you have in mind?"

Gloria smiled.

Part VIII

"Tyranny, like hell, is not easily conquered; yet we have this consolation with us, that the harder the conflict, the more glorious the triumph."
—*Thomas Paine*

They were legion; thousands of confused, lost souls waiting for direction. Over the internet, watching as Vlad filmed the entire event and broadcast it around the world, hundreds of thousands more—millions—waited. They sat in their bedrooms alone or in couples or threesomes. Groups had assembled at parties to watch it. Across Japan, Russia, Germany, Sweden and other countries, stadiums and concert arenas were filled with people watching on giant screens.

Gloria had become a celebrity thanks to Vlad. Hers was the world's fastest growing religion, and she was its spiritual leader. It had all begun with a young couple broadcasting sex on a webcam, followed by their joint-suicide in Gloria's name after reaching orgasm: slitting each other's carotid arteries and bleeding out while still in the act of coitus, all carefully planned and orchestrated by Vlad. This had spawned copycats. Couples fucking on camera then shooting each other, stabbing each other, taking sleeping pills, overdosing on heroin, all in the name of Gloria, with each death spread in living color on the internet.

Then Vlad had upped the ante by organizing the first suicide party. More than a hundred kids had come. A massive orgy watched by thousands around the world ending in a bloodbath as knives were passed out among the partiers, and blood was spilled all for the glory of Gloria.

More followed. Many more. It had become a world-wide epidemic of sex and death. After each event Gloria would come online to issue a statement, praising the suicides for their loyalty and promising them endless rewards in the afterlife, where she vowed she would soon join them. It had taken on a life of its own. Soon tapes were popping up from

201

every country showing similar orgy/suicides for Gloria—just as Vlad had said would happen. And Gloria praised each one in fiery speeches written by Vlad that she was getting better and better at delivering, whipping her followers into a frenzy and inspiring more sex/suicides. It had all culminated in this, the Mass Exodus as Vlad liked to call it. The lost and the damned from around the world had heeded her call. Midnight. Halloween. Corny but, as Vlad, had assured her, humans like the familiar. They like their rituals and traditions. That's why Christmas and Easter were celebrated during the winter and summer solstices, on Pagan holidays. The familiar. Tradition.

Her followers were everywhere, assembled before her. Around the world. Waiting. And Gloria was in place to guide them, instruct them. Lead them. She still felt so lost herself. She wasn't sure what would happen when she made it back to Hell. Vlad was acting confident but she wasn't even sure that he knew what would happen. She was making it up as she went, following her instincts and her anger. It didn't matter. They would follow blindly. They loved her. They called her a god. She was, at the least, a good surrogate. At least she was here. At least she had bothered to show herself. At least they could talk to her, touch her, fuck her. This made her far greater than the god many of them had grown up worshipping. God who wasn't there, who was never there. Had never been there.

They would follow her to the ends of Hell and earth. And it seemed to Gloria many of them had no idea just how literal this was going to be.

"You have exceeded the Masters' wildest expectations," Vlad said "They will be delighted."

"You know I'm not going back there for them."

"Oh, but you will be rewarded. You will be *handsomely* rewarded for all that you've done." Vlad wasn't stupid. Evil, petty, greedy, but not stupid.

She was sure he knew what she was planning. He just wanted to hear her say it. Once it was spoken aloud there would be no going back. "I don't want anything from them. I'm taking it all."

Vlad flashed his shark's grin. "All?"

202

"I'm not going to be a victim anymore. I'm never going to let anyone control me again. Not you. Not them. Not even God. I'm taking all of it. And you're going to help me."

"Oh, Gloria. You know that wasn't the plan."

"Plans change," she'd said. "I know what my mission is supposed to be, but I have to do this. If you aren't with me then you know what'll happen to you if I'm successful. All of those people who have gone to Hell for me already are waiting, and talking to the others about my coming, making more converts. Just like I told them to. And when I get there with a million souls backing me, it'll be like the second coming. All of Hell will bow before me."

Vlad was still smiling, still calculating. "Of course, you have my undying loyalty. I hope it all turns out like you think it will."

Vlad's smile bothered Gloria. There was something knowing about it, as if he knew something that he wasn't saying. Something vital, something that might change every-thing. But Vlad was a con-man and there was never any way of knowing when he was bluffing. This time, Gloria was positive his hand was empty.

Vlad was receptive to her ideas because they included him. Because they would mean great power for both. And because he was admittedly an opportunistic fuck, he was willing to try anything. Of course failure would mean an eternity of misery and suffering, but hey, what else was new? That perverted fuck had long ago learned to enjoy the miseries of Hell. And she had at least learned how to endure them.

The crowd had outgrown the small church, and in the middle of the night Gloria had taken them en masse to the Bandshell area inside Central Park. There they posted sentries around the perimeter, welcoming new worshippers and turning away protesters and those trying to stop the coming massacre. Anyone was welcome to join, but the few indigent stragglers or hapless late-night joggers that turned out to be more curious rubber-neckers than loyal followers were sucked in and forced to participate whether they wanted to or not. Once you were in, there was no leaving.

Gloria knew the police would be along at any time but didn't care. She could handle anything that came along, but she hated distractions. Cops would definitely be a pain in the ass she could do without.

Thousand of faces waited for Gloria to speak. Despite the volume of people it grew deathly quiet as Gloria stepped up on the Bandshell stage—where Duke Ellington, Irving Berlin and The Grateful Dead had once performed—and addressed her followers.

"We have a mission," she said, her voice booming loudly, heard by all without a microphone or speakers. "You know what you have to do."

The crowd nodded, muttered yes's, waited for more.

"Do you love me?"

"YES!" was the resounding, thunderous, overwhelming reply.

"Do you love this world?"

"NO!"

"And what about Him?" Gloria pointed up to the heavens. "Do you love Him?"

"NO!"

"Then come with me. It is, as they say, far better to rule in Hell than to serve in heaven. Follow me and I promise you, you will not suffer. We will rule eternity together and live forever in paradise! "

The crowd cheered, some screaming and crying and calling her name until she raised her hand for silence.

"You will fall into the Ocean of Fire. Some will be snatched away, delivered into Heaven. We will come for you. Prepare those you meet there for our arrival. There will be no more separation between Heaven and Hell. The reign of God and Satan has ended!"

She studied the faces in the crowd for a moment, looking for doubt, looking for anyone she felt might be considering Heaven as an alternative to doing her bidding. Satisfied, she continued. "Those of you who fall into the Ocean of Fire— and this will be most of you—climb to the banks and wait for me. Demons will grab you, but I will save you! We will all

204

save you! You are one of us now. We are all in this together and we cannot be stopped. We cannot be denied!"

The crowd cheered again, unable to help themselves, unbearably excited. It was a good speech. Vlad had done a great job writing it. He had a rare talent for manipulation. He had done an equally impressive job coaching her to read it, like he always did. Like he had been sent here to do. Gloria looked over at him. He was still grinning. She wondered if he had known that this was how it was going to end from the start, if he had somehow planned it all. Because if it was part of his plan then it was part of the Masters' plan and she was once more being used as a pawn in a game she couldn't understand. It would mean she was once again a victim.

Gloria paused. What if this *was* all part of some demonic divine plan? What should she do? She looked around at the throngs of teeming humanity, all assembled to follow her to Hell. Was it too late to turn back? She thought about all the hundreds of people she had already talked into committing suicide in her name, the deluded fools she'd fucked and murdered in her little basement temple, and the baby, the whore's baby, and Nathan. She looked back out at the crowd.

"We love you, Gloria!"

They had no idea what they were saying. They knew nothing about love. Neither did Gloria. She had thought she loved her husband and daughter but then she had left them for drugs and sex and the ridiculous idea of fame. She had thought that they had forgiven her, that they had still loved her, but then they had tricked her and sent her to Hell. She had even thought she loved the Masters… and Madria. But there was no such thing as love in her world. She knew that now. There was only lust and sex and pain and deceit. That was the only love she had ever known, the only love she had to give. It was too late. She had to see this through.

She leapt from the stage into the crowd, offering herself to them. And the orgy began.

She was kissed and licked, groped and caressed, sucked and fucked from one orgasm to the next. Penises of every size and description were thrust into her, eager to spend themselves

205

inside of her before she dispatched them with a swipe of her claws, disemboweling, dismembering, and decapitating her lovers one at a time, only to have them immediately replaced by another in an endless series of orgasm and death. All around her, her followers were enthusiastically fucking in every imaginable combination: heterosexual, bisexual, homosexual, couples, threesomes, foursomes, and more. Semen, saliva, blood and vaginal fluids glistened everywhere on naked flesh as they enjoyed their final climax on earth.

Sirens surrounded the park along with blue and red flashing lights. Two helicopters, a police helicopter and one she assumed was from one of the TV networks, circled above. The sound of gunshots rang out from all directions, followed by screams. There were gunbattles going on all over the park between the police and Gloria's followers. The cops were killing her lovers, her people. Some of the police were being pulled into the orgy. Everything was in danger of coming apart.

"Vlad?" she called. "Are you ready?"

Vlad nodded, and signaled groups of people stationed around the perimeter of the crowd. They guarded large trunks filled with knives and began passing them out amongst the crowds. Around the world, the thousands of others watching on the internet got the message and began pulling out their own knives and guns and pills and needles. More worshippers stationed at the foot of the stage guarded vats filled with a grape juice and cyanide mixture, and they were now carefully pouring the drink into small paper cups and handing them out as quickly as possible.

Without hesitation people began opening veins and arteries, cutting through their own throats and wrists, stabbing each other in the chest. Some opened their femoral arteries, bleeding out within minutes. Very few of them stopped fucking, even as they bled to death. Others drank, and lay on the ground immediately after. One by one they began to die. They were all on their way to Hell.

The ground turned muddy beneath her feet, the earth saturated with the blood of thousands. Everywhere she looked bodies littered the park floor. Some lay still, some were still twitching and convulsing, some moaning and crying out in pain, some still furiously copulating.

"Go, Vlad," she yelled. "Wait for them. Gather as many as you can. I'll follow when we're finished here."

"Don't keep me waiting" he said and with that, Vlad raked a claw across his throat, tearing out his esophagus, carotid artery, and jugular vein in one savage motion.

"I'll wait for you," he gurgled through a mouthful of blood as he collapsed to the muddy earth and disappeared.

"It won't be long." Gloria waited for the remaining followers to die. She began walking among the dying, dispatching those who remained with quick swipes of her claws.

There was a lesbian couple lying on one of the small park bridges. Gloria stepped onto the bridge and began making her way toward them, continuing to dispatch the occasional worshipper who had not yet found his way to Hell. Blood coated her skin in a fine sheen that made her amphibious complexion glimmer and shine. The slick ichorous life-fluids dripping from her arms, legs and torso, dribbling down her face, shimmered in the moonlight.

One of the women was already near death from a slash across her femoral artery that had emptied most of the blood from her veins and was still hard at work pumping out the rest of it. A sheet of blood poured from the bridge to the concrete below where Gloria had once watched street performers breakdance for tips. The dying woman's lover, a long, lean, redhead with small breasts but wide hips and a firm plump ass that porn producers would have loved for anal scenes, was still licking her pussy, sucking her clit, trying to bring the woman to one last orgasm before she died. Gloria looked at the cut on the redhead's thigh. It was too shallow. She had missed the artery.

"She's gone," Gloria said, startling the woman from her rapture.

"Gloria!" The redheaded woman scrambled from between her lovers legs and knelt down between Gloria's thighs. She began licking Gloria's clit. Gloria looked down at Red's lover, whose eyes had begun to glaze. Her chest had ceased its rise and fall. She was dead.

"Did you love her?"

The redhead stopped licking Gloria's cum-drenched snatch for a moment and looked up at her.

"Huh?"

"Did you love her?"

"We were in love. We got married last year in San Francisco. You know, before they repealed the law."

Gloria didn't know anything about the law. She had still been in Hell when the Supreme Court had given gays the right to marry and then when the constitution had been changed to outlaw it again. Even had she been on earth, she doubted she would have cared. It was a human thing and her humanity had been surgically excised by the Masters.

"Do you love me?" Gloria asked.

"I do. Of course, I do. You are my goddess.'"

"Will you let us both go to Hell alone?" Gloria asked, pointing to the feeble wound on Red's thigh.

"I-I can't. I'm afraid."

The NYPD were closing in on them with their guns drawn.

"Stop! Stop right there!"

"Don't you fucking move! You in the costume! Don't fucking move!"

"Hands in the air!"

"Get down on your knees!"

"Come with me," Gloria said, ignoring the cops swarming around her like gnats, reaching out her hand to the young lesbian.

The redheaded woman was still on her knees, smiling up at Gloria. On the bridge, it looked as if every cop in New York had assembled. There were hundreds of guns pointed at them.

The woman nodded. "Take me. Take me with you. I can't do it myself."

"Don't do it! Hands in the air! Hands in the air! Don't you fucking do it!"

Gloria raised her talons and slashed them across the

redhead's throat, severing her trachea, esophagus and cervical vertebrae, sending her head spinning off the bridge to the concrete below, her long mane of crimson hair twirling into the darkness.

The bullets began to hail down, pounding into Gloria's flesh. She took more than a hundred rounds before she finally dropped. A demon has so few vital organs, and nearly every part of her was expendable, replaceable. Except for that one tiny spot in the prefrontal lobe that housed her soul. Out of hundreds of rounds fired from the policemen's semi-automatic guns, a single bullet found that sweet spot. There was a moment of darkness and then an explosion of flames as Gloria found herself hurtling toward Hell.

Part IX

"It is better to conquer yourself than to win a thousand battles. Then the victory is yours. It cannot be taken from you, not by angels or by demons, heaven or hell."
    —Hindu Prince Gautama Siddharta, the founder of Buddhism, 563-483 B.C.

Gloria descended into Hell, plummeting into the Ocean of Fire, liquid fire burning her flesh without incinerating. The searing heat stung her skin as she swam to shore, where the beach for as far as she could see was filled with her followers. Vlad was nowhere in sight. So much for waiting for her. No doubt he'd run off to warn the Masters. She wondered if they had even needed his warning. They must have had some way of monitoring her movements on earth.

The demons who usually preyed at the edge of these waters for fallen souls found themselves overwhelmed. The ocean of Hell had overrun its banks and millions upon millions of souls were emerging from the flaming sea.

The sky was black with souls hurtling into the boiling ocean of protoplasm. Even the angels who normally patrolled the skies had retreated, as many of them had been pulled down into the Ocean of Fire by the sudden deluge of souls. The oceans flooded Hell with a tsunami of the damned. The humans were attacking anything they found that was not human, forcing those demons caught in the tide into the flaming waters. The war had begun.

Demons were pouring from the tunnels. They hacked through the human souls like scythes through wheat, but the humans were relentless. The demons attacked savagely, fighting with hatred and rage behind them, propelling them, giving them strength. Hundreds of thousands of demons attacked with studded clubs, planks of wood fitted with razors and knives, with carved-out skulls of past victims, bloody flesh still dripping gore, with anything they could grab and use as a weapon. But they were horribly outnumbered, and as Gloria herself had discovered during her tour in eternal torment, souls in hell regenerated.

There were millions of humans, and those who had just arrived with Gloria had not yet learned to fear the inferno and its masters. They were on a mission. They were determined to wrestle Hell from the demon's grasp in honor of their infernal lord, Gloria. And they learned quickly to attack the demons in hordes and relinquish them of their weapons.

The demons who wouldn't give up easily, like those caught by the shore, were soon overrun by the masses of newly-dead humans engulfing them like toxic waves from the flaming sea. Those in the way were trampled, torn to pieces, disemboweled, dismembered, pulverized beyond recognition despite their remarkable strength. The overwhelming force from the sheer *number* of humans shattered the ranks of demons. But the destruction done to them was temporary, because like the humans they had attempted to annihilate, the demons were spirits and could not be permanently destroyed.

And some believed they would ultimately be triumphant, that Gloria's insane coup was a *temporary* insanity. But those who fought back did so in vain. They quickly discovered there was no victory, not for Hell, not for them. And maybe they were right, they figured, and this was temporary. But even so, it made no sense to stick with the losing side. When this entire mess was finished, they'd lick their wounds and pledge eternal loyalty to the victor. It didn't matter to them who that might be.

The humans embraced them, converted them, made them loyal followers of Gloria. For now, at least. It suited the demons well to spend their days this way.

Those who refused to succumb were dragged off into the caverns deep within the bowels of Hell.

Time to make an example of the non-believers, it was decided. One demon with a ring of baby skulls adorning its belt was dragged across the dirt, his claws digging into the ground in a feeble attempt to gain purchase. His enormous antlers, filed down into dozens of deadly points was torn from his head. He was knocked down and he crashed to his knees, roaring as he fell, his knotty forehead smashing into the cave wall, a tusk snapping off, the thick scorpion tail protruding from the center of his spine snapping and cracking wildly until it was chopped off with an axe.

The mob descended on him and at first he held them at bay, smashing in their skulls with swipes from his massive fists but they kept coming and coming and when they retreated they took pieces with them. Like biting insects, relentless, pervasive, taking at first nips of flesh to aggravate until they were retreating with larger pieces, then with more vital pieces . . . gnawing, chomping, grinding away limbs, chunks of its distorted, freakish face, and they fled with these pieces, scattering them throughout the caves, dropping chunks of the demon into the bottomless pit of the Ocean of Fire.

The armless, legless, dickless torso demon began the arduous task of searching for his stolen body parts, unable to regenerate without them. It wobbled uselessly, like a turtle flipped on its back, trying desperately to move through the cave. After some time, the demon realized he had moved maybe an inch. He wanted to scream his rage, to demand they bring back his stolen body, but they had ripped out his tongue and vocal cords as well.

Torso demon began his endless trek through the passages of Hell and wondered who the fuck he was being loyal to and whether or not it was worth it.

***

Led by Gloria, humans and newly recruited demons, hellspawn, wraiths, fallen seraphim, fauns, nephilim, ghosts, the innocent and the damned thrown together in a stygian cesspool of primordial ooze seeping from the filthy walls swarmed the chambers, overtaking and overthrowing everything in their path.

The catacombs were soon littered with body parts of Hell's denizens torn apart in the fight, unable to find their own scattered limbs and organs to regenerate, and littered too with those too afraid to fight, too afraid to join the cause, swept up in the maelstrom and destroyed by the very force of it. Some feared the Masters more than they feared Gloria and her endless masses and they refused to succumb no matter what they were threatened with.

And some reminded Gloria what a fool she was, believing she could defeat the Masters—and Satan himself.

"Let Satan show himself!" Gloria exclaimed. "Let the almighty Morning Star join in the fight. Goddamned coward." She spat in the dirt.

Buried deep within the passages of Hell—a section Gloria had not seen before, not surprising considering the vastness of Hades—she began to discover various rooms, each filled with tortured souls in various stages of experimentation.

She freed those willing to join her—or those at least willing to lie and promise their eternal devotion in exchange for their freedom from their current state of misery and torment. She wasn't foolish enough to believe these converts were suddenly true devotees, but she had the strength and the numbers, and they would all fall into place or be destroyed. There was no third option, and she wasn't concerned.

The few stubborn idiots too foolish to lie were left to their various tortures. A disemboweled demon forced to slowly eat his own intestines, pulling through the lanky length of fiber and muscle and tissue like sausage through a skinny casing, sucking it back, devouring the ruined meat. Beside him, a human man watched helplessly while strapped into a chair as the ebola virus slowly ate away his flesh, leaving behind gangrenous holes oozing diseased pus, the putrid smell making him gag, the sight of his flesh dissolving into puddles of blood and liquid tissue making him vomit. Others were stretched on racks until joints popped out of their sockets, until flesh tore; eyes were repeatedly gouged out with scalpels the moment they regenerated, flicking the base, slowly carving out the ciliary muscle until a slight pop! was followed by unremitting pain, blood flooding the cheeks, filling the nostrils. One eye, the other, regenerate, repeat. Face covered with gore, screams bursting from chests until exhaustion set in, until they're unable to utter another sound. Orifices stretched to unrecognizable

213

proportions by medieval instruments. And this *still* was the better alternative to joining Gloria, some believed. She found their stupidity, their lack of faith mind-numbing. When Satan got wind of this, they taunted through agonized moans and shrieks, all Hell's gonna break loose, so to speak.

And somewhere in the back of her mind this worried Gloria, but there wasn't anything she could do about that now. She would face Satan when he finally decided to join this fight. She was quite surprised he hadn't joined in by now. What the hell was he waiting for?

Down another deserted corridor Gloria led another contingent. The rest of the massive crowd had been instructed to wait. Traveling through narrow tunnels with a massive force behind her was beginning to get a bit claustrophobic. Besides, they weren't actually *getting* anywhere. They had destroyed everything in their path that they hadn't absorbed. As far as Gloria knew, the only thing left in her way were the Masters. And Satan. Maybe Vlad, depending on which side he was on now, but that didn't worry her. Vlad was a spec in the grand scheme of things.

Beyond the antechamber a figure was outstretched as if in welcome, suspended from the rock walls like a monarch butterfly stretched out on a board. His face was contorted into an unnatural grimace. Here was a creature who had faced inexorable pain and suffering. Gloria couldn't tell if it was a human or a demon, it was so badly disfigured. She couldn't help but feel a twinge of compassion for it. She was surprised she still felt any *positive* emotions and wondered if she should be concerned. Compassion was a human emotion after all, something she shouldn't still experience? Did this somehow make her more human? No, she decided. She was a god and could experience any fucking emotion she desired. If she felt any twinge of compassion for another creature, so be it.

"Cut it down," she instructed, but before anyone moved a rustle of air from the suspended figure made her look up.

The thing wasn't dead, as she'd suspected it was. Slowly its eyes opened, and in them Gloria recognized something strange and beautiful: compassion. Impossible for a demon but this was definitely not a human. It was too big, too powerful. And just as slowly it began to move, slightly raising its badly beaten head. A delicate rustling began to grow in force, swelled from a gentle breeze to a gale force wind. Its gigantic wings expanded, until they were wrapped around the things horribly beaten body. The wings, once magnificent, were filthy, torn, shredded remnants of their former glory, streaked with dirt and piss and shit, trampled and stomped until they barely resembled wings anymore. This thing had once been an angel. The angel exhaled deeply, as if unfurling his wings brought him great relief.

"I know you," Gloria whispered, stepping closer to the demon/angel, bringing her hand up until it touched his chin. "Is it you?"

He nodded slightly.

"Can you talk?"

He shook his head. *No.*

Gloria longed to hear his angelic voice, the enigmatic voice of her former tormentor. His hideous appearance could hide many things, but not his original nature. She remembered how radiant he had looked when he'd first shrugged off his infernal flesh and had reassumed his angelic form. It had obviously been a mistake, one he had been paying for ever since.

"Cut him down!" she yelled. "Gently."

Half a dozen arms carefully supported the mutilated seraphim as they cut him down and lay him on the ground. Gloria knelt beside him. "We'll take care of you," she said, taking his clawed hand in hers. She owed him that much. He had saved her life once, had sacrificed himself so that she might experience some happiness. And this had been his reward: eternal torture and damnation. That was about to end. Gloria would see to that.

Gloria stood over the angel/demon and stared down at him. "Is he okay?" she asked no one in particular.

The woman beside her shook her head. "I have no idea. There's no way to—"

Gloria backhanded the woman, sending her flying off her feet, sending her smashing into the wall several feet away.

"Remember who you are addressing!" she snapped, whirling to face the group one at a time. "I am your God! Would you prefer Satan to me? Would you prefer the torments of Hell to my love? Then address me as you would Him!"

The group muttered apologies, and the woman Gloria had attacked slowly climbed to her feet, wiping the blood from her face and neck. "I'm sorry, Goddess. No disrespect intended."

"And the angel?" Gloria asked again. "What can be done for him?"

Everyone looked at Gloria but no one spoke. She'd felt it was necessary to keep this group submissive, but now she wondered if that had been a mistake. None of her followers acted as if they would betray her. She wondered if spending time in Hell had made her paranoid.

"Someone answer," she said. Still no one did. "You may answer!"

"Well," and this voice belonged to the same woman Gloria had struck. Gloria was beginning to gain respect for this woman. She had a set of stones on her. "It's not like there's an infirmary here. Is there really any way of knowing? I mean, the other demons don't die . . . why would he?"

"Because he's not a demon, not anymore." Gloria said. "He's an angel, was an angel . . . a fallen angel who became a demon. And then was redeemed . . . and so they did this to him, as punishment. He apparently became a pet project," she continued, stroking his battered wing. "They've fucked him up pretty badly . . . I don't know if he'll be able to recover. But I owe him. Help him."

Things had never been the same for her angel/demon, the one who had spent what had felt like an eternity torturing her, raping her, shredding the skin from her body over and over and over. Yet he had shown remorse, had set her free. Had tried to redeem himself from the pain he had inflicted, knowing that if he failed, he would be punished. And he had failed. Heaven still had not accepted him, and Hell wanted him to pay.

"We'll do the best we can, Goddess," another follower said, stepping up from the shadows. "We can stay with him. Try to, I don't know, nurse him back to health or something."

"Fine," Gloria said, nodding. "For now, the Ocean of Fire will be our home base, until we can figure out better communications in this place. If you have any news you need to report, get to the lake. If I'm not there, someone will always be able to find me."

"Yes, Goddess."

The group dispersed, some carrying her angel/demon to the shores, others . . . she didn't know where the others were going. She'd never asked, nor had she given directions. But they set out purposefully, as if on a mission, and she felt that if she asked, she would appear weak. How could she *not* know where they were going, what they were doing? To ask would be ridiculous. Still, this was unacceptable, this not knowing. Something she would have to fix.

She moved through the tunnels, watching the continuing slaughter, the onslaught of her people reducing Hell to scores of helpless demonic creatures.

"Vlad!" she yelled. If he was still loyal, he would hear her. He would come. He was never far from her. Not unless he was with the Masters.

Vlad appeared seconds later, and to her surprise fell to his knees before her.

"Goddess," he said. He stood up and grinned. "Have to make it look good for the others, now don't I?"

"Take me to the Masters," she said, shaking her head at his impudence. She *was* a goddess now. He should know better than to display such arrogance and sarcasm.

"That's . . . not such a good idea."

"I didn't ask for your opinion. I gave you a command."

"Look, lover. Things really aren't all that different. I don't buy into your line of bullshit." He crossed his arms over his chest, his elbows resting on his massive gut. "You may be *their* goddess, but you're my bitch."

Gloria backhanded Vlad and he went flying off his feet, smashing headfirst into the wall. "You got the better of me once, you fucking troll. Never again. I'll have my people on you faster than you could possibly imagine."

The corridor seemed to breathe on its own with the volume

of humans spilling through the caverns. "I only have to say the word and they'll have you in a thousand pieces, scattered all through Hell."

Vlad struggled to his feet and wiped the blood off the gaping wound on his crushed cheekbone. "Fine," he said, pig eyes staring hard. "But you have to listen to me. It's too soon to go after the Masters."

"Why?"

"You need a game plan."

"And you have one." Of course he would, she thought. One where he would undoubtedly set her up, sacrifice her to the Masters.

"You can't face them alone."

Gloria raised her arm, swept it across the cavern. "Does this look like I'd be alone?"

Vlad shook his head, then winced. "Them?! They're no match for the Masters! Even in mass numbers they couldn't win. The Masters aren't ordinary demons, Gloria. They're gods."

"And I'm a goddess."

"These humans made you a goddess. The Masters have always been as they are. One goddess fighting a dozen gods? Do you really like those odds?"

"I don't believe the Masters will fare any better than the rest of these demons. Their might is in their cunning and their seductiveness. They aren't fighters."

"Yes, and neither are you. You are as they are and they've been at it far longer. Do you really want to bring all these humans to meet the Masters? How long do you think it would be before they wooed all your precious followers away from you? They have been at this game for untold eons. You're new to this. You aren't even very good at it yet. "

"But I have something they don't. I represent change. They've been running Hell for untold eons, as you say. It's going to be hard for them to convince anyone that things would be better staying as they are then with me in control, not after what my fellow humans have seen and experienced here."

Vlad looked her up and down.

"But they are not 'your fellow humans.' Not anymore. You're not human anymore, Gloria. You are just like the Masters now, a god as you have anointed yourself. How are you going to convince your humans that you are any different from the Masters? And what makes you think you would be, with the reins of Hell in your hands? The power of billions of souls? Power corrupts and ultimate power corrupts ultimately. As you said, you're a god now."

Vlad was once again smiling that cocky vulture's grin that made her feel like she was something on the menu.

Gloria paused. What would she do with that much power? What would she become? What had she already become?

"And what are you, Vlad? Are you a god?"

"I was created, same as you. Don't you see? They can take that away."

"Then why haven't they?"

Vlad opened his mouth but shut it quickly. He cocked his head, as if considering her question.

"What I think," Gloria said, "is that *they* think all of these souls were brought to Hell by me to satisfy their request. I also think they can't undo what they've done to me. They just figure they can keep me under control."

"Or take the humans from you regardless of whether you intended them to or not. Like I told you, they are the master seducers, the master planners, the master schemers and manipulators. They are always ten steps ahead."

"Either way, Vlad," she said, stepping closer to him. "I really need to see those fuckers again. If I'm wrong . . . well, it's better to find out, now isn't it? I'd hate to have false hope." She smirked at him. She was ready for this.

A young girl staggered forward. She was no more than a teenager, with her face torn away, clawed down to the ectoplasmic bone, slowly regenerating, her vagina a ragged bloody hole that looked as if it had been cored out with a knife. "Goddess," she said, collapsing to her knees, "we have found the Masters."

A chill raced up Gloria's spine.

"Bring everyone."

The other humans looked around, uncertain.

"Everyone?"

"I want every soul in Hell here now! Send the word. Bring them all!"

Vlad was still smiling, Gloria tried her best to ignore him but she would have much rather smashed every tooth in his face. Then she noticed something she hadn't before. Vlad was sweating. This was more than his usual unctuousness. Beads of perspiration were rolling down his forehead.

The heat in the caverns had increased dramatically by legions of damned souls. But the increased heat and humidity was nothing for a demon, certainly nothing for a Master. Either Vlad had not been made as she had been or he was nervous, more than nervous, terrified.

The girl kneeling at Gloria's feet pointed the way and Gloria began to remember as they walked. It was all beginning to look familiar. The millions of feet behind her sounded like thunder as they marched through Hell toward the Masters' lair. They rounded a corner and Gloria stopped dead in her tracks. Behind her, her millions upon millions of marching feet came to an abrupt halt.

"Gloria. My sweet, Gloria."

That voice was like warm butter and honey and syrup and it made Gloria's legs weak. "Madria."

The demoness stood alone in the corridor. Her arms, all six of them, were spread in welcome. Her midnight skin made her almost invisible in the darkness of the tunnel. The only thing Gloria could see clearly was that smile, every bit a predatory as Vlad's but sensual in a way that Vlad's could never be. Those obsidian eyes reflected the little light in the tunnel and swirled it across the surface of her retinas in that hypnotic kaleidoscope of colors.

She came to Gloria and Gloria embraced her. They kissed and Madria's twin tongues slid into Gloria's mouth, licking her lips and tongue and then slipping out of her mouth and down her body, over her nipples and between her thighs. Gloria moaned and nearly swooned. Those smooth slippery hands overwhelmed her with sensations of pleasure. Madria's skin was somehow cool despite the unfathomable heat of inferno. Her skin felt luxuriously soothing against Gloria's. Soon Gloria felt herself being carried away, losing herself in the demoness' embrace. Madria's penis was slowly pushing its way inside of her and Gloria wanted to feel it so badly, wanted the beautiful demon to make love to her right there on the floor. She reached up and grabbed Madria's enormous breasts. The nipples were as erect as the penis pressing against Gloria's labia and they were already dripping with sweet, creamy milk. Gloria remembered how that milk had tasted, how gloriously intoxicating. She wanted to suck them, drain them dry, while Madria's hands and tongues and beautiful throbbing hard cock brought her to orgasm after orgasm. Then she heard the grumblings of the humans behind her.

Vlad had been right, the Masters could turn this all around in an instance and wrestle control of these souls away from her unless she could show them she was not like the other demons. Gloria backed away from that soft silken embrace before Madria could penetrate her and held the beautiful ebon demon at arm's length.

"Madria, take us to the Masters."

"Us?" Madria asked. "Are you with them?" she asked, looking beyond Gloria at the battered and bleeding souls in varying states of regeneration, amassed behind her. Madria laughed. "Or are you with us?"

She embraced Gloria again, this time quickly running her six hands over Gloria's face, throat, breasts, and up between her thighs.

Gloria shoved her away again with all her mental and emotional might. "No! Take us to them now! Or I'll have them tear you apart."

"Still choosing everyone else over me, Mother?"

"What did you just say?"

"You heard me, Mother. Don't you recognize your own flesh and blood?" Madria asked, stepping back so that Gloria could get a better look at her. "Although truthfully, none of my flesh or my blood is what it once was. I doubt we share a

221

single cell in common any longer."

"Angela?"

"Oh, not anymore. Not for a very long time and not ever again. But yes, that's who I was. Now, I am Madria, your lover, a Master of the inferno."

"You're a pawn, same as always, Angela. And I have no more time to waste on you and your games. Take me to the Masters or I will order my people to rip you apart."

"But don't you want to fuck me again?" She began to laugh and Gloria smacked her to the floor. Madria rose quickly and charged, and Gloria merely stepped aside and let the humans engulf her, sucking her into their midst and dragging her back into the tunnels, where more and more humans stretched for hundreds of miles through the caverns. Madria struggled and fought, but the farther back into the tunnels she was dragged the weaker she became as the humans dismembered her bit by bit as they passed her along. Her screams were terrible and seemed to go on without end.

Gloria had long ago ceased to care. She had done all she ever could or would for her child, and now it was time to cut the apron strings. "Goodbye, Angela."

Gloria turned and continued to walk, following the corridor, now surer than ever that she was headed in the right direction. When she looked over at Vlad, the smile had left his face.

The Masters' corridor came into view abruptly. One minute they were stumbling along in darkness and the next they were in the huge, brightly-lit antechamber, standing before those magnificent, beautiful demon-gods.

"Welcome home, Gloria." Mephisto stared at Gloria, unfazed as thousands of humans flooded the antechamber carrying swords and tusks and clubs and axes, prepared for war.

"You know why I'm here, Mephisto."

"You're here because I summoned you. You're here because I made you into the glorious creature you are and sent you back to earth to bring more souls to Hell, and you have done your job beyond anyone's wildest expectations.

Anyone's but mine. You have done precisely as I knew you would. You are here because I wanted you here."

Gloria felt a twinge of doubt. She looked around at the thousands of humans crowding the chamber and the hundreds more still pouring in, the millions more she knew were clogging the tunnels for miles in every direction, and she regained her confidence, her composure. With them behind her she was unstoppable.

"It's over, Mephisto. There are no more Masters in hell. Not after today. I want Satan. Take us to him."

They all laughed. All of them, except for Gloria and the humans that now surrounded them waiting for Gloria's command. Beside her, even Vlad was laughing. Mephisto looked at her like she was some lost imbecile who somehow did not get an obvious joke.

"I told you before, there is no such being. At least there wasn't . . . until now." Mephisto knelt before her, prostrating himself at her feet. All the other Masters followed suit.

"Satan!" they all cried as one by one they bowed to her.

"What? No!"

As Mephisto had said, she had fulfilled her role perfectly.

One of the Masters, the one with the rows of breasts that went from beneath his collarbone down to the nest of penises seething between his long girlish thighs, rose and crossed the room. The humans parted to let him pass. He disappeared among them for a moment, then reemerged carrying a crown of horns, massive black ram's horns that curled in a great semi-spiral. He handed the crown to Mephisto, who rose and placed it on Gloria's head.

"You are now the ruler of Hell."

"Hail, Gloria!" the crowd roared.

"Just like that?" Gloria said to Mephisto. "No fight? No protest?"

Mephisto shrugged. "As I said, there is nothing that I did not foresee. Nothing that I did not plan. We made you what you are. We made you for a purpose… and *this* is it!"

"Hail Satan!" the crowd echoed.

But Gloria wasn't finished. She had promised them more.

She had promised her followers that there would be no more division between Heaven and Hell. No more judgment. No more good and evil. No more punishment. She had to finish it. Perhaps this is what the Masters had created her for? Why she had been put through so much. Perhaps this was her destiny? To end the rule of gods, devils, angels, and demons over mankind.

Gloria thought about it for only a moment before deciding her next move. "We're going into the tunnel. To Heaven."

"For what?" Mephisto asked. His smile was unnerving. It was the same smile he had worn when she had called out Satan, as if he was humoring a confused and ignorant child.

"To take it over. To remove Him from His thrown."

"And which *Him* are you referring to?"

Gloria was growing impatient. "God!"

"Ahhhh. God. How can you be sure He'll be there? And Gloria . . . how do you know He even exists?"

Gloria faltered, confused, uncertain. "How do I know? Be-because of all of this! How can there be a Hell if there's no Heaven? Besides, I've seen it. I've seen the tunnel. I've seen the angels above the Ocean of Fire catching humans and taking them to Heaven."

"And what does all of that prove?"

"That God exists! That Heaven is real!"

"It proves nothing. What indication has this God you are looking for ever given you that he is capable of creating anything perfect? What indication has he ever given you that he is capable of creating a paradise? Because he created earth? Hell? What?"

"But there has to be. The tunnel?"

"It goes somewhere, a place they call Heaven, but it's not what you think it is. It's no Paradise, and there's no Jesus waiting for you.. Just more dead souls and more of us." He waved his thin muscular arms broadly, indicating the rest of the Masters. "Only in more . . . comely manifestations."

"The angels?"

Mephisto smiled.

"Bullshit! You're lying! There is a God. There has to be."

"There may be. But if so, just like on earth, He chooses not to show Himself."

"Bullshit! You're a liar! You're a demon, a devil, a deceiver. Why should I trust anything you say?"

"Why should I lie to you now? You've won. You're the ruler of all you survey. You are Satan."

"No!" Gloria ripped the crown from her head and tossed it to the ground. She pushed her way out of the chamber, shoving humans and demons alike as she ran back through the tunnels toward the one that led out of Hell.

The souls of the damned were packed so densely into the tunnels that Gloria was swimming through them, blind, unable to see inches in front of her, groping and pushing her way through the endless waves of humanity, fighting against the tide. Hours passed before she reached a part of the tunnel where the crowds had thinned. Gloria picked up her pace, heading in what she hoped was the direction of the tunnel. She had to find it, had to prove Mephisto wrong.

She passed dismembered demons, just pieces here and there, chunks of flesh still living and breathing and pulsating, still writhing in agony on the cave floor. As she ran further, she passed Madria/Angela's decapitated torso. Some of the humans were having their way with her remains. A slick sheen of semen covered her breasts, and globs of it leaked from her vagina. They cast hungry looks at Gloria and for a moment she feared she would be attacked as well, before some other humans nearby recognized her and bowed to her. Gloria could only imagine what they had done with Angela's head, what they were likely still doing with it somewhere. She wasn't sure the humans were any better than the demons had been. Now the lunatics were running the asylum.

Gloria struggled her way back to the huge chamber and the entrance to the tunnel. Some brave souls had already charged the tunnel and were making their way toward Heaven. Gloria followed them.

She didn't remember the tunnel being quite so long, but now that she was desperate to get to Heaven it seemed as if it was twice the distance it had been before.

Finally, Gloria emerged into that soft white light and followed it to the field where she had seen her mother. Her mother was there again and so were all the other damned souls who'd made the journey with her and their loved ones. Gloria stormed past them all. She could hear her mother calling to her as she ran across the field. Angels came from nowhere to try to stop her and soon she was running full speed, slashing angels open with her claws as they tried to stop her. The skies turned black with angels hurtling through the air in pursuit of her.

Gloria ran harder, faster, head down, demanding every ounce of speed and endurance her demonic body was capable of. She ran until the field ended and she came to a vast city. Gloria kept running deeper into the city.

When she finally came to a stop, her demon body spent, unable to give her anymore, Gloria finally looked around and began to scream. "It can't be. No. It can't be. No. No. *Nooooo!*"

The angels grabbed her, pulling her away, back across the fields, back to the tunnels. But it was too late. She had seen it. Homeless people crowding the sidewalks, drug dealers and addicts doing their transactions on the streets, police officers patrolling in cars—and prostitutes, prostitutes working the corners. It was exactly the same as earth.

There was no paradise.

"Where is *God*?" Gloria demanded of the angels who still bore her aloft, flying her back across through the tunnel, back to Hell. It made no sense at all. Everything she'd been through, all the pain, all the struggle. What did it all mean? What was the point?

"Where is He?" Gloria cried as she struggled in their grasp. "Where's God? Where is He? Where's God!"

If they knew, they never said a word.

Is God willing to prevent evil, but not able?
Then he is not omnipotent.
Is he able, but not willing?
Then he is malevolent.
Is he both able and willing?
Then whence cometh evil?
Is he neither able nor willing?
Then why call him God?
 —Epicurus, Greek philosopher, BC 341-270

ABOUT THE AUTHORS

MONICA J. O'ROURKE has published more than one hundred short stories in magazines such as Postscripts, Nasty Piece of Work, Fangoria, Flesh & Blood, Nemonymous, and Brutarian and anthologies such as HORROR FOR GOOD (for charity), THE MAMMOTH BOOK OF THE KAMA SUTRA, and The Best of Horrorfind. She is the author of POISONING EROS I and II, written with Wrath James White, SUFFER THE FLESH, and the new collection, IN THE END, ONLY DARKNESS. Watch for her new novel, WHAT HAPPENS IN THE DARKNESS, later this year from Sinister Grin Press. She works as a freelance editor, proofreader, and book coach. Her website is an ongoing and seemingly endless work in progress, so find her on www.facebook.com/MonicaJORourke in the meantime.

WRATH JAMES WHITE is a former World Class Heavyweight Kickboxer, a professional Kickboxing and Mixed Martial Arts trainer, distance runner, performance artist, and former street brawler, who is now known for creating some of the most disturbing works of fiction in print .

Wrath's two most recent novels are THE RESURRECTIONIST and YACCUB'S CURSE. He is also the author of SUCCULENT PREY, EVERYONE DIES FAMOUS IN A SMALL TOWN, THE BOOK OF A THOUSAND SINS, HIS PAIN and POPULATION ZERO. He is the coauthor of TERATOLOGIST cowritten with the king of extreme horror, Edward Lee, ORGY OF SOULS cowritten with Maurice Broaddus, HERO cowritten with J.F. Gonzalez, and POISONING EROS cowritten with Monica J. O'Rourke.

Wrath lives and works in Austin, Texas with his two daughters, Isis and Nala, his son Sultan and his wife Christie.

deadite press

"Header" Edward Lee - In the dark backwoods, where law enforcement doesn't dare tread, there exists a special type of revenge. Something so awful that it is only whispered about. Something so terrible that few believe it is real. Stewart Cummings is a government agent whose life is going to Hell. His wife is ill and to pay for her medication he turns to bootlegging. But things will get much worse when bodies begin showing up in his sleepy small town. Victims of an act known only as "a Header."

"Red Sky" Nate Southard - When a bank job goes horrifically wrong, career criminal Danny Black leads his crew from El Paso into the deserts of New Mexico in a desperate bid for escape. Danny soon finds himself with no choice but to hole up in an abandoned factory, the former home of Red Sky Manufacturing. Danny and his crew aren't the only living things in Red Sky, though. Something waits in the abandoned factory's shadows, something horrible and violent. Something hungry. And when the sun drops, it will feast.

"Zombies and Shit" Carlton Mellick III - Twenty people wake to find themselves in a boarded-up building in the middle of the zombie wasteland. They soon discover they have been chosen as contestants on a popular reality show called Zombie Survival. Each contestant is given a backpack of supplies and a unique weapon. Their goal: be the first to make it through the zombie-plagued city to the pick-up zone alive. But because there's only one seat available on the helicopter, the contestants not only have to fight against the hordes of the living dead, they must also fight each other.

"Muerte Con Carne" Shane McKenzie - Human flesh tacos, hardcore wrestling, and angry cannibal Mexicans, Welcome to the Border! Felix and Marta came to Mexico to film a documentary on illegal immigration. When Marta suddenly goes missing, Felix must find his lost love in the small border town. A dangerous place housing corrupt cops, borderline maniacs, and something much more worse than drug gangs, something to do with a strange Mexican food cart…

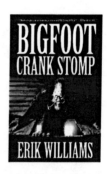

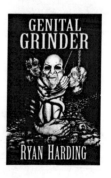

CPSIA information can be obtained at www.ICGtesting.com
Printed in the USA
BVOW04s1401201113

336823BV00012B/271/P